Edmund Crispin was born in 1921 and educated at Merchant Taylors' School and St John's College, Oxford, where he read Modern Languages and where for two years he was organist and choirmaster. After a brief spell of teaching (a fact to which he attributed, tongue-in-cheek, his knowledge of the criminal in human nature) he became a full-time writer and composer (especially of film music). Among other variegated activities in the same departments, he produced concert music, edited many science-fiction anthologies, and wrote for many periodicals and newspapers. For a number of years he was the regular crime-fiction reviewer for the London *Sunday Times*. Edmund Crispin (whose real name was Bruce Montgomery) once wrote of himself: 'He is of sedentary habit – his chief recreations being music, reading, church-going, and bridge. Like Rex Stout's Nero Wolfe he leaves his house as seldom as possible, in particular minimizing his visits to London, a rapidly decaying metropolis which since the war he has come to detest.' Until his death in 1978 Mr Crispin lived in Devon, in a quiet corner whose exploitation and development he did his utmost to oppose. His crime books include *Beware of the Trains*, *Buried for Pleasure*, *Fen Country*, *The Glimpses of the Moon*, *Holy Disorders*, *Love Lies Bleeding*, *The Moving Toyshop*, *Swan Song*, *Frequent Hearses* and *The Long Divorce*.

Edmund Crispin

The Case of the
Gilded Fly

Penguin Books

PENGUIN BOOKS

Published by the Penguin Group
27 Wrights Lane, London W8 5TZ, England
Viking Penguin Inc., 40 West 23rd Street, New York, New York 10010, USA
Penguin Books Australia Ltd, Ringwood, Victoria, Australia
Penguin Books Canada Ltd, 2801 John Street, Markham, Ontario, Canada L3R 1B4
Penguin Books (NZ) Ltd, 182–190 Wairau Road, Auckland 10, New Zealand

Penguin Books Ltd, Registered Offices: Harmondsworth, Middlesex, England

First published by Victor Gollancz 1944
Published in Penguin Books 1971
10 9 8 7 6 5 4 3

Printed in England by Clays Ltd, St Ives plc
Set in Linotype Times

For Muriel and John
donum memoriae causa

Contents

Note

As the setting of this story is a real place, more or less
realistically described, it must be emphasized that the
characters in it are quite imaginary and bear no relation to
any living person. Equally fictitious are the college, hotel
and theatre in which most of the action takes place, and
the repertory company I have portrayed bears no relation
to that at Oxford, or indeed anywhere else that I know of.

E.C.

1. Prologue in Railway Trains

> Hast thou done them? speak;
> Will every saviour breed a pang of death?
>
> *Marlowe*

To the unwary traveller, Didcot signifies the imminence of his arrival at Oxford; to the more experienced, another half-hour at least of frustration. And travellers in general are divided into these two classes; the first apologetically haul down their luggage from the racks on to the seats, where it remains until the end of the journey, an encumbrance and a mass of sharp, unexpected edges; the second continue to stare gloomily out of the window at the waste of woods and fields into which, by some witless godling, the station has been inexplicably dumped, and at the lines of goods trucks from all parts of the country, assembled like the isle of lost ships of current myth, in the middle of a Sargasso Sea. A persistent accompaniment of dark muttering and shouting, together with a brisk tearing of wood and metal reminiscent of early Walpurgis Night in a local cemetery, suggest to the more imaginative of the passengers that the engine is being dismantled and put together again. The delay in Didcot station amounts as a rule to twenty minutes or more.

Then there are about three *fausses sorties,* involving a tremendous crashing and jolting of machinery which buffets the passengers into a state of abject submission. With infinite reluctance, the cortège gets on the move at last, carrying its unhappy cargo in an extremely leisurely manner through the flat landscape. There are quite a surprising number of wayside stations and halts before you arrive at Oxford, and it misses none of these, often lingering at them beyond all reason, since no one gets either in or out; but perhaps the guard has seen someone hurrying belatedly down the station road, or has observed a local inhabitant asleep in his corner and is reluctant to wake him; perhaps there is a cow on the line, or the signal is against us – investigation, however, proves that there is no cow, nor even any signal, *pro* or *contra*.

Towards Oxford matters become a little more cheerful, within sight of the canal, say, or Tom Tower. An atmosphere of purposefulness begins to be felt; it requires the utmost strength of will to remain seated, and hatless, and coatless, with one's luggage still in the rack and one's ticket still in an inside pocket; and the more hopeful occupants are already clambering into the corridors. But sure enough, the train stops just outside the station, the monolithic apparitions of a gas-works on one side, a cemetery on the other, by which the engine lingers with ghoulish insistence, emitting sporadic shrieks and groans of necrophilous delight. A sense of wild, itching frustration sets in; there is Oxford, there, a few yards away, is the station, and here is the train, and passengers are not allowed to walk along the line, even if any of them had the initiative to do so; it is the whole torture of Tantalus in hell. This interlude of *memento mori*, during which the railway company reminds the golden lads and girls in its charge of their inevitable coming to dust, goes on usually for about ten minutes, after which the train proceeds grudgingly into that station so aptly called by Max Beerbohm 'the last relic of the Middle Ages'.

But if any traveller imagines that this is the end, he is mistaken. Upon arrival there, when even the most sceptical have begun to shift about, it is at once discovered that the train is not at a platform at all, but on one of the centre lines. On either side, waiting friends and relations, balked at the eleventh hour of their re-union, rush hither and thither waving and uttering little cries, or stand with glum, anxious faces trying to catch a glimpse of those they are supposed to be meeting. It is as if Charon's boat were to become inextricably marooned in the middle of the Styx, unable either to proceed towards the dead or to return to the living. Meanwhile, internal shudderings of seismic magnitude occur which throw the passengers and their luggage into impotent shouting heaps on the floors of the corridors. In a few moments, those on the station are surprised to see the train disappearing in the direction of Manchester, with a cloud of smoke and an evil smell. In due time it returns backwards, and, miraculously, the journey is over.

The passengers surge self-consciously through the ticket-barrier and disperse in search of taxis, which in wartime collect fares without regard of rank, age or precedence, but according to some strictly-adhered-to logic of their own. They thin out and disappear into the warren of relics, memorials, churches, colleges, libraries, hotels, pubs, tailors and bookshops which is Oxford, the wiser looking for an immediate drink, the more obstinate battling through to their ultimate destination. Of this agon there eventually remain only a solitary few who have got out to change, and who dawdle unhappily on the platform among the milk-cans.

To the ordeal described above the eleven persons, who, at different times and for different purposes, travelled from Paddington to Oxford during the week of 4–11 October 1940, reacted in different and characteristic ways.

Gervase Fen, Professor of English Language and Literature in the University of Oxford, frankly fidgeted. At no time a patient man, the delays drove him to distraction. He coughed and groaned and yawned and shuffled his feet and agitated his long, lanky body about in the corner where he sat. His cheerful, ruddy, clean-shaven face grew even ruddier than usual; his dark hair, sedulously plastered down with water, broke out into disaffected fragments towards the crown. In the circumstances his normal overplus of energy, which led him to undertake all manner of commitments and then gloomily to complain that he was overburdened with work and that nobody seemed to care, was simply a nuisance. And as his only distraction was one of his own books, on the minor satirists of the eighteenth century, which he was conscientiously re-reading in order to recall what were his opinions of these persons, he became in the later stages of the journey quite profoundly unhappy. He was returning to Oxford from one of those innumerable educational conferences which spring up like mushrooms to decide the future of this institution or that, and whose decisions, if any, are forgotten two days after they are over, and as the train proceeded on its snail-like way he contemplated with mournful resignation the series of lectures he was to deliver on William Dunbar and smoked a great many cigarettes and wondered if he would be allowed to investigate another murder, supposing one occurred. Later he recalled this wish without satisfaction, since it was to be granted in that heavily ironic fashion which the gods appear to consider amusing.

He travelled first-class because he had always wanted to be able to do so, but at the moment even this gave him little pleasure. Occasional pangs of conscience afflicted him over this display of comparative affluence; he had, however, succeeded in giving it some moral justification by means of a shaky economic argument, produced *extempore* for the benefit of one who had unwisely reproached him for his snobbishness. 'My dear fellow,' Gervase Fen had replied, 'the railway company has certain constant running costs; if those of us who can afford it didn't travel first, all the third-class fares would have to go up, to the benefit of nobody. Alter your economic system first,' he had added magnificently to the unfortunate, 'and then the problem will not arise.' Later he referred this argument in some triumph to the Professor of Economics, where it was met to his chagrin with dubious stammerings.

Now, as the train stopped at Culham, he lit a cigarette, threw aside his book, and sighed deeply. 'A crime!' he murmured. 'A really splendidly complicated crime!' And he began to invent imaginary crimes and solve them with unbelievable rapidity.

Sheila McGaw, the young woman who produced the plays at the repertory theatre in Oxford, travelled third-class. She did this because she thought that art must return to the people before it could again become vital, and she occupied herself with showing a volume of Gordon Craig designs to a farmer who was sitting next to her. She was a tall young woman, with trousers, sharp-cut features, a prominent nose, and straight flaxen hair cut to a bell. The farmer seemed uninterested in the techniques of contemporary stage-craft; an account of the disadvantages of a revolving stage failed to move him; he showed no emotion, except perhaps for a momentary disgust, on being told that in the Soviet Union actors were called People's Merited Artists and paid large sums of money by Josef Stalin. At the advent of Stanislavsky, seeing no opportunity of flight, he came off the defensive and attempted an outflanking movement. He described the methods used in farming; he waxed enthusiastic over silage, the bulling of cows, bunt, smut, and other seed-borne diseases, chain-harrows of an improved type, and similar subjects; he deplored with a wealth of detail, the activities of the Ministry of Agriculture. This harangue lasted until the train finally got into Oxford, when he bade Sheila a warm farewell and went away feeling slightly surprised at his own eloquence. Sheila, who had been somewhat taken aback at this outburst, eventually managed to persuade herself by a form of autohypnosis that it had all been very interesting. However it seemed likely, she reflected with regret, that a farming life bore little actual resemblance to Eugene O'Neill's *Desire under the Elms*.

Robert Warner and his Jewish mistress, Rachel West, travelled up together for the first performance of his new play *Metromania* at the Oxford Repertory Theatre. It had come as somewhat of a shock to his friends that a satirical dramatist as well known as Warner should have had to put on a new play in the provinces, but there were one or two excellent reasons for this. In the first place, his last London production had despite his reputation not been a success, and the managements, assailed by a first-class theatrical slump as a result of the blitz, had become extremely wary; and in the second place, it contained certain experimental elements which he was not entirely certain would come off. From all points of view, a try-out was indicated, and for reasons which I need not go into now, Oxford was chosen. Robert was to produce the play himself, with the company as it stood, but with Rachel, whose West End reputation was a more than adequate box-office draw, in one of the leads. The relationship between Robert and Rachel was an amiable and enduring one, and during the last year had become almost platonic; moreover it was backed by common interests and a genuine mutual esteem and sympathy. From Didcot onwards they sat in silence. Robert was in his late thirties, with rather coarse black hair (a rustic forelock drooping over his brow), heavy horn-rimmed spectacles shielding alert, intelligent eyes, tall, rather lanky and dressed inconspicuously in a dark lounge suit. But there was a certain authority in his bearing and an impression of severity, almost of asceticism in his movements. He reacted to the dallyings of the railway company with practised self-control, only getting up once, to go to the lavatory. Passing down the corridor, he caught a glimpse of Yseut and Helen Haskell two or three compartments away, but passed hurriedly on without attempting to speak to them and hoped they had not seen him. Returning, he told Rachel they were on the train.

'I like Helen,' said Rachel reasonably. 'She's a sweet child, and an extremely competent actress.'

'Yseut I abominate.'

'Well, we can easily miss them when we get to Oxford. I thought you liked Yseut.'

'I do *not* like Yseut.'

'You'll have to produce both of them on Tuesday, anyway. I don't see that it makes much difference whether we join up with them now or not.'

'The later the better, as far as I'm concerned. I could cheerfully murder that girl,' said Robert Warner from his corner. 'I could cheerfully murder that girl.'

Yseut Haskell was frankly bored; and as was her habit, she made no secret of the fact. But whereas Fen's impatience was a spontaneous, unselfconscious outburst, Yseut's was more in the nature of a display. To a considerable extent we are all of necessity preoccupied with ourselves, but with her the preoccupation was exclusive, and largely of a sexual nature into the bargain. She was still young – twenty-five or so – with full breasts and hips a little crudely emphasized by the clothes she wore, and a head of magnificent and much cared-for red hair. There, however – at least as far as the majority of people were concerned – her claims to attractiveness ended. Her features, pretty enough in a conventional way, bore little hints of the character within – a trifle of selfishness, a trifle of conceit; her conversation was intellectually pretentious and empty; her attitude to the other sex was too outspokenly come-hither to please more than a very few of them, and her attitude to her own malicious and spiteful. She was of that very large company of women who at an early age are sexually knowledgeable without being sexually experienced, and even now the adolescent outlook persisted. Within limits, she was charitable, within limits even conscientious about her acting, but here again it was the opportunity of personal display which chiefly interested her. Her career, after leaving dramatic school, had been mainly in repertory, though a rapid affair with a London manager had at one time got her a lead in a West End show, which for one reason and another was not a very great success. So that two years ago she had come to Oxford, and remained there ever since, talking about her agent and the state of the London stage and the probability of her returning thither at any moment, and in general showing a condescension which was not only totally unjustified by the facts but which also not unnaturally succeeded in infuriating everyone. Matters were not improved by a bewildering succession of affairs which alienated the other women in the company, caused a harassed and totally innocent undergraduate to be sent down, and left the men with that unsatisfied oh-well-it's-all-experience-I-suppose feeling which is generally the only discernible result of sexual promiscuity. She continued to be tolerated in the company because repertory companies, thanks to their special and frequently changing methods of work and precedence, exist emotionally on a very complex and excitable plane, which the slightest commotion will upset; with the result that the more sensible members of the company refrained from any overt expression of dislike, being well aware that unless at least superficially friendly relations are maintained, the apple cart goes over once and for all, hostile cliques are formed, and wholesale changes have to be made.

Robert Warner Yseut had known about a year before the events with which we are concerned, and moreover known intimately; but as he was a man who demanded a great deal more than mere bodily stimulation from his affairs, the relationship had been brutally cut short. In the normal way, Yseut preferred to break off these things herself, and the fact that Robert, wearied of her beyond endurance, had anticipated her on this occasion, had left her with a considerable dislike of him and, by a natural consequence, a strong desire to capture him again. As she travelled, she brooded over his coming visit to the theatre and wondered what could be done about it. In the meantime

15

she concentrated her attention on a young Captain in the Artillery, who was sitting in the corner opposite reading *No Orchids for Miss Blandish* and entirely unaware of the maddening dilatoriness of the train. She tried a few words of conversation with him, but he was not to be drawn, and after a short time returned to his book with a charming but distant smile. Yseut sat back in her corner with unconcealed disgust. 'Oh, hell!' she said. 'I wish this bloody train would get a move on.'

Helen was Yseut's half-sister. Their father, an expert on medieval French literature, and a man who showed little interest in anything else, had nevertheless had a sufficient sense of worldly affairs to marry a rich wife, and Yseut had been their first child. The mother had died three months after she was born, leaving half her fortune in trust for the child until she was twenty-one, with the result that Yseut was now considerably richer than was good for her. Before she died, however, there had been a furious quarrel over Yseut's outlandish name, on which the husband had with unexpected firmness insisted. He had spent the best years of his life in an intensive and entirely fruitless study of the French Tristan romances, and was determined that some symbol of this preoccupation should remain; and eventually he had somewhat to his own surprise had his own way. Two years later he married again, and two years later still Helen had been born, the second baptism causing his more sarcastic friends to suggest that if any further daughters appeared they should be called Nicolette, Heloise, Juliet and Cressida. When Helen was still three, however, both her parents had been killed in a railway accident, and she and Yseut were brought up by a distant and business-like cousin of her mother, who, when Yseut was twenty-one, persuaded her (by what means heaven alone knows, since Yseut disliked Helen intensely) to sign a deed leaving the whole of her money, in the event of death, to her half-sister.

The dislike was mutual. To begin with, Helen was different from Yseut in almost every way. She was short, blonde, slim, pretty (in a childish way which made her look much younger than she actually was), had big candid blue eyes, and was entirely sincere. Although not particularly intellectual in her tastes, she was able to talk intelligently, and with an intellectual humility which was charming and flattering. She was prepared to flirt, but only when the process did not interfere with her work, which she regarded with justifiable if slightly comic seriousness. In fact, she was for her age an extremely clever actress, and though she had none of the hard intellectual brilliance of the Shaw actress, she was charming in quieter parts, and two years previously had made an astonishing and very well deserved success as Juliet. Yseut was only too well aware of her sister's superiority in this respect, and the fact did nothing to create any additional cordiality between them.

Helen had not spoken since the journey began. She was reading *Cymbeline*, with a little frown of concentration, and was not sure that she was enjoying it very much. Occasionally, when the train halted for a particularly long time, she gave a little sigh and gazed out of the window; then returned to her book. 'A mortal mineral,' she thought: what on earth does that mean? And who is who's son, and why?

Sir Richard Freeman, Chief Constable of Oxford, was returning from a police conference at Scotland Yard. He sat back comfortably in the corner of his first-class compartment, his iron-grey hair carefully brushed back and a light of battle in his eye. He was holding a copy of Fen's *Minor Satirists of the XVIIIth Century* and was in process of registering emphatic disagreement with the opinions of that expert on the work of Charles Churchill. On hearing this criticism later, Fen was not impressed, since publicly at any rate he manifested nothing but a superb indifference for his subject. And in fact, the relation between the two men was a peculiar one, Sir Richard's chief interest being English literature, and Fen's police work. They would sit for hours expounding fantastic theories about each other's work, and developing a fine scorn for each other's competence, and where detective stories, of which Fen was an avid reader, were concerned, they frequently nearly came to blows since Fen would insist, maliciously but with some truth, that they were the only form of literature which carried on the true tradition of the English novel, while Sir Richard poured out his fury on the ridiculous methods used in solving them. Their relationship was further complicated by the fact that Fen had solved several cases in which the police had come to a dead end, while Sir Richard had published three books of literary criticism (on Shakespeare, Blake, and Chaucer) which were regarded by the more enthusiastic weekly papers as entirely outmoding conventional academic criticism of the sort which Fen produced. It was, however, the status of each as an amateur which accounted for their remarkable success; if they had ever changed places, as a mischievous old don in Fen's college once suggested, Fen would have found the routine police work as intolerable as Sir Richard the niggling niceties of textual criticism; there was a gracious and rather vague sweep about their hobbies which ignored such tedious details. Their friendship was a longstanding one, and they enjoyed each other's company enormously.

Sir Richard, absorbed in the author of the *Rosciad*, failed altogether to notice the erratic behaviour of the train. He alighted at Oxford with dignity, and acquired a porter and a taxi without difficulty. As he climbed in, Johnson's dictum on Churchill occurred to him. ' "A huge and fertile crab-tree",' he murmured, to the great surprise of the driver, ' "A huge and fertile crab-tree".' Then more abruptly: 'Don't sit there gaping man! Ramsden House.' The taxi swept away.

Donald Fellowes was on his way back from a happy weekend in London, which he had spent listening to services from organ lofts, and taking part in those endless discussions of music, organs, choir-boys, lay clerks and the peccadilloes and eccentricities of other organists which occur whenever church musicians come together. As the train moved out of Didcot he closed his eyes thoughtfully and wondered whether it would be a good thing to alter the pointing of the Benedictus and how long he would be able to go on taking the end of the Te Deum *pianissimo* without someone complaining. Donald was a quiet dark little person, addicted to bow ties and gin, and very inoffensive in manner (if anything, a little too unemphatic), and he was organist at Fen's college, which I shall call St Christopher's. As an undergraduate he had been so much occupied with his music that his tutors (he was reading history) had despaired, and as it turned out with reason, of ever getting him through anything; and after the fourth attempt both he and they had given it up with mutual feelings of relief. At the moment he was merely hanging about, carrying on with his organist's job, vaguely preparing for groups or sections, writing his B.Mus. exercise, and waiting for call-up. His remote contemplation of the canticles was frequently interrupted by a much less remote contemplation of Yseut, with whom he was, as Nicholas Barclay was later to put it, 'very gravely in love'. Abstractly, he was aware of all her shortcomings, but when he was with her they made no difference; he was completely and utterly enslaved and infatuated. As he thought of her, he felt suddenly acutely miserable, and the dallyings of the train added irritation to his misery. 'Damn the girl!' he said to himself. 'And damn this train. . . . I wonder if Ward is going to be able to get through that solo on Sunday. Damn all composers for writing top A's in solo parts.'

Nicholas Barclay and Jean Whitelegge left London together, after a morose and silent luncheon at Victor's. Both of them were interested in Donald Fellowes, Nicholas because he considered him a brilliant musician who was letting himself go to pieces over a girl, Jean because she was herself in love with him (and so, incidentally, had every reason to dislike Yseut). It is true that Nicholas was hardly qualified to criticize others for letting themselves go to pieces. As an undergraduate reading English a brilliant academic career had been prophesied for him, and he had bought, and read, all those immense annotated editions of the classics in which the greater part of every page is occupied with commentary (with a slight gesture to the author in the form of a thin trickle of text up at the top, towards the page number), and the study of which is considered essential to all those so audacious as to aim at a Fellowship. Unfortunately, several days before his final examination, it occurred to him to question the ultimate aims of academic scholarship. As book superseded book, and investigation investigation, would there ever come a time when the last word had been said on any one subject? And if not, then what was it all about? All very well, he had reasoned, if one derived personal pleasure from it; but personally, he did not. Then why continue? Finding these arguments unanswerable, he had taken the logical step of abandoning his work completely, and had taken to drinking, quite amiably, but persistently. Upon his failing to appear at his examination, and proving quite deaf to all remonstrances, he had been sent down, but as he had comfortable private means this did not perturb him in the least, and he moved between the bars of Oxford and London, cultivating a mildly sardonic sense of humour, making many friends, and confining his reading exclusively to Shakespeare, huge tracts of which he now knew by heart; in these circumstances even a book had become unnecessary, and he could simply sit and think Shakespeare, to the annoyance of his friends, who regarded this as the limit of idleness. As the train proceeded towards what he had once with an eye to its plethora of music described as the City of Screaming Choirs, Nicholas sipped cheerfully at a flask of whisky, and ran over whole scenes of *Macbeth* in his mind. 'Present fears are less than horrible imaginings: my thought, whose murder yet is but fantastical . . .'

Of Jean there is less to be said. Tall, dark, spectacled and rather plain, she had only two interests in life, Donald Fellowes and the Oxford University Theatre Club, an undergraduate body which produced uninterestingly experimental plays (as these bodies generally do), and of which she was secretary. Where the first of these two interests was concerned, she was frankly in the grip of an obsession. Donald, Donald, Donald, she thought, clutching tightly to the arm of her seat: Donald Fellowes. Oh hell! This must stop. He's in love with Yseut, anyway, not you . . . the bitch. The conceited, selfish bitch. If only she weren't . . . if only someone . . .

Nigel Blake was contented, and he thought of a great many things as the train crawled on its way: of the pleasure it would be to see Fen again; of his hard-won first in English three years ago; of his laborious, but quite interesting life as a journalist since then; of his belated fortnight's holiday, at least a week of which he would spend in Oxford; of seeing Robert Warner's new play, which was sure to be good; and above all, of Helen Haskell. Don't get excited, he told himself, you haven't met her yet. Go easy. It's dangerous to fall in love with people just from seeing them on the stage. She's probably conceited and horrible; or else engaged; or married. And anyway she's certainly surrounded with young men, and it's ridiculous to suppose that you're going to induce her to take any notice of you in the space of a week, when you don't even know her yet . . .

None the less, he added grimly to himself, you're going to have a damned good try.

The destinations of these people in Oxford were various: Fen and Donald Fellowes returned to St Christopher's; Sheila McGaw to her rooms in Walton Street; Sir Richard Freeman to his house on Boar's Hill; Jean Whitelegge to her college; Helen and Yseut to the theatre and subsequently to their rooms in Beaumont Street; Robert, Rachel, Nigel and Nicholas to the 'Mace and Sceptre' in the centre of the town. By Thursday, 11 October, they were all in Oxford.

And within the week that followed three of these eleven died by violence.

2. Yseut

Ahi! Yseut, fille de roi,
Franche, cortoise, bone foi . . .

Beroul

Nigel Blake arrived in Oxford at 5.20 in the afternoon, and
went straight to the 'Mace and Sceptre', where he had booked a
room. The hotel, he reflected sadly as his taxi drove up to it, was
not one of the architectural glories of Oxford. It was built in a
curious amalgam of styles which reminded him of nothing so
much as an enormously large and horribly depressing night-
club-cum-restaurant he had once visited near the Brandenbur-
ger Tor in Berlin, where every room impersonated some
different national style in an aggressive, romantic, and improbable way. His own room appeared to him like a grotesque
parody of the Baptistry in Pisa. He unpacked, washed off the
dirt and discomfort which a rail journey always involves, and
wandered downstairs in search of a drink.

By now it was half past six. In the bar and lounge, the civilized prolegomena to sex operated a restrained, objectionable
puppet-show; a corpse of painted gothic overlooked these proceedings. In general, the place was much the same as Nigel remembered it, though the undergraduate population had
dropped, and the military risen, considerably. A few belated
theological students of the arty type, who had remained presumably to work during the vacation or who had come up a few
days early, whined and gibbered in a discussion of the poetic
beauty of the conception of the Virgin Birth. A group of R.A.F.
officers by the bar swallowed their beer with noisy, jejune enthusiasm. There were one or two very old men, and a miscellaneous riff-raff of art students, schoolmasters, and visiting
celebrities, who sat about hoping to be noticed, and without
whom Oxford is never complete. A motley collection of women
attached to the younger men and for the most part engaged in
manipulating and focusing their attention upon themselves,

completed the gathering. One or two Indian students idled rather aggressively about, ostentatiously bearing volumes of the better-known contemporary poets.

Nigel found himself a drink and an empty chair and settled down with a little sigh of relief. Decidedly the place had not altered. In Oxford, he thought, the faces change, but the types persist, doing and saying identical things from one generation to the next. He lit a cigarette, stared about him, and wondered whether to go and see Fen that evening or not.

At twenty to seven Robert Warner and Rachel came in. Nigel knew Robert slightly – a tenuous acquaintance based on a series of literary luncheons, theatrical parties and first nights – and gave him a cheerful little wave.

'May we join you?' said Robert, 'or are you meditating?'

'Not at all,' replied Nigel ambiguously. 'Let me get you a drink.' And thanking heaven that Robert was not the kind of man immediately to clamour 'No, let *me* get *you* one', he found out what they wanted and went off to the bar.

On his return he found them talking to Nicholas Barclay. Introductions were performed, and Nigel trailed off again to the bar. Eventually they all got settled, and sat for a moment in silence, gazing expectantly at one another, and sipping their drinks.

'I'm looking forward enormously to seeing your play next week,' said Nigel to Robert. 'Though I must admit I'm a bit surprised that you're putting it on here.'

Robert gestured vaguely. 'It's a case of needs must,' he said. 'My last thing was such a miserable flop in the West End that I had to go to the provinces. The only consolation is that I shall be able to produce it myself, a thing I haven't been allowed to do for years.'

'Only a week's rehearsal on a new play?' said Nicholas. 'That's going to be a sweat.'

'It's a try-out really. Various agents and managers are coming down from London to confirm their belief that I am, in fact, a dandelion seed in the wind, and that I've lost all my mind. I hope to disappoint them. Though God knows what sort of a production it will be; this place has become a repository for callow children from the dramatic schools, with a substratum of old crocks and one or two of the most notorious hams in Europe. Whether I shall be able to beat them into a proper use of timing, gesture and intonation in a week I really can't imagine. But Rachel's going to be in it, and she'll help.'

'Frankly, I doubt it,' said Rachel. 'An outsider starring in repertory for box-office purposes creates more bad feeling than anything else. You know, muttering in corners.'

'What's the theatre like?' Nigel asked. 'I hardly went near the place while I was up here.'

'You worked!' put in Nicholas incredulously, who always pretended that he had not.

'It's not bad,' said Robert. 'An old place, put up somewhere in the eighteen-sixties, but modernized just before the war. I was working there about ten years ago, and my God, it was awful then: squeaky dimmers, erratic tabs, and flats that fell over at a touch. All that's been done away with now though. Some good soul with money and ambitions crammed the place with every technical device he could lay hands on, including a revolve –'

'A revolve?' said Nigel vaguely.

'Revolving stage. Like a circular turntable, divided across the middle. You set the next scene on the side hidden from the audience and then, when the time comes, just twiddle it round. It means you can't have flats projecting on to it from the wings, and that rather limits you in the composition of your sets. As a matter of fact, I don't think they use it much here – it's a sort of white elephant; certainly I shan't. But it's a nuisance, because you lose an enormous depth of stage you could very well do with.'

'And what,' said Nicholas, settling back more comfortably in his chair, 'is the play about? Or is that giving away trade secrets?'

'The play?' Robert seemed surprised at the question. 'It's a re-write of a thing of the same name by a very minor French dramatist called Piron. You probably know the story. About 1730, I think it was, Voltaire began to receive verses from a Mlle Malcrais de la Vigne, to which he gallantly responded, and a huge correspondence sprang up between them, all very amorous and literary. Later on, however, Mlle de la Vigne came to Paris, and turned out to Voltaire's fury and everyone else's delight to be a great fat youth called Desforgues-Maillard. Piron used this situation as the basis of his play, and I've taken it over and modified it, reversing the sexes though and making the chief character a woman novelist and her correspondent a mischievous woman journalist. I know it doesn't sound up to much,' he concluded apologetically, 'but that's really only the bare bones of the thing.'

'Who's playing the woman novelist?'

'Oh, Rachel of course,' said Robert cheerfully. 'Lovely part for her.'

'And the journalist?'

'Frankly, I'm still uncertain: I think Helen. Yseut's quite incapable of playing comedy, and anyway I dislike her so much I simply couldn't bear it. There's one other girl, apart from the older women, but I'm told she does such extraordinary things on the stage that I simply mustn't give her anything more than a bit part. I'm giving Yseut a bit part too – only on in the first act. But,' he added maliciously, a little smile creasing the corners of his mouth, 'I shall insist on her taking a curtain every night, so that she can't take off her make-up and go home.'

Nicholas whistled, took out a cigarette case, opened it, and balanced it on the table with a gesture of invitation. 'Yseut is really very unpopular,' he said. 'I've never met anyone who had a good word to say for her.'

Nigel, as he took a cigarette, flicked his lighter, and handed it round the little group, thought he saw a gleam of interest appear in Robert's eye.

'Who in particular dislikes her?' Robert queried.

Nicholas shrugged. 'Myself, for one, on more or less irrational grounds; though I have a friend who's making a bloody fool of himself over her. "I am as true as truth's simplicity, and simpler than the infancy of truth" – you know. Helen, for another – what a sister to have to drag about with one! Jean – oh, you don't know her of course; girl called Jean Whitelegge, because she's in love with the Troilus aforementioned – the humble village maiden waiting for her knight to stop fooling about with the wicked princess. Everyone in the company, because she's an intolerable little bitch. Sheila McGaw, because – Oh, God!'

He broke off abruptly. Looking up to see what had caused the interruption, Nigel saw Yseut come into the bar.

'Talk of the devil,' said Nicholas gloomily.

Nigel studied Yseut curiously as, with Donald Fellowes, she came into the bar, and was struck by her total lack of resemblance to Helen. The brief interchange he had just heard interested him, though for the moment he was inclined to be no more than superciliously amused at the antagonism which the girl seemed to arouse. She looked a compound of negative qualities – conceit, selfishness, coquetry – and little more besides (later he was to appreciate malice as a positive quality). She was dressed very simply, in a blue sweater and blue slacks which set off the red of her hair. Nigel noticed the almost imperceptible traces of disagreeableness in her features, and sighed: but for that, a model whom Rubens, or Renoir, would have delighted to paint. Certainly, Nigel admitted to himself with perhaps a little more than mere scientific interest, she had a magnificent body.

By comparison, Donald Fellowes seemed uninteresting; he moved awkwardly, and with little address. Nigel thought he recognized him; but where on earth had he come across him before? He made a futile, indefinite attempt to summon up the memory of his acquaintance during his years at Oxford, and as always happens on these occasions, could not remember a single one – only a phantom pantomime of blank, indistinguishable masks. Fortunately the problem was solved for him by a gleam of recognition which appeared in Donald's eye. Nigel smiled feebly, foreseeing a certain amount of gaucherie and embarrassment in the near future; he never had the courage simply to tell people that he didn't remember them.

There followed the ceremony of mumblings, apologies and recognitions which always occurs when a group of people only partially acquainted are brought together, and a great and complicated manoeuvring of chairs. Nigel, about to go off once again to the bar, was forestalled by Nicholas, who as he ordered pink gins contemplated with unconcealed glee the extremely uncomfortable relationships which were likely to be established within the next few minutes.

Yseut, after a perfunctory and apparently pejorative survey of Nigel, attached herself firmly to Robert; Rachel talked to Donald; and Nigel and Nicholas sat listening in comparative silence.

Yseut began by being solemnly reproachful. 'I wish you'd allowed me to play the journalist,' she said to Robert. 'I know it's silly to argue about casting, but frankly, I've had much more experience of that sort of thing than Helen. And I thought perhaps in view of the fact that we knew each other so well – '

'Did we know each so well?'

A trace of asperity appeared in Yseut's voice. 'I didn't think you'd have forgotten so quickly.'

'My dear child, it's not a question of forgetting.' Instinctively they both lowered their voices. 'You know damn well we never got on together. And as for bringing that up over a question of casting – '

'It's not just the casting, Robert, and you know that as well as I do.' She paused. 'You behaved damned badly to me, and I haven't had as much as a line from you since. In anyone else, it would have been intolerable.'

'Are you thinking of suing me for breach of promise? I assure you you'll have a job.'

'Oh, don't be such a bloody fool. No – I shouldn't have said that.' She was dramatizing freely with voice and gesture. 'I suppose in a way it was my fault that I couldn't keep you, even as your mistress.'

'I already had a mistress.' This conversation, thought Robert, is getting damned awkward: much worse than I expected. Aloud he said: 'And anyway, Yseut, I thought we agreed about all this long ago. It's had no influence on the casting, if that's what you mean.' (A lie, he thought, but if people will be so intolerable . . .!)

'I've missed you, Robert.'

'My dear, I've missed you too, in a way.' The conventions of polite behaviour were beginning to sap Robert's firmness.

Yseut looked at him with wide, innocent eyes in which there was a hint of tears; he half expected her to lisp when she spoke.

'Couldn't we take it up again, darling?'

'No, dear; I'm afraid we couldn't,' said Robert, recovering his firmness. 'Even if it were possible from my point of view, which it isn't, what about that young man Donald what's-his-name who's sitting there making sheep's eyes at you?'

Yseut flung herself back in her chair. 'Donald? My dear, surely you credit me with sufficient good taste not to take seriously a youth like that.'

'He's of the male gender; I thought that was your only requirement.'

'Don't be cynical, darling. It's very *vieux jeu* now.'

He marvelled at the lack of dignity which could have prompted her to such an offer. Half in curiosity, he began to probe again.

'And besides, Helen tells me he's very much in love with you. Surely you owe him sufficient consideration not to go about asking other men point-blank to go to bed with you.'

'I can't help it if people fall in love with me.' A toss of the hair, conventional mime for 'It is not *my* responsibility!'

'If you don't love him, make a clean break.'

She sneered. 'Oh, don't talk like a twopenny novelette, Robert. He's hopelessly young and silly and clumsy and inexperienced. And ridiculously jealous, too.' A hint of complacency came into her voice.

A pause. She went on:

'God, how I hate Oxford! How I hate the silly, bloody, fools who surround me here! And the theatre, and everything about the filthy place.'

'There's nothing to stop you leaving, I suppose. The West End is waiting tensely for you to decide what part you want to play, and opposite whom – '

'Damn you!' There was a sudden cold venom in her voice.

'Pleasant reminiscences?' inquired Nicholas from the middle distance, who had caught the last few phrases of the conversation.

'Shut up, Nick,' she said. 'As far as success is concerned, you're no shining light.'

Nigel saw Nicholas' expression harden. 'Dear Yseut,' he said silkily, 'how fortunate it is that I have no reason in the world to be polite to bitches like you.'

'You little – !' She was tense with fury now. 'Robert, are you going to let him talk to me like that?'

'Shut up, Yseut,' said Robert. 'And you shut up too, Nick. I've no wish to be surrounded by squabbling children all evening. Have a cigarette,' he added, waving his case about.

It was an unpleasant little incident, one of several such, destined to culminate in murder. But what had astonished Nigel had been the sight of Donald Fellowes during those few seconds. Literally, the man had been shaking with rage; his hand had trembled as he took a cigarette from Robert's case and lit it, throwing away the match without attempting to offer it to anyone else; the blood had drained from his face and the sweat had started out on his brow. Nigel was so alarmed that he half rose from his chair, afraid that Donald was going to smash at Nicholas with the first thing that came to hand. He had controlled himself – fortunately. But Nigel realized then how strong his passion for Yseut was, and marvelled.

It was Rachel who restored the situation. 'Are you going to be here long?' she said quietly to Nigel.

Nigel played up nobly. 'About a week, I think,' he said as casually as he could. 'A week of blessed rest from journalism. I'm reviving memories – ' his eye travelled uneasily round the gathering as he spoke, and he was relieved to see that they were all sulking – 'though of course there are very few people I know up now. It's funny how little the place has changed, despite the war.' There was a desperate pause. 'I wonder,' he said to Robert, 'if I might watch some of the rehearsals of your play? If the company doesn't object, that is. I know so little about the theatre, and I'm sure it would be good for me.'

'By all means,' said Robert a little absently. 'We run through the whole thing tomorrow (reading, of course), then Act 1 will be set on Wednesday, Acts 2 and 3 on Thursday, run-through on Friday and Saturday and dress-rehearsal on Sunday evening. Monday we piece together the fragments of the dress-rehearsal, and there we are. I dare say one or two of the older members of the company will object to having people hanging about, but they'll just have to lump it.'

'Oh, if it's going to be a nuisance – ' said Nigel hastily.

'Good heavens, no. Make yourself fairly inconspicuous, that's all. Donald what's-his-name is coming whenever he can get away from his choirboys, and so is a don I met yesterday – called Gervase Fen, of all the impossible names –'

Nigel was genuinely surprised. 'Oh, you've met Fen, have you?' he inquired rather unnecessarily.

'Yes. Is he a friend of yours?'

'He used to be my tutor. How did you come across him?'

'Quite by accident, in Blackwell's. He was reading a book off one of the shelves, and going to the rather extreme length of cutting the pages with a penknife.' Robert chuckled. 'When one of the assistants ticked him off, he said solemnly, "Young man, this bookshop was dunning me for enormous bills long before you were born. Go away at once, or I'll cut out all the pages and scatter them on the floor." The assistant went, in some dismay, and he turned to me and said, "Do you know, I was afraid I was going to have to." We chattered for a bit, and he seemed struck dumb on learning who I was and gaped at me and asked a lot of solemn and quite idiotic questions about how I thought of things and whether I enjoyed writing and whether I dictated my plays to a secretary. Is it a pose, by the way? I didn't think it was, but I was a bit taken aback.'

'No, it isn't,' said Nigel definitely. 'He's always had a sort of naïve enthusiasm for the celebrated. It's refreshing at first, but it becomes a bore, and one gets so ashamed of him at parties.'

'Anyway, the upshot of it was that I invited him to come along to rehearsals, for which he was quite pathetically grateful. However towards the end of our conversation he began to shuffle his feet and fidget about and look at his watch, so I politely took my leave, and he rushed away with tremendous strides saying "Oh dear, oh dear, I shall be too late!" like the White Rabbit in *Alice*, knocking over a pile of pamphlets on Russia, and absentmindedly taking with him the book he'd been looking at. Obviously he couldn't make out where it had come from, because later I saw him take it into Parker's and exchange it for a detective novel.'

Nigel emitted a sound which can only be described as an explosive snort. When he had recovered he said:

'I'm going in to see him after dinner tonight. Would you like to come?'

'Thanks, but it really can't be managed. I'm going on Friday, when I've got this play off my mind a bit.'

At this point there suddenly appeared at the table the young Artillery captain to whom Yseut had spoken in the train. He wore a bashful smile. Nigel had seen him at an adjacent table, his attention torn between the conclusion of *No Orchids for Miss Blandish* and the charms of Rachel, which had obviously smitten him severely.

'Excuse my butting in,' he said, addressing himself chiefly to Yseut, 'but we met in the train, and I was getting awfully bored sitting there all on me lone-e-o. You see, I don't know anyone in Oxford yet,' he added apologetically.

A confused clamour of invitation arose.

'I say, thanks awfully,' he said. 'Do let me get you all another drink.' And he rushed away and returned with his arms full of glasses, spilling the greater part of their contents on the floor. In the meantime Donald Fellowes rose abruptly and left without a word.

'All comes from practice,' said the Captain proudly, depositing the drinks in an unsteady manner on the table and sitting down with a bump. 'My name's Peter Graham,' he added. 'Captain Peter Graham, His Majesty's Royal Artillery, at your service.' He grinned at each of them in turn.

Rachel took charge of the introductions, and the conversation drifted into indifferent channels. Rachel, after a brief wink at Robert, resigned herself to the respectful attentions of Peter Graham, who was inquiring hopefully whether the reputation of actresses for immorality was justified. Robert was thrown back on Yseut again, while Nigel and Nicholas discussed their undergraduate days and found acquaintances in common. Eventually Peter Graham surged to his feet.

'I say,' he said, 'I wonder if you'd all like to come to a party in my rooms here on Wednesday night? After the bars have closed, of course. And bring lots of people. I think the hotel will let me have plenty to drink, so you needn't bring bottles.

'In the meantime,' he added, after they had all murmured expressions of delighted acquiescence, 'Rachel – I mean Miss

West and I are going to have dinner together, so I hope you'll excuse us.' (Here Robert shot a desperate glance at Rachel, who mischievously refused to notice it.) 'So long,' said Peter Graham cheerfully. 'I expect I shall see you all about,' he added, feeling that perhaps some justification was needed for this abrupt departure. 'I think I'm going to like Oxford.' And he had whisked Rachel out before anyone could say a word.

Nigel and Nicholas also began to make movements of departure. 'I must be off now,' Nicholas said firmly.

'No, don't go,' said Robert hurriedly. 'Stay and have dinner with us.' He waved his hand dejectedly in the direction of Yseut, and semaphored distress signals.

'I'd love to, but I'm afraid I'm dining with a friend in New College. And I'm late already.'

'What about you?' Robert addressed Nigel plaintively.

But Nigel had absolutely no wish to dine with Yseut. 'I'm sorry,' he said mendaciously, 'but I'm afraid I've got an engagement too.'

'Oh dear,' said Robert.

'By the way,' said Nigel as they turned to go, 'what time is the rehearsal tomorrow?'

'Ten o'clock,' answered Robert dismally. They left him sunk in gloom, and Yseut smiling like an overfed cat.

In the doorway a somewhat drunk R.A.F. officer cannoned into Nicholas, and recovering himself, stared at him blearily for a few seconds.

'Bloody type!' he announced technically. 'Why the hell aren't you in uniform – bloody type!'

'I'm part of the culture you're fighting to defend,' said Nicholas looking at him coolly; he had been invalided out of the army after Dunkirk.

'Bloody pongo!' said the R.A.F. officer, and feeling his vocabulary exhausted, went his way.

Nigel looked curiously at his companion as they left the hotel. 'I should imagine *Coriolanus* is one of your favourite plays,' he said.

Nicholas smiled. 'In a way you're right; "the common cry of curs", you mean. But it's not snobbishness; it's just a congenital inability to suffer fools gladly. I think that's the chief reason, not any moral scruples, why I so loathe that bitch Yseut. Someone is going to kill or mutilate that girl one day – and I for one shan't be sorry.'

Outside, Nigel left him. And as he strolled back to dine at his college, he was more than usually thoughtful.

3. Trying Tender Voices

An ancient fabric raised t' inform the sight
There stood of yore, and Barbican it hight ...
Where infant punks their tender voices try,
And little Maximins the gods defy.

Dryden

It was well after midnight when Nigel left Fen's room in St Christopher's to return to the 'Mace and Sceptre'. Their talk had been of old acquaintances, old days, of the present state of the college, and of the effects of the war on the university as a whole. 'Morons!' Fen had said of the present set of undergraduates, 'Sophomores!' And from the glimpses Nigel had had of them he was greatly inclined to agree. The average age of the college had been much reduced, and a sort of standard public-school prefect's common-room type had superseded the more adult eccentricities and individualities which had existed before the war. Then, again, there were more people reading science, and fewer reading arts, and this Nigel, with the instinctive snobbery of the arts man, deplored.

But throughout the evening he had been distrait. Something of the tangled implications of the Yseut situation had been conveyed to him by that brief conversation before dinner, and he was now less inclined to be amused than he had been at first. He remembered Donald Fellowes trembling with rage in his chair, Nicholas' cold sneer, Robert's instinctive, almost physical repugnance for the girl; and there were other threads which as yet he had not seen. A little vaguely, he wondered how the situation would resolve itself. Probably, like most of these *impasses*, it would melt away with the removal of one or more of its elements. Nigel, who was naturally lazy, deplored hasty decisions and decisive steps and always waited until the situation had been altered and the decision no longer had to be made. Doubtless it would all smooth itself out somehow.

He slept soundly and woke late, so that it was already 10.30 by the time he set out for the theatre, and he cursed himself for allowing himself to be so late.

The theatre was ten minutes' brisk walking from the hotel. It stood near the outskirts of the city, a little drawn back from a long, residential street which also served as the main road to a neighbouring town. Contemplating it in the fresh, clear autumn sunlight, Nigel wondered if we didn't sometimes do the Victorians an injustice by invariably condemning their architecture as graceless. Certainly in the present case the unknown architect had succeeded in conveying an impression of mellow, if slightly effeminate, charm to the building. It was a big place, built in soft yellow stone, and fronted by a wide lawn where on summer evenings the audience would stroll with drinks and cigarettes, during the intervals. The greater part of the building had been simply restored; only the proscenium, stage, dressing-rooms and bar had been completely modernized, the latter – which was on the first floor behind the circle, and to which two flights of steps led up from either side of the foyer – in a witty *pastiche* of the original style which blended charmingly with it. The two box-offices, too, had been provided with broad sheets of glass in place of the tiny roman arches through which transactions have to be carried on in the majority of old theatres.

Nigel slipped quietly into the darkened stalls, still feeling annoyed with himself for being so late. He had wanted to watch all the rehearsals and get some idea of how a play was actually built up to the first performance.

He was surprised, however, to find that next to nothing was happening (later he realized that this is the case with about a third of every repertory rehearsal). Under working lights on the stage a few people stood or sat inactively about in the middle of the current play's set, holding typed books and smoking or chattering in a subdued manner. A young woman whom Nigel took to be the stage manager was banging chairs and tables about so energetically that Nigel expected them to fall to pieces at any moment. Robert stood talking to someone beside the orchestra pit, across which an unsteady-looking plank was laid to provide a passage from the stage to the front of the house. A young man vaguely played a few bars of jazz on the piano in the orchestra pit.

'I wish we could get a move on,' he said to someone on the stage.

'Clive hasn't turned up yet.'

'Well, can't we do the second act?'

'He's on in all the acts.'

'Where in God's name is he?'

'He said he was catching the 8.30 from town. Either it's fantastically late or else he's missed it.'

'What does the man keep rushing up to town for anyway?'

'He goes up to see his wife.'

'Good heavens. Every night?'

'Yes.'

'Good heavens.'

It was all curiously unreal, thought Nigel. The effect of artificial light probably. It had not previously occurred to him how little actors and actresses see of the sun. He became suddenly aware that he was unintentionally eavesdropping the conversation of two people who were standing in the darkness near him.

'But darling, must you run about after him like that?'

'Don't be silly, darling, one's got to be nice to these people if one's going to get on at all.'

'You mean in the theatre you've got to use your sex to get yourself jobs!'

'Well, you surely don't imagine people get parts out of sheer acting ability.'

Someone in the electrician's gallery switched on a flood, and in the momentary dazzle Nigel saw that the two were Donald and Yseut. He felt uneasily that he ought to move, but curiosity compelled him to stay. Neither of them had noticed him.

'If only you wouldn't be so damnably jealous, darling . . .'

'Yseut, dear. You know how much I love you –'

'Oh, God, yes. I know.'

'Of course it's a damn nuisance for you when you're not in love with me.'

'Darling, I've told you I love you. But after all, there's my career as well.'

'Jane!' came Robert's voice suddenly from the front. 'Ring for Yseut, will you, dear? I want to run through her song with her.'

'It's all right, darling, I'm here,' said Yseut and went off down the gangway.

The little group on the stage began to disperse in various directions.

'Don't go away, people,' said Robert. 'Just clear the stage. This won't take long, and we've got to make a start afterwards whether Clive's arrived or not. Someone can read his part. Did you get a dance routine worked out?' he added to Yseut.

'Yes. But I didn't know how it was going to be set. Will it be as it is now?'

'Is that all right for the first act, Richard?' Robert appealed to the scenic designer.

'The flats in the O.P. will be further back,' said Richard. 'And there's no table – Jane! Jane dear!'

The stage manager appeared from the prompt corner like a rabbit out of a hat.

'Jane, that table's much further upstage.'

'I'm sorry, Richard, but if you remember it's fixed down. We can't take it up now – we had a hell of a job with it in the first place.'

'Oh, well, never mind,' said Robert, 'do the best you can for the moment. Bruce dear boy,' he added to the young man in the orchestra pit, 'you'll play it for the moment, won't you? Straight through, two choruses.'

The young man in the orchestra pit nodded gloomily. 'Why was I born?' he said. 'Why am I living?'

'That's right. It's an old song, but quite nice.' (To Yseut) 'Ready, dear? Now, what in God's name is the cue? Oh, yes. Clive says: "Well, get on and sing the thing if you must".'

'Quiet please!' A subdued murmuring from the wings ceased abruptly.

'WELL, GET ON AND SING THE DAMN THING IF YOU MUST!' roared Robert suddenly.

The pianist played a couple of bars' introduction, and Yseut began to sing.

> 'Why was I born,
> Why am – ?'

'Sorry, sorry, just a minute!' said Robert suddenly. The music ceased. 'Yseut dear, you'll be *upstage centre* at the beginning. We'll get the moves for the song set later; do what you like for the moment. All right "Get on and whatever-it-is, diddle-diddle-diddle." '

Robert retired backwards up the gangway, and the music began again.

Nigel went across to Donald. 'Hello!' he said.

Donald, whose eyes had been fixed on the stage, started violently, 'Oh, hello,' he answered. 'Couldn't think who it was for a moment. Let's go and sit down, shall we?'

When they had got settled, Nigel's attention went back to the stage again. Against his inclination, he was forced to admire the way Yseut sang, adopting for the occasion a slight American accent and a slight lisp. She put it across beautifully; it was all very provocatively sexy.

> 'Why was I born,
> Why am I livin'?
> What do I get,
> What am I givin'?
> Why do I want the things I dare not hope for?
> What can I hope for? I wish I knew!
>
> Why do I try
> To draw you near me?
> Why do I cry? –
> You never hear me!
> I'm a poor fool, but what can I do?
> Why was I born to love you?'

The song over, the young man at the piano played through another chorus with a bored expression, and Yseut danced. She danced well, with a sort of naïve seductiveness, but it did not seem to please Donald. 'Wretched display!' he muttered; and then, turning to Nigel: 'I can't think how these women can bring themselves to do that sort of thing. Yet they seem to love it.'

'It's quite harmless, you know,' said Nigel mildly. 'I suppose you mean the music.'

'No, I don't, I mean the sex. And they adore showing off that way.'

38

'Well, it's not very surprising,' replied Nigel, 'that a woman should enjoy making an elementary form of sexual advance to a roomful of men without the slightest chance, so to speak, of being taken at her word. It must be a most delightful feeling.'

'Wouldn't you mind if it were your wife?'

Nigel looked at him curiously. 'No,' he said slowly, 'I don't think – '

'Right!' The conversation was cut short by the conclusion of the song and Robert's voice. 'That's lovely, dear, thank you,' he said to Yseut.

'Did you really like it, darling?'

'One or two things may have to be altered when we get it properly set,' he said, sternly refusing to be drawn beyond the bounds of conventional politeness. 'Jane, dear!' he continued hastily, 'will you ring for everyone: we're going to do Act 1. . . . And Jane!'

'Yes?'

'Has Clive arrived yet?'

'Yes, he's just got in.'

'Thank God for that.'

The call bell clamoured vociferously all over the theatre. The company assembled little by little, including the miserable Clive, a bland young man in a black hat, who seemed quite unaware of the delay he had caused; and after a while the rehearsal was launched.

About half-way through the act, a girl approached Donald and Nigel whom Nigel had not met before. It was Jean Whitelegge, and with her appearance Nigel realized he had found yet another part of the tangle whose centre was Yseut, and which had been so aggravated by Robert's arrival. That the girl was madly in love with Donald there was no doubt: little tricks of speech, gestures, everything made it obvious to the very blindest. Nigel groaned inwardly; he couldn't imagine what Jean saw in Donald, whom he thought rather a silly little man, and even less could he imagine what Donald saw in Yseut. It was all very difficult. He inquired politely whether she were watching the rehearsal.

'No, I've been working here for the last few weeks,' she said. 'They let me do props out of term-time.'

Let you do props, indeed! thought Nigel, who knew enough about the theatre to be aware of the thanklessness of the job. Jean, he decided, was one of that all-too-large body of amateur actresses who get excited at the smallest contact with the professional stage, and fritter away their lives in useless jobs connected with it. But while he was still summoning up an interested grimace, she turned and began talking to Donald in a low voice. Donald, Nigel saw, was becoming irritable under a stream of reproaches. It's ordinary comedy, thought Nigel – a pure Restoration drama situation – but it refuses to be comic; it's bitter and dull and sordid and witless. Later he was to realize just how bitter these quarrels were, and to reproach himself for not paying more attention to them.

At a quarter to twelve they finished the act. And Nigel, who had been watching, fascinated, the way the thing came to life even with the players reading and frequent interruptions to arrange moves, was sorry to hear Robert say:

'All right, people, break for coffee! Quarter of an hour only!'

'There's coffee in the green room if you want it,' said Jean to Nigel. 'And by the way, have you got a 'cello?'

'Good heavens, no,' said Nigel in alarm.

'And you wouldn't lend it even if you had; I know. I've *got* to get a 'cello from somewhere for next week.' She disappeared down the gangway.

'Frankly,' said Donald, 'that girl's a nuisance.'

Something in his *sans façon*, man-of-the-world tone suddenly irritated Nigel.

'I thought her charming,' he said shortly, and went off down the gangway to see Robert, who was on the stage talking to the scenic designer and the stage manager.

The company had melted away like magic, the women to the green room for coffee, the men for the most part to the 'Aston Arms' across the road. Robert greeted Nigel a little absently.

'I imagine you're finding this very dull,' he said.

'Good heavens, no. It's fascinating. And a very' – Nigel hesitated for a moment over the adjective – 'delightful play, if I may say so.'

'I'm glad you like it.' Robert seemed genuinely pleased. 'But of course, this is only the skeleton of the whole thing. No business, no props. But the company's much better than I dared hope. If only they can be induced to learn their lines!'

Nigel was surprised. 'Are they likely not to?' he asked.

'I gather one or two of them make a point of drying about six times every night until the Friday. However, we shall see. Are you having coffee?'

'If I shan't be drinking someone else's.'

'Good Lord, no. Do you know where the green room is? If you don't, Jane will show you. I'll be down in a minute. We can't afford to break for long, I'm afraid.'

'Coming?' said Jane, who was a slim, attractive young woman of twenty or thereabouts.

'Right,' said Nigel, and looked round a little guiltily for Donald. But he had disappeared.

As they went out backstage, Nigel looked curiously about him, at the big electrician's gallery in the prompt corner, the flats stacked against the walls, and the circular line which marked the edge of the revolving stage. The backs of the flats, he noticed, were scrawled with pictures of animals, caricatures of members of the company, and lines from past plays – relics of a sudden exuberance before an entrance or at a dress rehearsal. Even in repertory, with a new play every week, the excitement of a first night never becomes insipid.

They went out of a swing door at the back (carefully sprung and padded to prevent banging) and up a short flight of stone stairs to the green room.

'Were you here for Yseut's song?' asked Jane.

'I was, actually.'

'And you liked it?'

'Very much,' he said, not without truth.

'I'm understudying for her, and I'm terrified I shall have to do it. I can't really sing a note, but Robert asked me to, so I suppose he anyway thinks I can. But it's going to be a bore having to learn lines for a thousand-to-one possibility.'

'Yes,' said Nigel non-committally; he was thinking of Helen, who had not appeared in the first act. He added: 'I suppose Helen Haskell's on at the beginning of the second act?'

'Helen? Yes, that's right, dear. She'll probably be in the green room now.'

Nigel was slightly taken aback. He was not yet used to the vague and indiscriminate terms of endearment which fly about in the theatre.

They entered the green room. It was tolerably full, and Jane was some time getting him some coffee. Having presented it to him, she abruptly disappeared, leaving him to his own devices.

It slightly hurt his vanity to find that nobody took any notice of him. But he saw Helen sitting by herself looking at a copy of *Metromania*, and decided to take the bull by the horns. He went over and sat down beside her.

'Hello!' he said, not without some trepidation.

'Hello!' she replied, giving him a charming smile.

'I hope I'm not interrupting you learning your words,' he pursued ungrammatically, somewhat emboldened.

She laughed. 'Good Lord, no, not at this time of the week.' She threw the book on to the chair beside her. 'Do tell me who you are,' she said. 'I hear you've been in front. It must have been dreary.'

Damn the woman! thought Nigel: she makes me feel a babe. And I'm sure I look awful (he automatically put up a hand to smooth back his hair). I wish she weren't so attractive – or do I?

He said more or less composedly: 'I'm Nigel Blake.'

'Oh, yes, of course! Robert has told me about you – and Gervase.'

Nigel's face assumed an expression of sedate alarm. 'I didn't know you knew Fen,' he said. 'Anyway, don't take any notice of anything he's told you about me. He just says the first thing that comes into his head.'

'Oh dear, what a pity! He was rather complimentary.' She put her head a little on one side. 'Still, when I know you better I shall be able to tell for myself.'

Nigel felt ridiculously elated. 'Will you have lunch with me?' he said.

'I'd love to, but I doubt if we shall finish much before half past two, and that's awfully late, isn't it?'

'Dinner, then.'

'Well, we go up at 7.45, and I have to be in fairly early to change and make up. I should have to rush madly away. Tea?' she added hopefully.

They both laughed.

'Supper,' said Nigel firmly, 'after the show. Tea's such a dull meal. Perhaps I can persuade the hotel to let us have it in my sitting-room.'

'La, sir, what a suggestion!'

'Oh, well, it doesn't matter where. I'll pick you up after the show. What time?'

'About half past ten.'

'Lovely.'

Robert came in, and, after a brief nod to Nigel, began talking to Helen about her part. So he wandered off on his own, precariously balancing his coffee-cup in his left hand. Donald, Yseut, and Jean Whitelegge were in a little group by one of the windows, and the atmosphere looked far from intimate. With a vague idea of pouring oil on troubled waters, Nigel walked over to join them.

'Hello, Nigel,' drawled Yseut as she saw him approaching. 'Have you been enjoying the masterpiece?'

'I like it,' said Nigel.

'How curious. So does little Jean here.' Jean began to speak, but Yseut interrupted. 'It's all appallingly superficial, of course, and no opportunities for real acting. But no doubt dear Rachel's name will bring them in, like wasps round a jam-pot.'

Mentally, Nigel added himself to the already over-burdened list of those who disliked Yseut Haskell.

To his own surprise, he found himself remarking dogmatically: 'Comedy is necessarily superficial. And the technique of comedy acting, even if it is different from the technique of acting in serious plays, isn't any less difficult.'

'Why Nigel!' said Yseut with exaggerated surprise, 'how

clever you are! And we all thought you knew nothing about the theatre!'

He flushed. 'I know very little about the theatre. But I've seen enough of actors and actresses to resent their assumption that they are the only people who know anything about it.'

Yseut, feeling that the possibilities of unpleasantness in this topic had been too rapidly exhausted, changed the subject. 'I see you've introduced yourself to my sister. Don't you think she's attractive?'

'I think she's very attractive.'

'So does Richard,' said Yseut. 'I think they're quite serious about one another, don't you?'

Nigel's heart sank. He knew Yseut was being malicious, but there must be some foundation for what she said. . . . He replied, as casually as he could:

'They're attached to one another, are they?'

'Oh, but of course. I thought everyone knew. But you've been here such a short time, why should you? And anyway, I'm sure it's a matter of complete indifference to you.'

Nigel, who was about to say 'It is', stopped himself in time. If he did, there was every possibility that Yseut would tell Helen at the earliest possible opportunity. Childish intriguing and hypocrisy! But Yseut's game was one which, temporarily at least, she compelled those with whom she came in contact to play. He said:

'On the contrary. As I said, I find your sister very attractive.'

He was relieved to hear a cool, sensible voice behind him. It was Rachel.

'Hello, Nigel,' she said. 'Are you enjoying this chaotic rehearsal? Silly question,' she added with a smile before he could reply. 'I expect everyone has asked you that and you're tired of answering it.'

'I've got quite used to saying "Yes, I am", and watching the polite incredulity on people's faces.'

'Oh, well, it'll brighten up towards the end of the week.' She took his arm and piloted him a little way away from the others. 'I don't think you like Yseut,' she said.

'Frankly, I don't. And you?'

'Nasty little creature.'

They both laughed, and the conversation drifted to other subjects. Robert's voice was suddenly heard saying:

'Jane, dear, go over to the "Aston" and bring the men back, will you? We're going to begin Act 2 almost immediately.'

Yseut stretched and yawned. 'Thank God I've finished. I shall have quite a pleasant week of doing next to nothing,' she said.

'Yseut,' said Jean Whitelegge abruptly, 'I want to talk to you about Donald.'

'Oh?' said Yseut with a slight sneer. 'And what is there to talk about, may I ask? Donald darling, you'd better go away; you'll get insufferably vain if you listen to two women fighting over you.'

'Oh, for God's sake, Jean – ' muttered Donald.

'Why don't you leave him alone?' Jean burst out suddenly. 'You know you're not interested in him, except when there's nothing else in trousers to go about with. Now you've got your precious Robert, stop playing about and leave him alone. Leave him alone, I say! You don't love him, and you never have. You don't love anything but your own vanity and conceit!'

'Jean, dear, don't,' said Donald uncomfortably.

She turned on him in a fury. 'Oh, don't be such a gutless little swine!' she cried. 'Can't you see it's for your own good – your own good, damn you!'

'Why, Jean dear,' said Yseut smoothly, 'I really believe you're jealous! But surely a pretty, intelligent girl like you has no need to worry about rivals; why, you've only got to lift a finger and Donald will do anything you say – '

Jean's face became convulsed. 'I hate you!' she sobbed. 'I hate you, you bloody little – ' She broke down and cried uncontrollably.

Rachel came over and grasped her tightly by the arm. 'Jean,' she said firmly, 'you know I'm going to want a big modern picture to bring on in the first act. Well, it's just occurred to me that you can get one from that little shop in the Turl which will do admirably – a reproduction of a Wyndham Lewis. I think it would be a good thing if you went and got it now.'

Jean nodded, and ran out of the room, still crying. In the

doorway she almost cannoned into Jane, who put her head in to say:

'Act 2 straight away, dear hearts!' Then *sotto voce* to Richard: 'Oh, Lord, what's happened now?' And disappeared.

'I think you might be more careful, Yseut,' said Rachel coldly. 'One or two more scenes like that and you'll have the whole company at loggerheads.'

'I've no intention of having my affairs criticized in public by a child like that,' said Yseut, 'and certainly it's no business of yours, in any case. Come on, Donald. Let's get out of this damned place. Apparently it's one of the latest rules of repertory that the producer's mistress can talk to the company anyhow she pleases.'

'What that child needs,' Rachel said to Nigel when she had gone, 'is a darned good spanking.'

The company reassembled on the stage, but a mood of depression had descended on the rehearsal. The news of Yseut's little scene with Jean had passed with lightning rapidity from mouth to mouth, and the always mercurial spirits of the company sank to the bottom. Nigel watched for some time longer, but he slipped away shortly before one o'clock and returned very thoughtfully to the 'Mace and Sceptre' for his lunch.

It was nearly a week later that he realized he had heard something that morning which would enable him to identify a murderer.

4. Wild Goose Overtaken

Pray for me, O my friends, a visitant
Is knocking his dire summons at my door,
The like of which, to scare me and to daunt,
Has never, never come to me before . . .

Newman

Nigel passed the rest of the day in various and not very interesting ways. His holiday was proving rather flat, largely owing to the fact that there were now so few people in Oxford whom he knew, while those he had met since his arrival were not only occupied with their job for most of the day, but got on so badly with one another that their company was generally anything but agreeable. If it hadn't been for Helen, he would probably have packed up and gone back to London straight away. He anticipated seeing Nicholas at lunch, but he had unexpectedly left Oxford and did not return until the next day. A walk round his old haunts, taken in the hope of its producing a few pleasant *frissons* of reminiscence, proved barren of amusement. And when the sky became overcast, and a thin, persistent drizzle set in, he gave it up in disgust and went to the pictures. After a late dinner, he sat gloomily reading in the lounge of the hotel until it was time to go and meet Helen.

Their supper-party succeeded in cheering him up a good deal. The rumour of her affair with Richard, to which Nigel led up with elephantine tact, Helen dismissed as quite baseless, and accused Nigel of being an innocent if he imagined that that sort of remark, coming from Yseut, had any relation to the facts. As they strolled back together to Helen's rooms, Nigel waxed sentimental, in terms which it is not necessary to speak of here; and went home so happy that we must suppose they were not ill received.

The next day, the day of Peter Graham's eventful party, brought with it a belated intimation of summer warmth which lasted until the end of the week. Peter Graham, who had spent Tuesday in dancing incessant and thoroughly inconvenient attendance on Rachel, devoted almost the whole of it to agitated preparations. In the morning, Nigel found him in the bar, laden with flowers and trying to cadge a couple of extra bottles of gin out of the barman. 'Cherries!' he was saying excitedly, 'I must have some cherries! And olives!' He greeted Nigel with delight, and rushed him away to the shops to buy a great quantity of unnecessary and expensive things for the party.

Within its limits, as Nigel afterwards admitted, it was a good party. There were unpleasantnesses, but he observed them through an agreeable alcoholic mist, and in any case he had become so used to unpleasantness during the past few days that he would have felt uneasy if none had occurred. The final incident, however – if something could be called an incident which passed completely unnoticed – did in fact disturb him.

He spent the earlier part of the evening at the theatre, watching a play in which a number of men and women committed a complex series of adulteries without any evident relish, to an accompaniment of jejune comment and cocktail glasses. He took some pleasure, however, in watching Yseut, and rather more, of a different kind, in watching Helen; and was somewhat irritated to find that he felt extremely possessive and proud whenever she came on to the stage, and had to suppress a desire to nudge his neighbours and win from them a similar approval. But the trivialities of the plot so wearied him that he slipped out before the end, and went home with hardly more than a thought as to how it would end. Doubtless they all succumbed to nervous diseases.

In consequence he arrived a little early at Peter Graham's room, to find that only Nicholas was there before him, comfortably settled in a corner and showing little inclination to move before the end of the party. Peter had certainly contrived an extraordinary display of bottles and glasses, and stood with a proprietorial air in the middle of them all, urging Nicholas, rather unnecessarily, to drink as much as he could before the others arrived. Nigel was astonished, though, how sober Nicholas remained throughout the evening; on reflection, he could not remember ever having seen anyone drink so much with so little effect.

After he had been there about ten minutes, Robert and

Rachel came in, to be greeted by Peter Graham with enthusiastic cries. A little later, two army officers, acquaintances of Peter's, also arrived, and later still, a considerable contingent from the theatre, in twos and threes.

'You asked us to invite a lot of people,' said Robert deprecatingly, 'and I think most of the company's coming. Except Clive,' he added gloomily, 'who's gone up to town to see his wife.' The marital preoccupations of Clive were beginning to prey on his mind.

Jean, Yseut, Helen, and Donald Fellowes all arrived together, with a motley collection of hangers-on from the theatre. A semblance at any rate of good feeling existed between them, though as the evening wore on Nigel noticed no real change in the situation at all; if anything, matters seemed to be worse. Richard, a tall, fair-haired young man in the late twenties, was there, and so was Jane, the stage manager. Nigel observed with some amusement a tendency on the part of Peter to gravitate away from Rachel towards Jane, a manoeuvre he accomplished rather clumsily; but Rachel was certainly more relieved than annoyed. The stage of polite conversation soon passed, and a horrible gaiety set in; fragments of speech were lifted high above the communal babble.

'Oh, Jane dear, you are a *slut*.'

'Tchekov, I assure you, began the disintegration of the drama by *disintegrating the hero* . . .'

'So I said that in my opinion you should play the whole of *Othello* in just one green spot . . .'

'. . . wanted to do Wycherly in modern dress, but the Lord Chamberlain stepped in . . .'

'Diana? Where's Diana?'

'You see that awful boy over there. ¡¡¡ Well, my dear, don't let it go any further, but he's – '

'I feel sick.'

'. . . no possibility of reviving the drama now that *the hero's been disintegrated* . . .'

'Have another drink, old boy.'

'Thanks, I've had one, old man.'

'Well, have another.'

'Thanks.'

'. . . bit arty, some of these people, aren't they?'

'I really do feel awfully sick.'

'Well, go outside then.'

'Tchekov . . . disintegration of . . .'

'. . . an appallingly earthy play about a farm with a *great flock of chickens* all over the stage . . . my dear, they were *uncontrollable* . . . whenever one went into one's dressing-room, there they were, *roosting* in the number nine . . .'

'. . . arrived at Manchester in pouring rain and found the theatre had been bombed the night before. So we had to go straight on to Bradford and open about an hour after the train came in . . .'

'. . . so my agent said to Gielgud: "A splendid reliable all-round man. He can do anything, except act . . ." '

'Bit of a bloody type, eh, old man? . . .'

'Oh, well; takes all sorts, you know . . .'

'. . . then Shaw *re-integrated* the hero . . .'

'I *wish* I didn't feel so sick . . .' .

Nicholas sat immovably in his corner, talking to Richard about Berkeleyan metaphysics; whenever one of the younger women came near him, he beckoned her solemnly over, kissed her equally solemnly on the lips, and then dismissed her with an airy wave of his hand and continued the conversation. Donald Fellowes was sulking on his own. Yseut was attached to Robert, saying:

'Darling, you must be nice to me this evening, you must! Please don't spoil the party for me, Robert darling! Darling!' She was already very drunk.

Nigel sought out Helen early in the evening, and with a few breaks stayed with her until the end. The row and the heat of the room were beginning to give him a headache. There was a good deal of horse-play going on, and he had no wish to become involved in it. He looked at his watch, discovered that he had already been there two hours, and suggested to Helen that they should go.

'In a minute, darling. I must look after Yseut; she'll never get home on her own.'

Nigel looked for Yseut, and was alarmed to see her in the middle of a large group, waving a heavy army revolver.

'Look what I've found,' she was shouting, 'look what little me's found!'

Peter Graham elbowed his way through the group.

'Now, Yseut dear,' he said, 'you'd better give me that; damn dangerous, you know.'

'Nonsense, 's not dangerous! Hasn't got 'ny bullets in.'

'All the same, old girl, better let me have it. Never know what'll happen.' He took it away from her, more or less by force, and said soothingly: 'Now, we'll put it away in the drawer with the cartridges, and forget all about it. There!'

'Beast!' said Yseut glumly; then suddenly turned on him and tried to claw viciously at his face with her long nails.

'Now, now!' he said, catching hold of her arms. 'Can't have that sort of thing, you know. All friends here,' he added a trifle vaguely.

Yseut became petulant. 'Let me go!' she said, tugging her arms away from him. 'Let me go, you great – lout!' She turned suddenly to Robert and flung her arms round his neck.

'Darling,' she whined, 'did you see what the swine did to me, darling? He tried to – to – molest me, darling.' She grinned foolishly. 'Go 'n – knock him down – if you're a man. Go 'n knock the swine down.'

Robert, acutely embarrassed, tried to detach her arms, but she was so far gone that she would have dropped if he let her go. Helen went across to her.

'Come on, Yseut,' she said brusquely. 'We're going now. Hang on to me.' She supported Yseut to the door, refusing vague and unenthusiastic offers of assistance. 'Good night, everyone,' she said with remarkable *sang-froid*. 'Thank you, Peter, for a lovely party.' And went.

Nigel followed to see if he could help. He met them coming out of the lavatory, Yseut pale, sweating and shivering. Helen flushed with sudden embarrassment when she saw him.

'Here, let me help,' said Nigel.

'No, thanks, Nigel. I can manage. You go back and enjoy yourself.' None the less, he went with them to the door of the hotel.

'Good night, darling,' said Helen, pressing his hand. 'If this doesn't cure me of going to parties, nothing will.'

'It was pretty beastly. Are you sure you can manage?'

'Yes. It's not far.' She made as if to go; then, turning, said hesitantly:

'Yseut's not bad, you know. Just silly.' A slight smile lit up her face. On an impulse, he went up to her and pressed her hand. Yseut, clinging to her arm, was mumbling inanely.

'God bless you, my very dearest,' he said. And then they were gone.

When he got upstairs again, the party was already beginning to break up. The guests went down the stairs in twos and threes, yawning and chattering. Nigel found Rachel standing by herself while Robert gave Jean some instructions for the next morning.

'How dare that girl make a fool of Robert like that, in front of everybody!' she exclaimed.

'Of course nobody blames Robert,' he answered. 'Why should they? It's not his fault.'

'I don't think he's altogether averse to having her hanging on to him,' she said with a sudden venom that astonished him.

'But surely you don't think – ?'

She dismissed the subject with an impatient gesture. 'Robert's like all other men: any change is a change for the better. But if he, or she, imagines I'm going to sit by and play the tolerant – '

She stopped abruptly. Nigel felt acutely uncomfortable. Another thread! he thought. This situation is certainly getting unpleasantly complicated.

After the farrago of 'good nights' Nigel and Nicholas found themselves alone with Peter Graham. The amount of drink he had had suddenly took effect in an unexpected manner, and while they were still talking to him he collapsed into a chair and began to snore profoundly. Nicholas sighed.

'Now, I suppose, we shall have to put him to bed,' he said.

This with some difficulty they accomplished. When they came out into the sitting-room again, Nicholas looked about him in disgust, at the empty bottles, dirty glasses, flowers scattered or broken, furniture disarranged, a blue haze of cigarette smoke and innumerable cigarette stubs, more or less concentrated round ash-trays. 'What a filthy mess this place is in,' he said. 'I pity the poor devil who has to clear it up.' He yawned and stretched. 'Oh, well, bed, I suppose. Coming?' Nigel nodded.

When they were out in the corridor, Nicholas said: 'Oh Lord, I've got a foul headache. If I don't get some fresh air I shall never sleep. I'm going out for a stroll. What about you?'

'No, thanks. If I want any fresh air I shall stick my head out of the window.'

'Right you are,' said Nicholas amiably. 'But mind the black-out. By the way,' he added, 'what was that Rachel was saying to you before she left? I thought I heard some strictures on our admirable sex.'

'The usual paean in praise of Yseut.'

'Oh, that!' Nicholas laughed. 'Rachel hates that girl. The "cool, sensible woman" pose wouldn't deceive a babe. She loathes her.'

'*Is* it a pose?' Nigel ventured.

Nicholas shrugged. 'Who knows? I think it is, anyway. "Men are all the same",' he quoted mockingly. ' "Any change is a change for the better." '

'Isn't that so?'

'Any change, however good, is a change for the worse,' said Nicholas firmly. 'Enough of this chatter, anyway. Good night to ye.' He went off downstairs, and Nigel returned to his room and began to undress.

In the long corridors of the hotel, the main lights had long since been extinguished; only a few pale, widely-spaced glims remained. Peter Graham groaned, and turned uneasily in his sleep. In the big entrance hall, lit only by a single bulb in the roof, the night porter dozed uncomfortably in his box, and so failed to see either the person who flitted silently up the big staircase to Peter Graham's room, or what that person was carrying on its return. The swing-doors creaked a little, and the night porter half awoke; then, seeing nobody dozed again. In his bedroom, Nigel dropped a collar-stud under the dressing-table.

'Damn!' said Nigel.

He was inexplicably uneasy; something was crying out to be investigated. Cool reason told him to forget it and go to bed.

But an irrational fear and premonition proved to be stronger than cool reason. 'This is a damned silly wild goose chase,' he said to himself as he slipped on his dressing-gown. Two minutes later he was opening the door of Peter Graham's sitting-room.

He switched on the light. Nothing was different; the haze of cigarette smoke still hung about, the ash remained as it had been, trodden into the carpet. Cursing himself for a superstitious fool, he went softly over to the drawer where the revolver had been put. His scalp tingled unpleasantly as he opened it and looked in.

The drawer was empty. Revolver and cartridges were gone.

He closed it again, and on a sudden wild impulse wiped the handle where he had touched it, with a corner of his dressing-gown. Then he went over to the bedroom door, and pushed it a little ajar. A shaft of light cut into the darkness beyond. From the room came the heavy breathing of one who sleeps deeply. He closed the door softly and went back to his own room.

Nigel slept only fitfully that night. For long stages at a time he was awake, smoking, and thinking over what he had discovered. Nicholas, whose room was next door to Nigel's, returned late, and made what Nigel thought an unnecessary amount of noise in getting to bed. But that was the least of his worries. In itself there was nothing so particularly disturbing about the disappearance of the gun, which might have been taken as a joke, or might, for all he knew, have been lent by Peter Graham to someone at the party. Yet he had watched them all leave, and could have sworn that nobody had it hidden on his or her person – it was a heavy, bulky thing, a Colt .38. The only conclusion he could come to, then – and it was not a pleasant one – was that someone had slipped back and taken it after the party was over, between the time, that is, when Nicholas left him and the time when he returned to the room. Nicholas? He seemed the most likely person, but anyone could have done it.

He rose and breakfasted early, wondering as he did so what the more riotous members of the party must be feeling like.

Then at half past nine he went back to his room to get a book. His way led him through the corridor where Robert's and Rachel's rooms were situated, and made him a party to coincidence which afterwards proved to have been of some considerable importance. As he passed Rachel's room, she came out on her way down to breakfast.

And it was at that precise moment that Yseut emerged from Robert's room opposite.

All three of them stopped dead; and to Nigel at any rate the implications of Yseut's presence were obvious. To say that he was astonished would have been the wildest understatement; he was very nearly stupefied. It was unbelievable that Robert had slept with Yseut that night – particularly in view of her condition when Helen took her home. But what else could one think? Rachel apparently was of the same opinion, and the expression on her face was not pleasant to see. Besides, Yseut's appearance shocked Nigel unutterably. She was slovenly dressed in a blouse and slacks, carrying a bag and a thin red notebook; and in her eyes was an expression of mingled fear and satisfaction which was repellent to a degree.

They looked at one another in silence for a moment. Then Yseut, with a slight sneer, went off downstairs. Not a word had been spoken.

Rachel made to go into Robert's room, but Nigel caught her arm.

'Is that wise?' he said.

After an almost imperceptible pause she nodded; and followed Yseut slowly downstairs.

Nigel went on to his room frankly bewildered. The whole business was inconceivable. Troilus' words came unbidden to his mind.

> 'O madness of discourse,
> That cause sets up with and against itself!
> Bi-fold authority! where reason can revolt
> Without perdition, and loss assume all reason
> Without revolt . . .'

Of course it was none of his business; of course it was nothing to make such a hell of a fuss about. And yet speculation refused to be quieted, and an unformed fear hovered persistently at the back of his consciousness. It was with difficulty that he persuaded himself to think of other things.

When he next saw Yseut he had been sitting in the bar since ten o'clock with Robert, talking rather awkwardly about indifferent things. About ten past ten Donald Fellowes had come in, deposited an armful of organ music on top of a radiator, and joined them. He was not pleasant company that morning – in fact he seemed to have relapsed into a permanent state of sullenness. He very ostentatiously directed his conversation towards Nigel, an attitude which succeeded in making Robert, who two days ago would have considered it merely amusing, extremely irritable; and since he talked mainly about music, a subject of which Nigel knew little and wished to know even less, conversation soon became merely sporadic all round. All three of them refused obstinately to refer to personal matters, which precluded more than a few vaguely conventional remarks about the previous night's party. And Donald was obviously suffering from a hang-over.

The rehearsal that morning was not until eleven o'clock. After the first rehearsal Nigel had not been to the theatre, and felt on the whole disinclined to do so before at any rate the dress-rehearsal.

'We shall have an hour's break for lunch this morning,' Robert said, 'and then go on through the afternoon.'

'Would you tell Helen I'd be glad to see her if she cares to lunch with me? I shall be in the lounge here from twelve o'clock onwards.'

'Helen? Yes, by all means.'

It was then that Yseut entered the bar. She was dressed as untidily as when Nigel had first seen her that morning, and still carried her bag and her notebook. He saw that as she came in an expression of black anger appeared on Robert's face, and that he half started up from his chair; then relaxed, and sat back looking extremely uncomfortable. 'Afraid she'll hang about his neck in public and make the whole thing obvious with a lot of dreary innuendoes,' thought Nigel, and added the mental footnote: 'which is exactly what she will do.' Yseut met Robert's eyes with a look in which triumph and defiance were oddly mingled, flung down her things, and swaggered to the bar. None of the three men moved to get her a drink, but she watched them closely as she ordered brandy and walked back with it.

'Well, my children,' she said, 'how are you all feeling after last night's carouse? Poor Donald, you look a bit green.'

'I think it would be more appropriate for us to ask you that question,' Nigel said drily.

'Was I very tight last night?' She laughed unconvincingly. 'Well, one's only young once, as the dreary cliché has it. I – er – went to your room this morning, Robert dear. I was so sorry not to find you in. I'm afraid when dear Nigel saw me coming out he thought the most dreadful things. And Rachel as well. Such a pity I had to run into her: I thought I was being so discreet.' She picked up her glass with a shaky hand and swallowed half the contents at a gulp. 'Still, I found what I went for.' She smiled silkily.

'I'm delighted,' Robert said. 'And as you say, what a pity I missed you.'

'Never mind – darling.'

(The innuendoes have begun, thought Nigel gloomily.)

Robert continued: 'Of course, I shan't see you at rehearsal today, but as I imagine there's something you'd like to talk to me about – '

She raised her eyebrows. 'I, darling? Nothing in the world. You sound so conspiratorial – doesn't he, Nigel? As though you wanted to slip me a cheque for blackmail. If you do, I'm sure the others won't mind. But of course. I'm not accepting any cheques or doing any blackmail; it's so unwise, and it's much, much better that the truth should be known.'

'What are you talking about, Yseut?' demanded Donald abruptly.

'Nothing, darling. Only a joke. A private joke.'

'I've got to go now,' Donald muttered awkwardly.

'Oh, must you, Donald? Are you going to practise your organ? Be sure and play nicely.'

Donald rose, picked up his music, and stood looking at her for a moment. Then with a brusque movement he turned on his heel and went. Yseut smiled after him.

'A sweet boy,' she said, 'but just a tiny bit gauche. Let me get you both another drink.'

Nigel rose automatically.

'What are you having? Rye and dry? Come to the bar with me, Nigel, and help me carry them back.'

On the way to the bar Yseut continued to look back over her shoulder and smiled at Robert. Arrived there, she propped herself up with her back to it and left Nigel to do the ordering.

Unfortunately, just as the barman was giving Nigel Yseut's brandy, it slipped from his fingers and spilt on the bar. He hurriedly pulled her away, but was not in time to prevent some of it running on to her blouse.

'Blast!' she said. 'You clumsy fool! For God's sake give me a handkerchief to wipe it off.'

Nigel gave her the handkerchief, without finding himself able to feel a shred of remorse at the incident, and ordered another brandy while she scrubbed ineffectually at the cloth. He suddenly felt extremely ill – no doubt a belated after-effect of the party – and very, very weary of Yseut and everyone who had to do with her. A fit of morose irritability seized him: I wish to God they'd all go and hang themselves, he thought.

They went back to Robert with the drinks (for which Yseut had conveniently forgotten to pay). Nigel saw her take a swift look about her, and then stiffen and flush furiously. She looked at Robert with eyes so full of hatred that tears sprang into them against her will.

'Damn you!' she said. And literally throwing her drink on to the table she snatched up her bag and left.

There was genuine bewilderment on Robert's face.

'Well, for heaven's sake!' he exclaimed. 'What on earth – ?'

Nigel grunted and sat down. 'Good riddance,' he said wearily, and swallowed a double whisky neat. Not unnaturally, this made him feel more sick than ever, and he was relieved when Rachel came in and he could decently excuse himself. Obviously she wanted to talk to Robert alone, and the conversation was perfunctory until he rose to go.

'You won't forget my message to Helen?' he said.

'Message?' answered Robert vaguely. 'Oh, yes, of course. No, I won't forget.'

'Good-bye, then.'

Rachel gave him a ghost of a smile.

'Arrivederci,' said Robert.

'Arrivederci,' he echoed; and went.

A hypocritical farewell, he said savagely to himself, as he pushed through the swing-doors into the street and made for St Christopher's: I should be delighted if I never saw any of them again. Let them all squabble their beastly heads off. Let them shoot each other with stolen revolvers, and I'm damned if I shall care. But they won't have the guts even to do that. It's all superficial and conventional and merely stupid. They wouldn't have the guts.

But he was wrong. For now on the borders of the mind the jackals and hyenas went back to their lairs, and soft-footed wolves began to stalk, in circles that grew ever narrower towards a point where they fell upon a struggling, screaming form and silenced it. The bickering and squabbling became transmuted by a sudden hidden alchemy into physical terror and physical agony and violent death. That afternoon Nigel left Oxford and returned to London; he came back the following evening, and heard a shot.

When he next saw Yseut she was dead.

5. 'Cave Ne Exeat'

I have seen phantoms there that were as men,
And men that were as phantoms flit and roam.

Thomson

'Intuition,' said Gervase Fen firmly, 'that's all it amounts to in
the end – intuition.'

He glared about the assembled company, as if challenging
anyone to contradict him. But nobody did; it was his room, to
begin with, and they were all heavy with Senior Common
Room port for which he had paid, so it seemed impolite to
argue. Moreover, it was exceedingly hot, and Nigel at any rate
felt little inclined to do anything but relax. It was eight o'clock
of the Friday evening, and only three hours ago he had completed the abominable journey down from town. He was tired.
He stretched out his legs and prepared to absorb anything Fen
had to say on his favourite topic.

The room was a large one, stretching the whole width of the
southernmost parallel of the second quadrangle in St Christopher's, and facing on to the garden on one side and the quadrangle itself on the other. It was on the first floor, and was
reached by a flight of steps leading up from the open passageway which led through into the garden. Austerely but comfortably furnished, the cool cream of the walls – set off by the
dark green of the carpet and curtains – was decorated only by a
few Chinese miniatures and by the meticulously arranged rows
of books on low shelves which occupied every side of the room.
On the mantelpiece were a few dilapidated plaques and busts of
the greater masters of English literature, and a huge desk, its
surface covered with an untidy mellay of books and papers,
dominated the north wall. Fen's wife, a plain, spectacled, sensible little woman incongruously called Dolly, sat at one corner
of the fireplace, in which a few embers glowed unnecessarily,
Fen himself sat at the other, while variously spaced between
them were Nigel, Sir Richard Freeman, and a very old don

called Wilkes, who had attached himself to the party for no particular reason some minutes before. On his arrival Fen had been extremely rude to him – but then he was habitually rude to everyone; it was a natural consequence, Nigel decided, of his monstrous and excessive vitality.

'Oh, and what can I do for you?' he had inquired. But Wilkes had settled himself down and demanded whisky with every evidence of a determination to stay long and leave late.

'I'm rather sorry you've come, you know,' Fen had pursued. 'I'm afraid you're going to be very bored with all these people.' To whose derogation this remark was intended it was impossible to tell.

Wilkes, however, who was rather deaf, was not in the least taken aback by these comments, and merely smiled benignly upon all and sundry and repeated his demand for whisky. Fen got it for him with painful reluctance, and contented himself henceforth with uttering in a penetrating whisper various slanders against the old man, to the acute embarrassment of everyone except Mrs Fen, who was apparently quite used to it and who said 'Now, Gervase!' in an objurgatory but automatic manner every few minutes.

It was getting dark. On one side a brief prospect of Inigo Jones, on the other the great lawn flanked with trees and flowerbeds, were melting away in shadow. On the horizon, three searchlights began to form their complex trigonometrical patterns. While in the quadrangle below, a little clique of rowdy undergraduates were singing a student song to words not usually supplied in the printed versions.

Sir Richard Freeman coughed disapprovingly as Fen became launched on his logomachy; he had heard it all before. But Fen was oblivious to such mild innuendoes, and proceeded with irrepressible verve to enlarge on his ideas.

'As I always tell you, Dick,' he was saying, 'detection and literary criticism really come to the same thing: intuition – that miserable and degraded counter of our modern pseudo-philosophies. ... However,' he went on, dismissing the intrusive digression with obvious reluctance, 'that is not the point. The point is that, to put it simply, the relation between one clue and another – I should say the nature of the relation between one

61

clue and another – occurs to your detective in exactly the same way – whether it be accelerated logic or some entirely extra-rational faculty – as the nature of the relation between, say, Ben Jonson and Dryden, occurs to the literary critic.'

He paused rather dubiously, scenting perhaps an inherent weakness in the instance, but trod hot-foot over it and returned to the safer regions of abstract peroration.

'Then once the idea has occurred to you, you can work on substantiating it from the text – or from the remainder of the clues. You get led astray occasionally, of course, but there's always logic to confirm or refute you. It follows,' he said, grinning cheerfully and shuffling his feet about, 'that although detectives aren't necessarily good literary critics' (and he waved happily at Sir Richard) 'good literary critics, if they bother to acquire the elementary technical equipment required in police work' (here Sir Richard groaned) 'are always good detectives. I'm a very good detective myself,' he concluded modestly. 'In fact I'm the only literary critic turned detective in the whole of fiction.'

The company considered this claim for a moment in silence. But any comment they might have wished to make on it was cut short by the sudden ringing of one of the telephones on Fen's desk. He bounded to his feet like a jack-in-the-box and strode exuberantly across to it. The rest sat with that half embarrassment which comes from being compelled to listen to a private telephone conversation. Wilkes began singing the opening theme of Strauss's *Heldenleben*, which took him through three and a half octaves and resulted in the most extraordinary series of sounds. A ghostly echo, of a wireless or gramophone, carried on with it from somewhere outside, and it occurred to Nigel that Wilkes was not very deaf if he could hear that. Through the din Fen's voice was heard apostrophizing the instrument:

'Who? . . . Yes, certainly. Send him over straight away.' He put down the receiver and returned rubbing his hands excitedly. 'That was the lodge,' he announced. 'Robert Warner the playwright is coming up to see me. It will be nice to have the opportunity of hearing just what he feels like when he's writing, and how he sets about it.'

A general groan of dismay went up; Fen's habit of cross-examining reluctant people about their jobs was not one of his more agreeable characteristics.

'We literary critics must get down to fundamentals, you know,' he added. Then his eye fell on Wilkes, and he said wistfully: 'Would you like to go now, Wilkes? I'm afraid you'll find it a bit beyond you.'

'No, I would not like to go,' replied the aged Wilkes with sudden asperity. 'I have only just arrived. For heaven's sake sit down, man,' he squeaked, 'and stop fidgeting about.'

This so abashed Fen that he sat down and openly sulked until, a few moments later, Robert Warner came in.

He greeted Nigel pleasantly and was introduced to the others, preserving a remarkable *sang-froid* while Fen bustled about finding him a chair and a drink and offering him a box of cigarettes, half of which he dropped all over the floor. When they had finished helping him pick them up they were all very breathless and red in the face, and sat in silence for a moment. This was unexpectedly broken by Wilkes saying in a determined voice:

'I am now going to tell you a ghost story.'

'No, no!' cried Fen, starting up in alarm. 'That's really not necessary, Wilkes. We can, I hope, succeed in keeping the conversation going without that.'

'I think it will be of interest,' Wilkes went on inexorably, 'not only because it concerns this college, but because it happens to be true. Furthermore, unlike the majority of true ghost stories, it is interesting and even a little thrilling. But of course if it will bore you – ' He stared blandly about the gathering.

'Certainly it won't bore us,' said Sir Richard, attracting to himself a baleful glance from Fen. 'Personally, I need a little relaxation.' He yawned. 'I feel sleepy.'

'We all do,' said Nigel, and added hastily: 'need a little relaxation.'

'Then it will be agreeable to you if I go ahead?' asked Wilkes.

Vague murmurs, quite undistinguishable.

'You are quite sure none of you object?'

More murmurs, perhaps vaguer.

'Very well then. To a limited extent, this narrative is based on my own experience. I was an undergraduate at the time – towards the close of the last century – and although the minor furore which the affair caused was kept very close indeed, I knew personally several of the people concerned. There were, of course, no Societies for Physical Research in those days, that is to say that although Sidgwick and Myers did start one in 1882, it had little credit – and I have the impression that if any investigation along those lines had been attempted, crucifixes and pentagrams notwithstanding, it could have done little but make a bad business into a worse one. As it was, the President of that time, Sir Arthur Hobbes, took the commonsense view and did the commonsense thing; though whether we succeeded in shutting it in again I suppose we shall never know. Certainly nothing of the same kind has happened since, but somewhere or other there may be a jack-in-the-box waiting for someone to slip the catch a second – no, a third, – time.'

He paused, and Nigel looked quickly round at the others. Fen, who had begun by fidgeting, was now immobile; Sir Richard lay back with his eyes closed and his hands folded; Robert was listening attentively and smoking, but Nigel had the impression that a corner of his mind was occupied with more important things; Mrs Fen was bent over her knitting. Wilkes went on:

'It began when they pulled down a wall in the antechapel, which, as you know, is situated at the north-east corner of the chancel in our college chapel. The whole of the chapel was restored at that time by a not incompetent architect from London, and eventually left as we have it now. Certainly at the time the fabric was extremely unsound, and could not be left, and on the whole there was little damage done to the original beauty of the building. In any case there was a certain up-and-coming spirit in those days which a little puts to shame our frantic and endless modern attempts at preservation – symbolic, no doubt, of our consciousness of our inability to create new forms of art – and I don't think any of the Fellows or the chapel committee objected to the renovations, with the exception of old Dr Beddoes, who objected to everything as a matter of habit and was easily enough overruled.

'The history of the college buildings is poorly documented,

and we had always been under the impression that the ante-chapel had been added by one of our Presidents under Charles I as a burial place for himself and his very numerous family. Substantially this proved to be correct, except that the ante-chapel turned out to be a rebuilding, in part, of an older place, possibly the robing-room of the Benedictine monks whose monastery originally stood on this site, and of which a few fragments still survive in the north quadrangle and the chapel. At all events, the removal of the facing from the north wall of the antechapel – which came down, the workmen said, with almost alarming ease once a start had been made on it – disclosed a much older wall, with a single rough stone slab set in the centre, and which could hardly have been later in date than 1300. Of course this caused a great deal of excitement, and people interested in such things came from all over Oxford to look at it, though the Chaplain, who was holding services in the nave during the restorations, was heard to complain that something or other had succeeded in making the chapel extremely damp, and indeed went down with bronchitis a day later, so that the services had to be taken by the President, and he was so unused to it that as often as not the liturgy and the thirty-fourth article went completely by the board.

'The slab of which I have spoken had been inset a good deal later than the construction of the wall, and had on it four brief inscriptions – or rather three inscriptions and a later addition in indelible chalk or ink. First of all there was the date – 1556 – which showed it to have been erected about the time of the martyrdoms. Then a single name: Johannes Kettenburgus. The librarian, who was fairly well up in the college records, easily traced a reference to one John Kettenburgh, a student of the college from 1554, who had been an enthusiastic supporter of the Reformation party, and who, as far as could be judged from a somewhat guarded contemporary document, had been hunted through the college by a band of infuriated townsmen and fellow-students – he must have publicized his views rather too aggressively – and beaten to death against one of the chapel walls. You can have a look at the document any time you like, though of course it's locked away now. What happened to the delinquents it doesn't say, but presumably in the circumstances there was little in the way of reprisals. And one supposes the slab was set up as soon as the Anglican reforms were finally established, though there is no mention of that either.'

He paused again, and Nigel suddenly had a sickeningly vivid picture of a young man crouching like a hunted animal by the wall of the antechapel, of the breaking of the bones in his wrists and fingers, and of the final blow which smashed a corner of the skull and drove its jagged edge into his brain. Despite the warmth of the evening, he felt suddenly cold, and was glad of the comforting pressure of the broad armchair against his back.

'But it was the third inscription which was the most interesting,' Wilkes continued. 'It consisted simply of the words *"Quaeram dum inveniam"*, which means, I suppose, "I shall seek until I find it". While the fourth, scrawled on in a much later hand, and apparently in a great hurry, was *"Cave ne exeat".'*

' "Do not let it get out",' said Nigel.

'Exactly. Who, or why, not specified, you notice, though later we had some suspicions of the answer to the first question. There was a good deal of excited speculation about the inscriptions, but no one could come to any definite conclusion, except that it seemed fairly obvious that the facing of the wall had been down once before and that the fourth inscription had been added on that occasion, before it was put back again. A Fellow of Magdalen, who was an expert on such things, identified the writing – from the formation of the letters and the material used, the details of which I can't for the moment remember – as being of the eighteenth century; and the librarian spent what little spare time he had in going through the not inconsiderable mass of documents and account books relating to that period.

'Nothing much happened for a day or two, except that the workmen showed an unaccountable repugnance for working in the antechapel, and one of the Decani boys had hysterics during the Venite one morning, for no very good reason that he was afterwards able to remember, and had to be taken out. Also the plaster dust which had been created by the demolitions showed little inclination to settle, although there was next to no draught in the chapel, and hung about in miniature fogs and clouds, seeming to get thicker and more obtrusive every day, so that the emergency services had to be given up altogether; much to the disgust of the Chaplain, who had formed his own opinions on the matter, and who announced from his sickbed that they had had at least a preventive value; but he was politely ignored.

'We come then to Mr Archer, the Dean, an estimable man very much in the intellectual vanguard of his time, which vanguard consisted of an uncompromising adherence to rationalism, and a concomitant admiration of men such as Spencer, Darwin, "B.V.", and William Morris. His favourite reading, I imagine, was Gibbon on Christianity and the more solemn parts of Voltaire, and not unnaturally he had shown little interest, one way or the other, in the restoration of the chapel, only remarking, *sotto voce*, that he would not consider it any great loss if they knocked it down altogether. It seems that one evening (I only had this at second hand, from a don who was an intimate of his) he sat up late reading, and after knocking out his pipe preparatory for bed, put out his light and looked out of the window into the garden beyond. It was a windless night, with a few clouds and a pale, anaemic moon (to which, I believe, he quoted the appropriate lines from Shelley), and at once something unusual about the aspect of the place struck him. When questioned later, he could only say that he had the impression of a furious *search*. All over the garden, bushes seemed thrust aside as if by a sudden gust of wind, and his eye, fascinated and horrified, traced an irregular movement from one to another – as of someone darting between them – which was too methodical and purposive to be at all pleasant. It is fairly obvious that he was, for the moment, badly frightened, and it is much to his credit that he stayed where he was rather than go and find more agreeable company than whatever was in the garden. After a few minutes his obstinacy was rewarded. He saw a dark figure emerge from the bushes at the further end of the great lawn, peer about it, and begin to run at a tremendous pace towards the college. As the figure drew nearer, he saw that it was Parks, the undergraduate who was organ scholar at the time, and that his face was distorted with fear. He gained the buildings in safety, however, and when Archer looked up again the garden seemed restored to normal, and nothing was moving; only out of the corner of his eye he thought he caught a glimpse of something white lying by the south side of the chapel, where it looks on to the garden. But when, with some reluctance, he put his head out of the window to observe it more closely, he saw that if there had been anything there at all, it was now gone.

'Well now, what was to be done? It was past one o'clock, and quite evidently Parks had been using the less normal means of entry to the college supplied by the tall, crenellated wall at the bottom of the garden. And a disciplinary reproach on the spot, as it were, would provide an excuse for discovering what had frightened him so. I ought perhaps to mention that this was the Dean's room at that time, and that then as now, the room below this, which Fellowes has, was occupied by the organ scholar.'

Fen grunted. Nigel looked quickly out of the window at which Archer must have stood, fifty years ago or more, and felt less comfortable than he would have believed possible. The room was very dark now, yet no one suggested turning on the lights. He very much wished someone would.

'Anyway, Archer went down to see Parks, and, to cut a long story short, found him pale and shaken, but with something of his confidence restored. He admitted quite openly that he had stayed late at a beer party and had come in over the wall. But when pressed as to what it was that had disturbed him he became a good deal less coherent and seemed very little inclined to speak of it. It seems that he had climbed the outside of the wall without any special difficulty (Archer made a mental note to see about this), but that on jumping from the top of it into the garden he had found himself almost in the arms of something which was waiting for him there, and of which he could say no more than that there had been bones and teeth, that a number of these appeared to be broken, and that it had moved shamblingly, dragging one leg behind it. This, he supposed, was why it had been unable to catch up with him; though Archer, who had watched the searching, was inclined to make a private reservation on this point.

'The long and the short of it was that Archer went back to

bed again, a little worried at leaving Parks alone for the night and not too pleased at being alone himself, but convinced that the encounter was a chance one and that for the moment, at any rate, there was nothing more to be feared. He read a chapter of Bradlaugh before putting out his light, but it failed to give him his usual satisfaction, and sleep came with difficulty. The next morning Parks proved to be still sound in wind and limb, and even a little uppish about his adventure, since in the circumstances the Dean had thought it unwise to penalize him in any way. Late that same evening, however, a terrible screaming was heard from his room. Naturally, help was forthcoming immediately, with Archer well in the van, but it was too late. They found him lying with his head battered in, though of weapon there was no trace.'

'Good God!' said Sir Richard. 'Murder!'

'If you care to call it that, yes. It seems that all of his cries which were distinguishable consisted of the one word "*arce*", which if my memory serves me right is the latin for "keep it off". And in fact all those who had heard him were agreed on this one word, though why he should have spoken in latin, faced with what he had been faced with, no one could imagine, since he was not even a classical scholar. It could only be supposed that he had been impressed by the inscriptions found in the chapel – and in fact he had shown a keen interest in them – and that after his adventure of the night before he had thought of the phrase as a kind of talisman in case another such meeting should take place. It was, I think, established that the word does play an important part in a goetic ritual of exorcism, and he may have imagined it would be of some use, though heaven knows, it let him down badly enough.'

'Was anything ever discovered?' inquired Nigel.

'Naturally there was a police investigation, but nothing came of it, and the coroner's jury returned a verdict of murder by person or persons unknown.'

'And what is your opinion?'

Wilkes shrugged. 'I tend to be of the opinion of the college authorities. After only a very brief consultation, they ordered the wall to be covered up again, which was very quickly done, and the anonymous eighteenth-century warning transferred to a little plaque on the outside, which is there now. The librarian, by the way, discovered a brief record of the earlier demolition – made to facilitate the erection of a tomb – and it appears that apart from the actual death something of the same sort happened then. I asked the Chaplain, a man who had a healthy respect for the foul fiend as well as his more normal preoccupation with Omnipotence, what he thought the object of the search was. "There is a reference in the Bible," he said shortly, "to one who goes about seeking what he may devour", but refused to pursue the matter further. I think his Anglican soul was shocked at the thought that an early member of his persuasion should have turned sour, as it were.'

'And nothing further occurred?' asked Robert.

'Nothing, except that to everyone's surprise the Dean began to attend chapel, and ended his life, I believe, a staunch churchman. Oh, there is one thing which perhaps I should have mentioned: in the document which gives the account of the killing of John Kettenburgh, the ringleader is mentioned as being one Richard Pegwell, who was organist at the time. But whether that has any bearing on the matter I couldn't say.'

They sat in silence while Fen did the black-out and turned on the lights. Robert slipped up to him and made a whispered inquiry as to the whereabout of the nearest lavatory.

'Bottom of the stairs on the right, my dear fellow. You will come back, won't you?'

'Of course. I shan't be a moment.' Robert nodded and slipped out.

'A very pleasant story,' said Sir Richard. 'Or, conversely, a very unpleasant story. What did you think of it, Mrs Fen? I'm sure you're the most sensible one of us here.'

'I thought it was a good story,' said Mrs Fen, 'and very well told, Mr Wilkes. But it sounded, if you'll forgive me, a little too neat and artificial to be true. As Mr Wilkes said, real ghosts appear to be tedious and unenterprising, though I'm sure I've never come across one myself, and never want to.' She resumed her knitting.

Fen gazed at her with something of the triumphant and sentimental pride of a dog-owner whose pet has succeeded in balancing a biscuit on its nose.

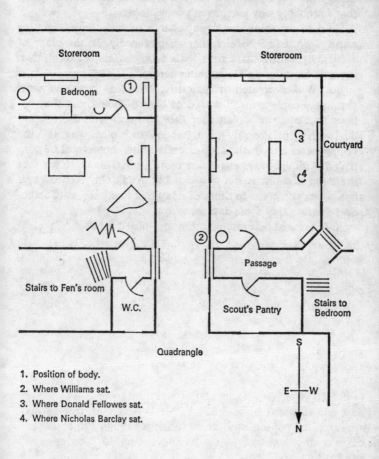

Gardens

Storeroom

Bedroom

① ⃞

Storeroom

Courtyard

③

④

② ○

Passage

Stairs to Fen's room

W.C.

Scout's Pantry

Stairs to Bedroom

Quadrangle

S

E — W

N

1. Position of body.
2. Where Williams sat.
3. Where Donald Fellowes sat.
4. Where Nicholas Barclay sat.

'Exactly my opinion!' he said. Then somewhat suspiciously: 'By the way, Wilkes, how is it I've never heard this story before? You haven't been making it up, have you?'

Rather to Nigel's surprise, Wilkes shook his head. 'No,' he said, 'I haven't been making it up. There are still a few people alive who can confirm it. As I say, it was kept pretty quiet; that's probably why you haven't come across it.'

'And do you think there's any chance of the – thing's – getting out again?' asked Nigel rather shamefacedly. In the blaze of electric light the remark sounded a good deal more foolish than it would have done a few minutes before.

But Wilkes treated it seriously. 'Not in the same way, perhaps. People are still scared of bags of bones, but they believe that one way or another they can understand them and deal with them. Possibly it will happen some other way. It is the killing, after all, which is the essential thing, however it be contrived. Killing always engenders more killing, that is to say that the debit account is never wiped off. And John Kettenburgh has, when you come to think of it, a great many scores to settle. So I dare say that some day, somehow – '

And it was at that moment that they heard the shot.

6. Farewell Earth's Bliss

The nudity of flesh will blush though tameless,
The extreme nudity of bone grins shameless,
The unsexed skeleton mocks shroud and pall.

Thomson

The room had grown so quiet that for a moment the noise of it
seemed deafening. It was only when Nigel had recovered from
his initial stupefaction that he realized it had come from below
– Donald Fellowes' room. In conjunction with the story they
had been hearing it was not an inspiriting sound. Even the
phlegmatic Sir Richard sat up sharply. He said:

'Is that some of your fool undergraduates messing about,
Fen?'

'If it is,' said Fen, rising in a determined manner, 'they're
going to hear about it. You wait here, dear,' he said to his wife,
'and I'll go and find out what's happened.'

'I'll come with you,' said Sir Richard.

'Me, too,' said Nigel ungrammatically.

Fen's wife nodded, and went on with her knitting. Wilkes said
nothing, but stared absently at the dying embers of the fire. As
they left the room, looking, as Nigel said afterwards, very determined and grim, Sir Richard took out his watch and turned to
Nigel.

'What do you make the time?' he said.

'8.24 exactly,' said Nigel after a brief glance at his own.

'Right. We've been about a minute so far. 8.23 is near
enough.'

'Aren't you anticipating rather?' asked Nigel.

'It's as well to know,' said the other briefly. And they followed Fen down the stairs.

At the bottom they met Robert Warner, who was coming out
of the lavatory with a ludicrously anxious expression on his
face.

'What on earth was that din?' he inquired. 'Sounded like a
shot to me.'

73

'That's what we're going to find out,' said Fen. 'I think I'm right in saying it came from in here.'

The door of the sitting-room on their left, which had the inscription 'Mr D. A. Fellowes' in white over the top, was ajar. Fen pushed it open and they all followed him in. The room presented nothing of particular interest. Like most college rooms, it was scantily furnished, and the only unusual feature was a grand piano to the right of the doorway. To the left was a screen, intended presumably to trap draughts, which as Nigel well remembered tend to be numerous in the majority of college rooms, but a cursory glance failed to discover anyone or anything concealed behind it. Over by the far window, on the right, was a small flat-topped desk; a table with one or two uncomfortable chairs stood in the middle of a threadbare carpet; and the fireplace, over on the left, was flanked by a couple of chintz-covered armchairs. The only other item of furniture was an enormous bookcase, which contained on one of its shelves a few lonely looking volumes and on another a large pile of music, hymn-books, anthems and services. The walls, which were disagreeably panelled in dark oak, were scarcely relieved by a few very small reproductions of modern paintings, and in the dusk the general effect was one of profound gloom. But the room was typical of many such, and as it had no occupant, Donald Fellowes or any other, Nigel gave it no more than a brief glance, and hurried on after Fen and Sir Richard to the door in the wall opposite, which led to the bedroom.

This also was ajar, and entering, they found themselves in a cold, comfortless, coffin-shaped room, furnished even more sparsely than the sitting-room they had just left. But for the moment they had eyes for none of the details.

For beside the doorway stood a man, looking down at Yseut Haskell, who lay on the floor with a black hole in the centre of her forehead, and the whole of the top part of her face blackened and scorched.

Like most people, Nigel had often tried to imagine how he would feel in the presence of violent death. Like most people, he had thought of himself as being calm, collected, almost indifferent. So the conscious part of him was totally unprepared for the sudden acute spasm of nausea which seized him at the sight of that motionless, lifeless form. He went quickly back to the sitting-room, and sat down with his face in his hands. Through the uncontrollable whirl of his thoughts and suspicions, he heard Sir Richard say, with a politeness which he remembered thinking excessive:

'Will you please tell me who you are and what you're doing here?'

It was a sensible homely voice which replied.

'Yessir, o' course, and the Professor here'll confirm what I say. Me name's Joe Williams, an' I bin workin' on repairin' the stonework in the archway opposite there. I was jest downin' tools an' makin' ready to be orf 'ome, when I 'ears that bloody racket – beggin' your pardon – and 'ops in 'ere quick as lightnin' to investigate. Must a' bin only a minute afore you gentlemen.'

'You haven't touched anything, have you?'

The voice replied with some scorn:

'Not likely. But I 'ad a good dekko round this room, and the other, and there ain't no one 'idin' in either of them, unless in that wardrobe there. An' you can be sure I kep' me eye on *that*. No one's come art o' this room since I bin 'ere. That's right, ain't it, Professor?'

'Williams is all right, Dick,' said Fen. 'He's been employed in the college for years on odd jobs about the place, and I don't think he's liable to fits of homicidal mania.'

'Not me.'

'Turn on the light, Fen,' said Sir Richard.

'Black-out,' said Fen gloomily.

'Oh, blast the black-out. We mustn't touch anything.'

'Black-out none the less.'

'Oh, very well.' Nigel heard the sound of curtains being drawn over the single window, and a shaft of light cut into the sitting-room from the half-open door. He pulled himself together abruptly and went and blacked out the room, wondering as he did so whether he were likely to be destroying valuable evidence.

From inside the bedroom Sir Richard was saying: 'Well, I must get on to the station before I do anything else. Where's the nearest telephone?'

'My room,' Fen replied. 'The lodge will put you through. You'd better tell Wilkes and my wife what's happened, but don't let them come down here. Tell Dolly if she likes to wait a while I'll be up as soon as I can get away for a moment. Wilkes had better go home, the old nuisance.'

'All right. Keep an eye on things while I'm away, and for God's sake don't mess about.'

'I never mess about,' said Fen in a pained voice.

'Williams, you'd better go across to the lodge and wait there. We shall want you for questioning later.'

'Right you are,' replied Williams cheerfully. 'Hour and a 'alf afore they close yet, anyway. P'raps you can get me over first,' he added hopefully.

'Tell Parsons on my authority to see that you get some beer from the buttery,' said Fen.

'Oh, thank you sir, I'm sure.' And Williams came out of the bedroom. He stopped as he saw Nigel and whistled. 'Well, if it isn't Mr Blake! 'Ow are you, sir, after all this time? Very glad to see you again, I'm sure.'

'I'm fine, Williams, thank you. And you?'

'Might be worse, sir, might be worse. Just able to sit up and take nourishment, as you might say.' Then, lowering his voice: 'Nasty business, this, sir. Pretty young thing, too. Friend of Mr Fellowes. I seen 'er come in 'ere several times afore. Only twenty minutes ago she come in 'ere, and 'er give me a "good evening" pretty as you like.'

'You saw her come in? That may be important.'

'No doubt about it, sir, no doubt about it. Still, mustn't talk about the case before the police get at it, I s'pose. Not that they'll 'ave much of a job. It's suicide, plain as mustard.'

'Do you think so?'

'What else can it be? No one come in or out o' this room for last 'alf hour except 'er. An' she couldn't 'a bin shot through the winder, 'cos it was shut when I arrived.'

Nigel felt a profound feeling of relief sweep over him. 'I'm glad of that, anyway,' he said. 'It means no one else is involved.'

'Ar, that's right. But what could 'ave induced 'er to do such a thing, I should like to know? Such a pretty, polite girl, I always thought, without a care in the world as one could tell. Well, I must be getting along. See you later, sir, I've no doubt.' He saluted and went out, his heavy boots clumping down the steps and into the quadrangle.

One man at least has retained his illusions about Yseut, thought Nigel bitterly. There must be few of her acquaintance who would be sorry to hear her dead. He wondered where Donald was, and how he would take the news. Then he went and joined the others, though for the moment he carefully refrained from looking again at the body.

Fen and Sir Richard were engaged in a brief muttered colloquy. Robert Warner stood nearby, looking about him with an air of methodical concentration. It was almost with a sense of shock that Nigel realized his presence. They had come in together less than five minutes ago, but the shock of seeing Yseut had driven everything else from his mind. He ventured to look again at the body, and was relieved to find that his first sickness did not return.

Sir Richard turned to Robert. 'I don't want to detain you, Mr Warner,' he said.

'I'm so sorry,' Robert replied. 'Of course you don't want a lot of people hanging around. It was only that – well, this has come as such a shock, and that I feel – well, responsible for the girl, in a way.'

'You know who she is?' said Sir Richard sharply.

'Oh, yes. Her name is Yseut Haskell, and she's an actress at the Repertory Theatre here.'

'I see,' said Sir Richard more cordially. 'In that case, no doubt you'll be able to help us. But I'd be glad if you didn't stop here. Perhaps you wouldn't mind waiting in Fen's room for a bit – I can't do anything until the local people arrive. If you smoke his cigarettes and drink his whisky I'm sure he won't mind.'

'No, no, make yourself at home,' said Fen vaguely. He was wandering about the room staring glumly at the furniture. 'These rooms are damp,' he added. 'Something ought to be done about them. I'll speak to the Domestic Bursar.'

'And Mr Blake –' said Sir Richard, turning to Nigel.

'Oh, don't send Nigel away,' Fen interrupted. 'I want him to stand guard with me. I suppose,' he continued rather wistfully, 'that I'm to be allowed to help?'

Sir Richard grinned. 'By all means. But I don't think you'll have much detecting to do in this case. Suicide is the obvious verdict.'

'Yes?' said Fen, looking at him curiously. 'I'll keep an eye on things, just the same, if you don't mind.'

'Just as you like. I must go and phone. Don't let anyone in.' And he went off upstairs with Robert.

Now for the first time Nigel had leisure to look about him. Yseut was lying on her side, with her legs bent up under her, her left arm pinioned under her, and the right flung out with palm upwards. Near it lay a heavy, blue-metal revolver, and on one of the fingers was a ring of curious design. She was wearing a dark brown coat and a green skirt, brown shoes and silk stockings, but was apparently without hat or gloves or bag. She lay in front of a chest of drawers, one of whose drawers was open with the contents untidily displayed, and on which lay a hand-mirror, a brush and comb and an expensive-looking bottle of hair-lotion. The rest of the room offered little to Nigel's inexperienced eye. There was a bed, a wash-stand and a wardrobe, a rug beside the bed, a bedside table with a lamp, a book and an ashtray containing one or two stale cigarette stubs, and several odd shoes were scattered about the floor. A shirt had been tossed carelessly on to the chair at the foot of the bed. The smell of gunpowder still hung on the air. The window, apparently, was shut, but at the moment that could not be investigated.

So Nigel turned his attention back to what was left of Yseut. It was curious, he thought, how completely death had drained her of personality. And yet not curious: for her personality had centred entirely on her sex, and now that life was gone, that too had vanished, leaving her a neuter, an uninteresting construction of clay, suddenly pathetic. She *had been* an attractive girl. But that 'had been' was not a conventional gesture to the fact of death. It was an honest admission that without life the most beautiful body is an object of no interest. We are not bodies, thought Nigel, we are lives. And oddly, there came to him at that moment a new and firm conviction of the nature of love.

He looked again; remembered Yseut singing and dancing; remembered Helen's 'She's not bad, you know; just silly'; and with all his heart, and despite the discomfort she had caused, wished her alive again.

> 'Ay, but to die, and go we know not where;
> To lie in cold obstruction and to rot . . .'

Just as for Claudio the fact of virginity had been nothing compared with the fact of death, so for Nigel all other considerations paled beside it. . . . He shook himself irritably; this was not a time for literary quotation. If Yseut had been murdered. . . . He looked inquiringly at Fen, but that expert, guessing the unspoken question, merely said non-committally: 'It looks like suicide', and continued his perplexed examination of the floor round the body.

Sir Richard came back rubbing his hands together. 'Your wife is going to wait,' he told Fen. 'She's talking to Warner at the moment. And I've managed to pack old Wilkes off to his room. The police are going to be here as soon as they can get, which will put an end, officially, to my responsibility, thank heaven.'

Fen nodded. Then said abruptly: 'Where on earth is that noise coming from? Nigel, go and tell them to shut it off.'

Nigel realized that 'The Hero's Works of Peace' were being trumpeted forth on the evening air, apparently from the room opposite. He had forgotten about the radio he had heard earlier in the evening. He went across and tapped on the door; then, being convinced that if there was a reply he would never hear it above the din, walked straight in.

He was more than surprised to discover that the two occupants of the room were Donald Fellowes and Nicholas Barclay. They were sitting in armchairs by the fire, listening to a radio which stood on a table beside them. Nigel stopped short on seeing them, and Nicholas performed an elaborate pantomime to demand silence, but Nigel waved him impatiently aside.

'Yseut's dead,' he said with unnecessary abruptness, and added to Donald: 'In your room. And for God's sake turn that thing off. I can't hear myself speak.' Nicholas turned it off. 'Well, well, well!' was his only comment.

Donald sat silent. He showed no reaction at all that Nigel could see, except to go a little pale. 'How do you mean, dead?' he muttered. 'And why in my room?'

'She's been shot in the head.'

'Murdered?' asked Nicholas, and added callously: 'Can't say I'm surprised. Did you do it, Donald?' he inquired with interest.

'No, damn you, I didn't.'

'The indications,' said Nigel, 'point to suicide.'

Donald showed his first sign of genuine emotion. 'Suicide?' he queried.

'You seem to be surprised.'

Donald went red and stammered. 'I – well – she wasn't well liked, you know. And she didn't seem the sort to – kill herself.' He suddenly buried his face in his hands. 'Oh God!' he said.

Nigel felt uncomfortable and at a loss as to what to say.

'I suppose I ought to come across,' said Donald after a moment.

'You can please yourself about that, I imagine. It's your room. And no doubt the police will want to ask you some questions when they arrive.'

'Oh!' said Nicholas. 'So they're not here yet? When did this happen?'

'About ten minutes ago. Sir Richard Freeman is in charge at the moment, and Fen's helping him.'

Nicholas pursed his lips and looked solemn. 'The college's tame detective, eh? So they think it's suicide. Ten minutes ago; that must have been the noise we heard, Donald. But the Battle section was making such an infernal row that we didn't take any notice; and you said it was only a group of second-year men fooling about. Do you think they'll want to see me?' he asked Nigel. 'Or can I go home?'

'I imagine that sooner or later they'll want to see everyone who had any connection with Yseut. So you may as well stay.'

'I shan't go back,' said Donald suddenly. 'I – don't – want – to – see –'

'All right, laddie,' said Nicholas. 'We'll stop here and console one another. And if either of us tries to do a bunk for the next boat-train to Ostend, the other can stop him. See you later, Nigel.'

Nigel nodded and went out. The reactions of both of them, he thought, had been typical: Nicholas' flippancy was habitual. He was struck, though, by the lack of surprise with which they had received the news. It was almost as though they had been expecting it.

He found Fen and Sir Richard in the sitting-room, endeavouring to keep up a pretence of activity, though until the doctor and the fingerprint and photograph people had got finished, there was practically nothing they could do. Nigel told them of the whereabouts of Nicholas and Donald, and Sir Richard, after a few questions concerning their identity and their connection with Yseut, nodded his approval of the arrangement he had made.

'We can't possibly keep an eye on everyone,' he said, 'and if anyone other than the girl herself is responsible, they'd be mad to try and clear out.'

A quarter of an hour later the police arrived, and were made *au fait* with the situation. The Inspector, an alert, sharp-eyed little man with a harsh voice, called Cordery, asked the ordinary pertinent questions and took a brief look round. Then he went into conference with Sir Richard, while the Sergeants who dealt with fingerprints and photography went about their business. The police surgeon, a tall, laconic, deep-voiced man, made a cursory inspection of the body and then waited patiently for them to finish.

'You'd better fingerprint anything likely,' the Inspector had said. 'For the moment, of course, we shan't have anything except the girl's prints for purposes of comparison.'

The doctor's preliminary report was brief and to the point. 'Death anything from twenty minutes to half an hour ago,' he announced. 'Cause of death the obvious one, unless there are any poisons unknown to science lurking around. The bullet's presumably lodged somewhere at the back of the cerebellum. Angle of penetration about horizontal, I should say. Can't tell you any more until I've had a proper look – and of course there'll have to be a P.M.'

Nigel, who had stood for a minute or two watching one of the Sergeants playing about with insufflator powder, camel-hair brushes, plates of glass and unpleasant-smelling ointments, became quickly bored, and wandered back to talk to Fen.

The change in Fen, he told himself, was astonishing. His usual slightly fantastic naivety had completely disappeared, and its place was taken by a rather formidable, ice-cold concentration. Sir Richard, who knew the signs, looked up from his conference with the Inspector and sighed. At the opening of an investigation, the mood was invariable, as always when Fen was concentrating particularly hard; when he was not interested in what was going on, he relapsed into an excessively irritating form of boisterous gaiety; when he had discovered anything of importance, he 'quickly became melancholy', after the manner of the young lady whose folly induced her to sit on a holly; and when an investigation was finally concluded, he became sunk in such a state of profound gloom that it was days before he could be aroused from it. Moreover these perverse and chameleon-like habits tended not unnaturally to get on people's nerves.

The fingerprint Sergeant put his head out of the bedroom door. 'What about the window, sir?' he said addressing the company at large with a fine impartiality. 'Am I to do that?'

'Yes, Sergeant,' said Sir Richard. 'We can't leave it all night for anyone to mess about with. Never mind the black-out – there isn't an alert, and I'll take the responsibility – but get finished as quickly as you can.'

'Right you are, sir,' said the Sergeant, and disappeared again. A moment later a flood of light went up into the heavens. A passing Free French pilot shook his head mournfully. 'Le black-out anglais,' he said to himself with the air of one whose worst suspicions have been confirmed.

It was not long before the fingerprinting was finished, and the doctor went back to make a second and more detailed examination. Before he went, however, Fen crossed the room and said something to him in a low voice. The doctor looked inquiringly at Sir Richard.

'That's all right, Henderson,' said Sir Richard. 'The Professor is helping us over the case.'

The doctor nodded and disappeared into the bedroom; the

82

second examination did not take him long. 'Not much to add,' he said when he emerged again. 'Slight abrasions on the left buttock and the left side of the head, caused presumably by the fall. Nothing else that I can see for the moment.' He turned to Fen. 'And you were quite right. The tendons of both knees are badly strained.'

The Inspector looked sharply at Fen, but for the moment refrained from comment.

'Oh, and there's one other thing; I don't know whether you noticed it,' the doctor continued. 'The ring on the fourth finger of the right hand is jammed over the knuckle, rather as if it had been put on after death; though what could induce anyone to do such a thing I can't imagine. It makes the idea of suicide a bit doubtful, you know. People don't go about wearing their rings in an uncomfortable position like that.'

The Inspector grunted. 'Go and take it off, Spencer,' he said to the Sergeant. 'It may be useful. You've tested it for prints, I suppose?'

'Yes, sir. Nothing, I'm afraid.' Spencer went into the bedroom.

'That in itself is odd,' said the Inspector. 'The girl's left-hand prints should be on it if she put it on. However, we'll cross that bridge when we come to it.'

'With all due deference to that well-worn metaphor,' said Fen, 'I have never quite been able to see how you can cross a bridge before you come to it,' and attracted to himself a malignant glare from the Inspector.

'If you've finished all your flapdoodle,' said the doctor, though it was not at all clear to what exactly he was referring, 'will it be all right for me to take the girl away?'

Fen and Sir Richard and the Inspector looked inquiringly at one another, but no one raised any objection, and Fen appeared to have lost interest in the proceedings altogether.

'Yes, take her away,' said the Inspector wearily. And the doctor went out, to return with two constables and a stretcher, on which the body was deposited and borne out to a waiting ambulance.

In the meantime, Sergeant Spencer had returned with the ring, which he laid on the table in front of the Inspector, and at which they all gazed with some interest. It was a heavy, gilt affair of some size, the oval set with a curious, formalized pattern representing some kind of insect with wings.

'Looks Egyptian to me,' said the Inspector. 'It's not gold, I suppose?' he inquired generally.

'No, gilded,' said Nigel. 'Not of much value, I imagine.'

'I think it is Egyptian,' said Fen, 'or, at any rate, an imitation of an Egyptian model. I can easily find out if you think it's important,' – his expression indicated that he did not – 'because the Professor of Egyptology is a Fellow here, and I think he's in college tonight. At all events he was in hall.'

'It might be as well, sir,' said the Inspector. 'If the ring proves not to have belonged to Miss Haskell, we shall have to try and trace it, you know,'

'Um. Yes,' said Fen dubiously. 'Nigel, go and see if you can find Burrows, will you? You know where his room is.'

Burrows was discovered without difficulty, and expressed himself delighted to assist a murder investigation in any way he could. The ring, he said, was a reproduction of a piece of jewellery of the twelfth dynasty at present in the British Museum. Asked if it was usual for such objects to be copied in modern jewellery, he replied that the question was somewhat outside his sphere, but that he imagined not, and that in any case it would be an expensive business, and would presumably have required special permission from the trustees of the Museum. The Inspector made a note of this last fact, and reflected that it would make the job of tracing the ring a good deal easier. Sir Richard, afflicted apparently by a sudden disinterested passion for knowledge, asked what sort of insect it was supposed to represent, and was told somewhat pityingly that it was a fly. On his remarking that the wings pointed forwards, and not backwards as with the majority of flies, he was further informed that as far as it was possible to judge from such a formalized representation, it was intended to be a gold-girdled fly, *chrysotoxum bicinctum*. Some reference was made at this point to the Professor of Entomology, but the Inspector, feeling that matters were getting a little out of hand, hastily brought the discussion to a close, and Burrows retired amid expressions of thanks, looking intensely pleased with himself.

A sort of round-table conference, involving an initial summing-up of the case, now took place. And the next object to which they turned their attention was the gun.

'Well now, Spencer,' said the Inspector, leaning back in his chair with a sigh, 'what about fingerprints?'

But Nigel interrupted before the Sergeant could speak. 'I think,' he said, 'I can tell you where the gun came from.' And he recounted the incident at the party, and his discovery that the gun was missing. 'Of course,' he concluded, 'I've no means of telling for certain whether that's the same one, but if you get on to the owner he'll know.'

'Ah, thank you, sir,' said the Inspector. 'That's very helpful – very helpful indeed. Although,' he added somewhat suspiciously, 'I don't quite see what made you go back to see if the gun was gone.'

Nigel felt somewhat ridiculous, and thanked his stars that he had a cast iron alibi for the time of the murder. He muttered something about an impulse.

'A sudden impulse – quite so,' said the Inspector, making an unnecessary note on the subject. 'We all act from such impulses upon occasion,' he continued pedantically, with the air of one who has propounded a metaphysical theory of startling originality and importance. 'Now, what time would it have been when you went back and found that the gun was gone?'

'Let's see now – I left Nicholas in the corridor about 1.30,' said Nigel. 'And I can't have spent more than ten minutes or so undressing. Say 1.40.'

'1.40 a.m. approximately,' repeated the Inspector, making another note. 'And the name of the owner of the gun – the gentleman who gave the party?'

'Captain Peter Graham.'

'Ah, yes. Elbow!' the Inspector called to the constable on duty at the door. 'Ring up the "Mace and Sceptre", will you, and ask Captain Graham if he'd be so kind as to step over here some time during the evening, as soon as he can conveniently manage.' Elbow vanished on this mission. 'Now, Spencer,' said the Inspector, relaxing again. 'The fingerprints.'

'Yes, sir. A few old prints on the barrel and chambers, which of course I haven't been able to identify. Nothing on the cartridges. And nothing on the butt and trigger except the prints of the young lady's right hand: thumb on the trigger, fingers round the back and the right side of the butt.'

'That's a curious arrangement, isn't it?' asked Sir Richard.

'Not if you come to think of it, sir,' said the Inspector. He picked up the gun and pointed it at his forehead, holding it round the back of the butt and with his thumb on the trigger. 'Only comfortable way to hold it, really, if you're going to shoot yourself as she apparently did.'

'Were there any prints on the hammer?' asked Fen. 'Any indication that the gun had been cocked, that is?'

'Well, sir, it's a bit difficult. There's a sort of criss-cross pattern on the hammer which doesn't take prints. But I think I can safely say it hasn't been touched.' Fen nodded and became gloomy.

'Anything else in the room?' asked the Inspector.

'A lot of old marks which I suppose belong to whoever lives in here.' The Sergeant looked about him with distaste, as though he expected to see some bearded hermit, indescribably filthy, cavorting in a corner. 'The girl's prints on both doorknobs, on the drawers of the desk in here, and on the drawers of the chest of drawers by the window in the bedroom.'

'H'm. It appears she must have been looking for something. There are such things as gloves, of course,' the Inspector added rather obviously. 'But apart from the business of the ring, which I grant you is queer, it looks up to now like a pretty plain case of suicide.'

'No, no, Inspector,' said Fen, who had been gazing reflectively at an unattractive Modigliani which was hanging on the wall near him, 'I'm afraid I can't agree.'

The Inspector looked at him gloomily for a moment. Then he said: 'Well, sir?' in a longsuffering voice.

'Everything militates against it. Leaving aside for a moment the question of why the girl should have wanted to commit suicide in any case, why she didn't leave a suicide note, why she should have chosen a singularly unattractive bedroom not belonging to her to do it in, and why, moreover, she should have interrupted herself in the middle – not at the end, mind – of a particularly intensive search to do it – you remember one of the drawers was still open – '

'Well, sir,' the Inspector put in, 'isn't it possible that she came across the gun in that very drawer – we don't know who took it – and shot herself on an impulse, as it were?'

'I don't say it's impossible; but I think it's extremely unlikely. Anyway, look at the material evidence. And use your common sense,' Fen added somewhat frantically. 'Oh Lord! Look – wait a moment and I'll show you what I mean.' And he rushed out of the room and returned a minute later with his wife. After she had greeted the Inspector with a slow, pleasant smile, Fen seized up the gun and handed it to her, saying:

'Dolly, would you mind committing suicide for a moment?'

'Certainly,' Mrs Fen remained unperturbed at this alarming request, and took the gun in her right hand, with her forefinger on the trigger; then she pointed it at her right temple.

'There!' said Fen triumphantly.

'Shall I pull the trigger?' asked Mrs Fen.

'By all means,' he said absently, but Sir Richard surged up from his chair crying hoarsely: 'Don't! It's loaded!' and snatched the gun away from her. She smiled at him. 'Thank you, Sir Richard,' she said benignly, 'but Gervase is hopelessly forgetful, and I shouldn't have dreamed of doing such a thing. Is that all I can do for you gentlemen?'

The Inspector nodded dumbly, and glared at Fen, who remained unmoved by the incident.

'Very well then,' said Mrs Fen. 'In that case, Gervase, I'm going home now. Try not to be late, and don't disturb the children when you come in.' She bestowed an approving smile on each of them in turn, and went.

Fen cut Sir Richard's expostulations short by saying: 'You see what I mean? Try it with any woman you like, and they'll all do the same thing.* The other way is psychologically impossible, though I agree that abstractly one wouldn't think it so; and someone has obviously been a little too clever. Besides, look at the weight of the thing, and the comparatively big leverage you have to put on the trigger. Try and pull it when you're holding

* If the reader cares to try this experiment for himself, Fen's assertion will be found to be correct. – E.C.

the thing in the position suggested by the prints, and you'll find you have the devil of a job. And then think of yourself committing suicide in that laborious and nerve-racking manner, and you'll realize it's hopelessly improbable. The only way to eliminate the difficulty would be to cock the gun, which makes the trigger into a hair trigger. And as Spencer has told us, that simply wasn't done.'

'That's right, sir,' said Spencer, seeming to feel that something was expected of him.

'Well, sir,' said the Inspector, who was beginning to look unhappy, 'I agree with that, as far as it goes. But what else?'

'Then, of course, there's the ring. Can you in your wildest imaginings suppose that anyone is going to commit suicide with a ring in that foully uncomfortable position on the hand in which they're holding the gun? Of course not. Suicides invariably take the utmost pains to make themselves comfortable. So quite obviously, for heaven knows what purpose, someone crammed that ring on to the girl's finger after she was dead, and someone in very much of a hurry, too, if I'm not mistaken.

'And finally, there's the fact that the girl was *kneeling* when she was shot; kneeling by the chest of drawers, which as you saw is rather a low one.'

The Inspector leaned forward. 'How do you make that out?'

'Look at the position of the body, man. If she'd been standing when she was shot, one leg might have been doubled up under her by the fall, but not both of them, neatly folded up like that. And then consider the effect of the impact of a heavy-calibre bullet on a person kneeling: they'd be thrown brusquely back with the knees as pivot. I asked the doctor to see if the tendons of the knees were strained, and lo, they were. *Et voilà.*'

Nigel gaped, the Inspector looked even more unhappy, and Sir Richard nodded. 'Good for you, Gervase,' he said. 'Well, where do we go from here?'

'Accident?' suggested Nigel tentatively.

The Inspector, relieved at this fortunate manifestation of an intelligence lower than his own, regarded him with disdain.

'*Hardly*, sir,' he said. 'The bullet entered horizontally, remember. It would have to be a pretty fantastic set of circumstances.'

'If the circumstances weren't fantastic, accidents wouldn't happen,' Nigel persisted doggedly, not liking to think of the third possibility. 'People take ordinary precautions.'

'No, Nigel, it won't do,' said Fen, 'there's no evidence for it at all.' Nigel relapsed into a mild fit of sulks.

'And that,' said Sir Richard thoughtfully, 'leaves us with just one thing.'

There was an uneasy silence at his words. It was broken by the Inspector suddenly banging excitedly on the table and saying:

'But, good heavens, it can't be that either! This man Williams says that nobody followed the girl in here from outside. No one came down from your room, Professor – '

'Here, wait a minute!' Nigel interrupted. 'Someone did. Robert Warner came down here to the lavatory two or three minutes before we heard the shot.'

'Um,' was the Inspector's only reaction to this intelligence.

'Yes, exactly, Inspector,' said Sir Richard. 'No one could possibly have shot the girl and done all that faking in the half-minute or so before Williams came in, or for that matter even in the minute-and-a-half before we arrived. Besides, I'm sure Warner's alibi is genuine. I heard him pull the plug as we were coming downstairs, and he unbolted the door and came out just as we reached the bottom.'

Nigel grunted agreement.

'There was no one hidden in the room when we arrived, and even if anyone had been waiting here when the girl came in, he couldn't have got away again afterwards.'

Nigel had a third idea. 'The window,' he said, unabashed by two previous failures.

'Ye-es,' said the Inspector dubiously. 'You mean whoever did it would conceal himself in here early on, kill the girl, wait until he saw Williams coming in, and then, with the guard outside removed, as it were, pop out again. But it would be devilish risky.'

'And it still doesn't get you over the difficulty that he'd have no time to do the faking,' added Sir Richard. Nigel sighed, and ventured no further ideas.

'However,' said the Inspector, 'it's worth looking into a bit more closely. Anyone getting out of the window would certainly have left marks. Apart from that, I don't quite know – '

'Suicide,' said Sir Richard, 'we've agreed is most unlikely, because of the ring, and the fact that the girl was kneeling, and the whole business about the gun; quite apart from the problem of why she should elect to do it here. Accident practically impossible. And murder, apparently, quite impossible. So the only conclusion is – '

'The only conclusion is,' put in the Inspector, 'that the thing never happened at all. *Quia*,' he added gloomily, with a sudden recollection of his schooldays, '*absurdum est*.'

7. Assessment of Motives

Who can tell what thief or foe,
In the covert of the night,
For his prey will work my woe,
Or through wicked foul despite?

Campion

'Well,' said Sir Richard resolutely, 'that means there's something we've missed. We shall have to go ahead and find out what it is, that's all.'

The Inspector sighed. A cast-iron suicide case had vanished to the winds, and he envisaged much tedium in the near future. He merely said: 'Where do we begin, then, apart from routine investigation of times and so on, from the porter and this man Williams?'

'Investigation, like charity, begins at home,' said Fen tediously.

'As far as I can see,' continued the Inspector, 'we shall have to discover who, if anyone, had a motive for killing the girl, and put them through it.'

'Wouldn't it be better to keep an open mind?' suggested Sir Richard. 'After all, we don't *know* she was murdered.'

'Well, sir,' said the Inspector a trifle impatiently, 'what other basis do you think we should take?'

Sir Richard stared at him as though he had just emerged from a cocoon, but refrained from producing an answer, for the very good reason that he could think of none.

'I think that's a very good idea, Inspector,' put in Fen drowsily. 'But not in this dreary hole, for heaven's sake. Let's go back to my room.'

'Isn't this Mr Warner up there?'

'Oh Lord, yes. Well, suppose we take Williams and the porter down here, and then go up and deal with Warner, and get rid of him, and have the other two up there afterwards.'

'Mr Fellowes and Mr Barclay: that seems reasonable.' The Inspector manifested a guarded approval. 'But I'm not sure it isn't better to question witnesses in the more uncomfortable surroundings.'

'True in a way,' said Fen even more drowsily. 'But if they're telling any lies, they're far more likely to relax and elaborate them and make them obvious from the depths of an armchair. What a dismal business it all is!' he concluded in a rather surprised tone.

'Then there's another thing,' said the Inspector. 'The next of kin must be informed. Has the girl any relations here in Oxford?'

Nigel remembered Helen for the first time that evening. The two sisters were so dissimilar, and moreover had got on so badly together, that it was not surprising he had forgotten the relationship between them. His heart sank. 'There's a sister,' he blurted out. 'Helen. She works at the rep. too.'

The Inspector made the inevitable note. 'We shall have to communicate with her. I suppose the theatre's on the telephone?'

'Yes, but – do you think there's any objection to my breaking the news to her? We're very good friends, you see and – '

The Inspector looked severe but proved amenable. 'Very well, sir,' he said, 'but I shouldn't say too much about the circumstances if I were you. Naturally, she'll have to be asked a few questions. I suppose' – he gazed earnestly at a tiny, effeminate wrist-watch – 'she'll be working at the moment.'

'Yes. And as far as I can see there's no point in telling her before the show's over.'

'Not that I can see, sir. Are there any parents?' He asked the question as though he suspected some form of autogenesis.

'Not living. A distant aunt, I gather, who acted as their guardian – but I've known them such a short time I really know very little about it. And of course they're both of age now.'

The Inspector nodded and made vague noises in his nose, since he could think of nothing to say. Fen, who had by now dozed off completely, was nudged by Sir Richard, and waking up, like the Dormouse, with a little shriek, said hurriedly:

'I propose that Nigel now tells us something about this girl, her immediate circle, and the relations between them, as far as he's been able to make out during the last few days. I'm taking it,' he said, addressing the Inspector, 'that he himself is not under suspicion, since he has a fool-proof alibi from Sir Richard and me, and, barring a contraption with pulleys and electromagnets, couldn't possibly have done the deed.'

The others uttered affirmative grunts, and after Fen had waved his cigarette-case about in front of them and they had all begun to smoke, Nigel told his story.*

They listened attentively, even Fen, who had recovered from his previous stupor. And although he shuffled and fidgeted and became increasingly gloomy as time went on, it was obvious that he missed nothing. Nigel's journalist's experience of précis-making stood him in good stead, and he spoke fluently and easily, remembering details of conversations without difficulty. None the less, it took some time, and it was close on ten o'clock when he had finished. The Inspector took notes with wearisome persistency. Sir Richard fiddled with his moustache and listened with half his mind, the other half being suddenly beset by a new theory regarding the dramatic abilities of Massinger.

' – So you see,' Nigel concluded, 'There's plenty of motive to choose from, if the girl was murdered.' And he sat back relieved that his job was over, drew a deep breath, and lit another cigarette.

'I say, how late it's getting,' said Sir Richard reproachfully. 'We shall have to leave a lot over to the morning, Cordery.'

'Yes, sir, I agree with you there. I suggest we get the times settled as exactly as we can, and see Mr Warner, as he's been kind enough to wait. As for the other two gentlemen' – he looked dubious – 'I think we might leave them till tomorrow. Perhaps if Mr Blake wouldn't mind acquainting them – '

'Fellowes will be in college all night,' Fen interrupted. 'He can't get out now, unless he climbs over the wall, by the bicycle shed or goes through the President's garden.' He looked apologetic. 'It all comes of having a system which is half monastic and half not,' he added aggrievedly and irrelevantly.

'Oh, very well, then,' said the Inspector a trifle peevishly. 'We'll see him tonight too. But there's no reason for this Mr

---

* Nigel Blake's account was a shortened version of that given in chapters 2–4. Nothing was omitted and nothing added. – E.C.

Barclay to stay if he doesn't want.' He began to feel slightly confused. 'Who is this Mr Barclay, anyway?' he inquired with pardonable irritation. 'And what has he got to do with it?'

'That's all right,' said Sir Richard, with the nervous air of one soothing a neurotic and excitable child. 'It's only that he was a friend of the dead girl's, and happened to be in the college when the thing happened.'

'I see,' said the Inspector unmollified. 'Well, if Mr Blake –'

'Yes, yes, Inspector,' said Nigel hurriedly and returned to the room opposite, wondering why it was always he who was deputed to act as call-boy. He found Donald and Nicholas surrounded by beer bottles and playing bezique, Donald ill-tempered and considerably the worse for wear, Nicholas with his habitual expression of urbanity on his lean, dark face. Nigel was beginning to find his mannerisms extremely irritating.

'Well?' he said, raising an eyebrow as Nigel came in. 'How is everything going, and is there an arrest yet? "An thou hadst been set i' the stocks for that question, thou hadst well deserved it",' he added to himself, raising one hand in a trite, effeminate gesture.

'The indications,' Nigel lied, 'still point to suicide.'

Nicholas, sensing the dislike in his voice, shrugged and was silent.

'And there's no particular reason for you to stay, now, if you don't want to.'

'My dear man,' answered Nicholas, 'I should have left long ago if I'd wished. As it is, I shall stay. I'm interested.'

'Just as you like,' returned Nigel shortly, and went out, cursing Nicholas under his breath. Also, he had not liked the look of Donald, who he suspected would be fairly drunk by the time they came to question him. That would make a bad impression, but he would probably be easy to pump. And yet what reason had he for suspecting Donald – or for that matter for suspecting anyone of anything? He realized that if it had not been for Fen, the whole thing would have been written off as suicide by now. For a moment he doubted Fen's reputation – wasn't he, after all, trying to make something out of nothing? And yet when he remembered the almost supernatural gleam of concentration in

Fen's eye and re-considered the evidence, he was forced to the conclusion that there was something undoubtedly wrong about the whole business. Racking his brains for a solution, he hurried back.

The Inspector was awaiting him, gazing with a theatrical air of concentration at his notebook. He received the news of Nicholas' decision without enthusiasm, and wondered inwardly whether he would ever get to bed that night. He had had a hard day at the station, and moreover had recently married a young wife, so this attitude was pardonable. He applied himself once again, resolutely but with regret, to his duty.

'Now, sir,' he said, 'according to your statement, a number of people had reasons for disliking the young lady who was killed. Let me detail them.' And he ticked them off on his fingers.

'(1) Mr Robert Warner. He knew Miss Haskell at some earlier time, and you think had had an affair with her.'

He summoned up a rumbled expression of disapproval, but suddenly feeling that it might be inappropriate, hastily converted it into a lengthy and unconvincing cough.

'In addition,' he went on, 'the young lady had been very persistent with him since his arrival, and apparently, the night before last, placed him in a compromising position, he being attached to another young lady, Miss Rachel West.' He paused, aghast at these erotic complications, and went on to the next person on his list.

'(2) Miss West herself, for the reasons aforesaid – that is to say, she was jealous of Miss Haskell on account of Mr Warner.

'(3) Mr Donald Fellowes, who although in love with Miss Haskell, was enraged at her deserting him in favour of Mr Warner, and moreover disapproved of her risqué behaviour on the stage.'

'Oh, come!' murmured Nigel at this alarming piece of characterization, but the Inspector swept on.

'(4) Miss Jean Whitelegge, who is in love with Mr Fellowes, and, while resenting his infatuation for Miss Haskell, considered also that she (Miss Haskell) was trifling with his (Mr Fellowes') affections.' He contemplated this further evidence of the activities of the Venus Pandemos with increasing dismay. Nigel suppressed a desire to giggle.

'(5) Mr Nicholas Barclay, who considered that Mr Fellowes was wasting his talents over this infatuation with Miss Haskell, and moreover disliked her on general grounds. That hardly seems to be a motive, sir,' he said, abandoning the official manner. 'And as to the first part of it, I confess I don't see what you mean.'

Sir Richard, about to embark on a disquisition on the value of the artist to society, thought better of it and was silent.

'Well, no,' admitted Nigel. 'That was only my impression, you understand. And of course there may be other people I know nothing about who had much stronger reasons for disliking Yseut. She was not popular.'

'So I gather. But I think perhaps we have enough to go on with for the moment.'

'I suppose,' said Nigel, 'that I haven't laid myself open to half a dozen slander actions by saying all this?'

'No, no, sir. You were officially asked to give your impressions, and you gave them, and that's all there is to it. No blame attaches to you even if those impressions prove to have been incorrect.' And he looked at Nigel with the severity of a medieval inquisitioner trying to wring a recantation from an intransigent Cathar. Nigel, however, remained unmoved.

At this point the constable put his head in at the door. 'Captain Graham, sir,' he said. 'Will you see him now?'

'Yes, Elbow. Show him in.'

Peter Graham looked much chastened. His youthful buoyancy had gone, and the lines of an unpractised and therefore slightly incongruous earnestness furrowed his brow. He greeted Nigel anxiously, and sat down on the edge of a chair with his hands in his lap.

Yes, the gun, he said, was his. He had discovered that it was missing on the day after the party, when he was tidying up his room. He had had, he explained irrelevantly but not surprisingly, an appalling hang-over, and had been very much distressed to find it gone. Yes, he had heard what had happened, poor little devil, and held himself partly responsible. But dash it, one didn't anticipate these things, and doubtless it would have happened somehow even if no one had known he possessed the thing. It was not he, he added, who had taken it out and waved it about for everyone to see. Asked why he had not reported the loss to the police, he said that first, he had felt very ill for the past few days, and second, that someone might have taken it as a joke, and would return it. Asked if he had any notion who might have taken it, he said he had none.

Some questions were then put about his relationship with Yseut, but beyond the fact that she had talked to him in the train, that he had seen her in the bar on Monday evening, and that she had come to his party, he had no information to give. He had not thought about her very much at all, he said, though he supposed she was attractive. Of her private affairs he knew nothing. She had seemed very drunk at the party, and had got into a temper with him when he took the gun away from her, but then parties were parties, and alcohol, he averred, did queer things to women. He was quite bewildered about the whole thing, he said, and could think of no reason why she should commit suicide, or for that matter why she should not.

And in fact, thought Nigel, he does look genuinely bewildered. Rising to go, he asked if he could have his gun back, but was told it must be kept as evidence. When Spencer had finished taking his prints, he went out with an expression of profound unhappiness on his face.

'All that will have to be confirmed,' said the Inspector after he had gone. 'It's possible, I suppose, that he knows more about the girl than he'll admit, but we must look for the obvious first, and go into the other things afterwards. I must admit that the attack the girl made on him seems queer on the face of it.' He sighed: it was wearing, he reflected, having to conduct a case with the Chief Constable sitting over you all the time.

Fen had asked no question during the interview, though he had listened to it with some care. But his manner had become markedly cheerful, and Sir Richard, with the blind faith of the early Christian martyrs, had in consequence paid no attention at all.

'His prints are the old ones on the barrel and chambers,' said Spencer, who had been comparing them. 'And there are some latent prints belonging to the girl, presumably when she handled the gun at the party.'

Williams was next questioned, somewhat the worse for a couple of hours of college beer, and inclined to be boisterous. The girl had come in, he thought, about twenty minutes before he heard the shot, but at what time exactly he could not say. She had said 'good evening' to him, and since he thought her an attractive bit of goods (though not wishing to speak ill of the dead, he added rather oddly), he had returned the compliment with what he described as a winsome smile.

'Did anyone else pass down the passage between the time she came in and the time you heard the shot?'

'Yes, sir, one gentleman, tall an' dark an' a bit lanky. But I takes a look at 'im over me shoulder, and 'e goes straight on up the stairs to the Professor's room.'

'Robert Warner,' put in Sir Richard.

'What time would that have been?'

'Abaht five or ten minutes after the young lady, I s'pose. Couldn't say for certain.'

'And you saw no one else during that interval – you'd be prepared to swear to that?'

Williams ruminated this question for a moment, making remote sucking noises with his teeth. Then he said: 'No, sir, no one else. I'm certain of that.'

The Inspector turned to Fen. 'Where does the archway opposite lead, sir? Just to another set of rooms?'

'There's a scout's pantry on the right as you go in,' said Fen, 'a sitting-room on the left, a staircase up to a small bedroom over the pantry, and then a way through to a paved courtyard beyond.'

'And that leads where?'

'It's enclosed, except for a small door on the west side, which leads out into the street.'

'That door is left open, then, I take it?'

'Until nine o'clock at night, yes.'

'Ah.' The Inspector seemed pleased. 'Now, Williams. No one came through from that courtyard, I suppose, during the time I mentioned?'

Williams looked indignant. 'Not likely. They'd 'ave 'ad to fall over me if they 'ad. Mr Fellowes an' another gentleman come over from 'ere and into the other sittin'-room earlier in the evenin', just afore you gentlemen come in from dinner, but that was all.'

'Well, tell us what you did when you heard the shot.'

'Nipped in 'ere quick as lightnin' an' fahnd the young lady as you saw 'er,' replied Williams promptly.

'Be more precise,' said Fen. 'What do you mean by "quick as lightning"? Exactly, and in detail, what did you do?'

'Well, sir, I was just abaht to knock orf work, as it was getting too dark to do anythin' further, when I 'eard it. So I lifts up me 'ead and says to meself "Did you 'ear what you thought you 'eard?" and then I puts me tools away in me bag and leaves it on the steps and comes straight over 'ere.'

'I don't call that "quick as lightning",' objected Sir Richard. 'How long did it take you to put your tools away?'

Williams looked uncomfortable. 'Couldn't say, sir, I'm afraid.'

'I'll put it another way, then: how long were you in the bedroom before we came down?'

'Oh, only a moment or two, sir.'

'H'm. And it was just under two minutes by the time we arrived. It seems as if your account needs revising a bit, Williams.'

Williams looked as alarmed as if he had been found with the weapon smoking in his hand.

'Tell me, Williams,' said Fen. 'Could you see into the windows of this room or of the rooms opposite?'

'Can't say as 'ow I looked, sir. But any'ow, it was so dark I shouldn't 'a' been able to see nothin' if I 'ad.'

Fen nodded. 'Did the shot sound very loud?'

'Well, sir, the wireless was makin' a lot o' noise, if you remember. No, I can't say as 'ow it sounded very loud. Not to make yer jump, like.'

'Did you see, or hear, Mr Warner come down to the lavatory?'

'No, sir, I didn't, but there's a carpet on them stairs, an' I was facin' the opposite direction, so I wouldn't 'a' done. I may 'ave 'eard the door shut be'ind 'im, but I wouldn't swear to it.'

'That's not very helpful,' said the Inspector when he had finally been dismissed. 'But I suppose we needn't have expected that it would be. There's one thing, though – we've established that no one came into this room after the girl.'

'We're assuming, you know,' said Fen, 'that she remained in one or other of these rooms from the time she came in to the time she was shot.'

'Where else could she have gone?'

'She might have gone up the staircase to the door of my room (without coming in), or she might have gone into the lavatory.'

The Inspector contemplated this new complication with unconcealed gloom. 'That will have to be investigated,' he admitted reluctantly, though if pressed as to how he was to set about it he would not have had the slightest idea – 'that will have to be investigated, but later, I think. For the moment we'd better see Parsons the porter, and try and get these times settled.'

Nigel seized the opportunity of going up to Fen's room and ringing Helen. He found Robert reading there when he arrived, but he only nodded and returned to his book.

Helen herself answered the stage-door telephone. Nigel told her without beating about the bush what had happened. There was a long silence at the other end. Then she said softly:

'Oh, my God! How did it happen?'

'At the moment it looks like suicide,' Nigel lied for the second time that evening.

'But – why?'

'Heaven knows, darling. I don't.' There was another silence. Then Helen said slowly:

'I can't say I'm really sorry, though I suppose I ought to be. It's – it's just the shock. Do they know when it happened? Everything's been in a frightful mess here, and Jane had to go on in her place, and dried every few seconds. Sheila's furious.'

'It was about two hours ago.'

There was a little gasp. 'Two hours – oh, my God!'

'Helen darling: are you all right? Shall I come round?'

'No, dearest, I'll be all right. I suppose the police will want to ask me questions?'

'I'm afraid so. They're coming round in the morning.'

'All right, Nigel. I must go now, and finish taking my make-up off. It's cold here, and I've got next to nothing on.'

'God bless, darling. See you in the morning?'

'Yes, dear, of course.' Nigel rang off and returned downstairs.

Parsons, the porter, was on the point of leaving when he arrived. He was as Nigel remembered him – a large formidable man with horn-rimmed glasses, whose attitude of invariable ferocity and aggressiveness combined ill with his status in the college. Like all the other college porters, he had read, Nigel suspected, in innumerable books on Oxford the statement that the porter is the uncrowned king of his college, and this conception had deeply affected his outlook, refusing to be eradicated by many years of bitter experience to the contrary. His attitude to undergraduates was one of overt intimidation incongruously combined with the conventional expressions of servility, and he respected none of them except those who declined to be intimidated. In any generation these were few in number, but Nigel had been one of them, and was greeted with warmth on his appearance.

His evidence was brief and to the point. Yseut had entered the college at six minutes to eight – he had looked automatically at the clock, since women were not allowed in after nine – and had gone, as far as he had been able to see, direct to Mr Fellowes' room. Robert Warner had come in at five past, and inquired his way to Fen's room, also going there direct, after he had ascertained that he was expected. No other strangers had come in since dinner, though Mr Fellowes had brought a guest to hall earlier in the evening – about half past six, he thought. Members of the college had been in and out as usual, but he could not remember who or at what times. He retired with dignity, leaving the Inspector looking a little better pleased with himself.

'Well, that's that,' said Fen, who had been growing increasingly fidgety. 'Thank heavens we can go up to my room now and sit in comfort.' And they all decamped.

Robert put down his book and rose to his feet as they appeared. He greeted them in turn, and asked a few amiable questions about how things were going. Fen collapsed into an armchair and pleaded with him to pour out some whisky for them all. The others settled down more austerely. Spencer bustled about taking Robert's fingerprints.

'Now, Mr Warner,' said the Inspector. 'Just a few things, if you don't mind.'

'By all means.'

'You were acquainted with the – with Miss Haskell?'

'Yes. I met her in town at a first-night party rather more than a year ago. We were friendly for a few weeks, and then she left to come back here. We did not communicate with each other, but of course we met again when I came here.'

'What is your business in Oxford, Mr Warner?'

'I'm producing a new play of mine at the Repertory Theatre.'

'Quite so. And you arrived when?'

'Sunday. Rehearsals didn't begin till Tuesday, but I wanted a day to look round and get acquainted with the company.'

'And your relations with Miss Haskell were – '

Robert looked uneasy. 'Extremely poor. She wasn't the sort of person to make herself liked at the best of times, and when I arrived she threw herself at my head and wanted to re-open our previous affair. I'd no desire to do anything of the sort, so naturally things became a bit difficult. Also, she was a poor actress, couldn't or wouldn't take direction, and constantly criticized the play and the production behind my back. In general, I frankly admit that she was a damned nuisance to me in every way.'

The Inspector was slightly overwhelmed at this outburst of frankness, which he vaguely felt was in some way indecent.

'*De mortuis nil nisi malum,*' added Robert as an afterthought.

'I understand, then, sir, that you gave the young lady no encouragement in her – er – attachment to you?'

'None whatever.'

'She did not visit your room on Wednesday night? You must forgive my asking such a personal question, but I can assure you that unless your answer is in anyway relevant to the case it will go no further.'

Robert looked surprised, but Nigel was unable to decide

whether the surprise was genuine or not. 'No,' he said, 'unless she crept in while I was asleep. At all events I saw nothing of her.'

'On that Wednesday night, Mr Warner, did you – er, were you – ?'

'The Inspector wishes to ask,' put in Sir Richard, cutting short his desperate search for a suitable euphemism, 'whether you were sleeping with Miss West on that night.'

'No,' said Robert, unperturbed, 'as a matter of fact I wasn't.'

'Now, sir,' pursued the Inspector. 'You were present at the party. No doubt you observed the incident with the revolver?'

'Oh God, yes. In fact, I was a party to it. The little – ' He checked himself, and went on: 'Yseut insisted that I should knock Graham down for taking it away from her. She was pretty tight by that time.'

'Quite so. What did you do when the party was over? Were you one of the last to leave?'

'I think so; yes. Rachel and I went straight to our rooms, muttered a few commonplaces about the unpleasantness of parties in general and Yseut in particular, and said good night. Then I undressed, went to the bathroom, took some aspirin to get rid of any after-effects' – characteristic of the man, thought Nigel – 'and went to bed. I read for half an hour or so, and then went to sleep.'

'Were you up early next morning?'

'At eight o'clock, if you count that early. I don't.'

'I asked for you when I came down,' put in Nigel, suddenly suspicious. 'The porter said he hadn't seen you, and the head waiter said you hadn't been in to breakfast.'

'Oh?' queried Robert coolly. 'I went straight out for a walk, as it happens, and I very seldom eat breakfast.'

'You didn't return to your room at any time before ten o'clock?' asked the Inspector.

'No. Why should I? Rachel, unlike myself, never gets up early, and I didn't expect to see her before half past ten.'

'Did you see anyone on your walk?'

'There were a few people about. No one I knew. And I may

say, Inspector,' he added rather unpleasantly, 'that if you're trying to prove I spent the night with Yseut, you're going to have a hard job of it.'

'You are aware that Miss Haskell went to your room the following morning?' said the Inspector, unruffled.

'So she told me.'

'Have you any idea why she went there?'

'Not the slightest.'

'You're sure, sir?'

Robert suddenly became angry. 'Yes, damn you,' he said.

'Very well, sir.' The Inspector smiled slightly. 'Now as to this evening. Would you mind detailing your movements during the later part of today?'

'Rehearsal finished at 4.30. I went back with Rachel to the hotel and we had tea together. At six o'clock we went and had a drink in the bar with Donald Fellowes and Nicholas Barclay, who went off just before half past. Rachel left shortly afterwards to have dinner with some friends in North Oxford, and I dined alone at the hotel. Then I returned to the bar, and some time towards eight left to come here.'

'Were you in the bar after dinner with anyone you knew?'

'No.'

'And you don't know exactly what time you left?'

'Good heavens, no. Is it important?'

'It may be, sir, and then again it may not,' said the Inspector heavily. 'We're simply trying to collect what details we can. Can you tell me how Miss West reacted to Miss Haskell's advances to yourself?'

Robert looked suddenly worried. 'I was surprised to find she was very annoyed, though usually she's extremely sensible about these things; and it wasn't as if the "advances", as you call them, were being reciprocated. Yes, she was annoyed both with me and with Yseut.'

'Though with no justification in the former case?' said the Inspector quickly.

Two red spots burned in Robert's cheeks, but he said levelly: 'None whatever.'

'If she was generally "sensible about these things", as you put it, then surely – '

'I say she had no justification whatever.'

The Inspector leaned back with a rather fatuous smile of complacency. 'And on arriving here?'

'I stopped at the lodge to ask my way to this room, as I didn't know the place at all, came straight up here, listened to a pleasant little ghost story for ten minutes or so, and then slipped out for a minute to go to the lavatory. While I was in there I heard an explosion close at hand, and when I came out I met the others coming down the stairs. The rest you know.'

'Were you carrying gloves, Mr Warner?'

'Gloves? Good Lord, no, not in this heat.'

'Thank you, sir. I think that's all for the moment. Sir Richard, Professor: have you anything you'd like to ask?'

Sir Richard shook his head and looked inquiringly at Fen.

'Just one thing,' said Fen comfortably from behind a glass of whisky. 'Do you know anything about Egypt, Warner?'

Robert looked puzzled. 'I was there before the war,' he said. 'But I only know tourist's stuff – the sort of thing anyone can pick up.'

'Nothing about the symbolism of ancient Egyptian religion, for example?'

Robert looked at him intently for a moment. 'No,' he said slowly. 'Nothing at all, I'm afraid.'

'Well, sir, that'll be all then,' said the Inspector.

'In that case,' said Robert, getting up, 'I'll be on my way.'

Fen, becoming belatedly aware of his duties as host, surged hurriedly to his feet. 'My dear fellow,' he cried, 'I really must apologize for giving you a most abominable evening. I'm afraid you'll never want to come here again. And I did so want to talk to you about your play. But I shall see it on Monday night, and I'd like to come to the rehearsal tomorrow, if I may.'

'By all means,' said Robert agreeably. 'And for heaven's sake don't apologize. It's not your fault if a murder's committed under our noses. I wish you joy of it. Anything more I can do, let me know.'

'I'm afraid this business is going to make things very difficult for you,' said Fen. 'You'll have to find someone at short notice to play the girl's part.'

'I'm not worried,' said Robert. 'Jane, who's understudying her, is perfectly competent.'

Fen nodded, and Robert, after bowing slightly to Sir Richard, Nigel and the Inspector, went to the door. There he turned and looked back.

'By the way,' he said, 'am I right in supposing that the gun which killed Yseut is the one she was playing about with at the party? It seems the most likely thing.'

'Yes, Mr Warner,' the Inspector answered. 'Someone – we don't know who – went back after the party and removed it.'

'In that case,' said Robert, 'I can help you a little more. You see, I saw the person who took it.'

'You what!' exclaimed the Inspector, sitting up abruptly.

'Of course I didn't realize what they were up to until this evening. But as I went to the bathroom, on my way to bed, I saw someone slip into Graham's room without turning on the light, and come out again carrying something which at the time I didn't recognize. I simply thought that a guest at the party had left something behind.'

'Yes, yes!' the Inspector almost shouted. 'And that person was – ?'

'Jean Whitelegge,' said Robert.

8. A Fine and Private Place

The grave's a fine and private place,
But none, I think, do there embrace.
Marvell

The Inspector gazed at Robert severely. One felt that this surprising piece of information had existed all along at the bottom of his mind in a pure and immaterial form, and that he was offended at this brutal thrusting of it into the coarse and limited medium of words. He regarded Robert as a man might be regarded who has capped a peculiarly subtle and appropriate literary allusion with the hackneyed banality of a proverb.

'You would swear to that?' he inquired automatically. The question was a perfectly rhetorical one, and manifestly he had no notion that the method of compelling truth which it involved was something like three centuries outworn.

'Well,' said Robert kindly, relapsing into the constatation of obvious extenuating circumstances which is employed in instructing the very unsophisticated, 'I'd swear to the fact that she went back to that room. Naturally I can't be certain that she took the gun away with her.'

The Inspector dismissed this cautious and scholarly emendation with a slight frown. 'We may draw our own conclusions about that, sir,' he said, with the aggressive air of one claiming a prerogative. 'Thank you, Mr Warner, you have been very helpful – very helpful indeed,' he added more emphatically, feeling the expression to be inadequate. Robert vanished almost imperceptibly from the room. The Inspector cast about in his mind for words suitably expressive of gratified surprise, and finding none, abandoned the responsibility of comment and asked of the company in general:

'Well, now: and what have we to say to that?'

Nigel at least had nothing to say. There was the fact, and there seemed to be nothing further to say about it at the moment; doubtless it was interesting. 'Interesting.' He proffered the opinion with a certain gloom, conscious of its futility.

'Entirely valueless,' opined Fen infuriatingly.

'Something to be investigated,' said Sir Richard prosaically.

This last comment appeared adequately to fill a disturbing blank in the Inspector's mind. 'And investigated it shall be,' he said with something of the procrastinating valour of Achilles when required to fight against the Trojans. 'As to the rest of the interview, to *me* at any rate' – he underlined the pronoun as though challenging anyone to submit it to pejorative scrutiny – 'it appears obvious that Mr Warner *did* spend that Wednesday night with Miss Haskell.' He breathed heavily.

'If you think that has anything to do with the case, Cordery,' said Sir Richard coldly, 'doubtless you were right to be as persistent as you were. But you must remember that you are a policeman, and not a Watch Committee.'

The Inspector received the rebuke with appropriately qualified penitence. 'None the less, sir,' he said, 'you must admit it may very well have some bearing on the matter in hand.'

'I'm getting very bored with all this,' interposed Fen suddenly. 'I shall go away if it continues. We have completely lost the point in a maze of routine investigation.' He became minatory. 'There are only two points to decide: first, whether this was suicide – I have given the reasons why it obviously was not (incidentally, did you notice there was no dent in the soft pinewood floor where the gun fell? Another slip). And second, since it was evidently murder, how it was done.' He became plaintive. 'There are only a few relevant questions to be asked, and the whole thing's over. Yet they have to be submerged in a mass of irrelevant – *stuff*.' He pronounced the word with a disgust intensified by his inability to think of a better one. 'That's all very well in a detective novel, where it has to be put in to camouflage the significant things – though I must say I think some more entertaining form of camouflage might be devised – '

Sir Richard roused himself acerbly. 'Really, Gervase: if there's anything I profoundly dislike, it is the sort of detective story in which one of the characters propounds views on how detective stories should be written. It's bad enough having a detective who *reads* the things – they all do – '

A gust of overwhelming fury smote the Inspector. 'Now it is you,' he cried hoarsely, 'who are wandering from the point. The problem is not to decide how the murder was done, though that may have its importance. The problem is to decide who did it.'

'But we know that, don't we?' said Fen with deliberate malice.

The Inspector paused. He appeared to be summoning up his resources for a titanic counterblast to this offensive suggestion. His lower jaw dropped and the blood rushed pinkly to his cheeks. No adequate rhetoric, however, was at his disposal, and regretfully dismissing the impulse of violent physical expression, he resorted to a heavy, subliminal irony. '*You* may know, sir,' he said ineffectually at last.

'I do,' said Fen simply.

Sir Richard was at once the incarnation of bluff, hearty common sense. 'Nonsense, Gervase!'

'I *do* know.' Fen adopted the theatrical wail of those who believe themselves to be everlastingly misunderstood by their fellows. 'I knew three minutes after we arrived in that room.'

'Three mi – !' Curiosity struggled with indignation in Sir Richard's mind, and curiosity abruptly won. 'Who then?'

'Ah!'

Sir Richard lifted both hands, palms outward, in the conventional mime for despair. 'Oh Lord!' he said. 'Mystification again. I know: it can't come out till the last chapter.'

'Nothing of the sort,' said Fen huffily. 'The case isn't complete yet. I cannot imagine, in the first place, *why* this person should do such a thing.'

'Good heavens! Aren't there enough motives hanging around?'

'All sexual motives, my dear Dick. I don't believe in the *crime passionnel,* particularly when the passion appears, as in this case, to be chiefly frustration. Money, vengeance, security: there are your plausible motives, and I shall look for one of them. I confess, too, that certain details, though probably inessential, still puzzle me.'

'Well, that's a relief, anyway,' said the Inspector with a sudden access of unconvincing jocosity. 'I think,' he added cautiously, apparently fearful of opposition, 'that we'd better see Mr Fellowes next.' This exercise of initiative appeared to console him somewhat.

'He'll be up in a moment,' said Nicholas, who had appeared opportunely on the Inspector's words. 'At the moment he is on my instigation engaged in being violently and repeatedly sick. He holds his liquor ill. It's my opinion that he shouldn't be allowed to drink at all, or only very little.'

He smiled benevolently round the gathering, seeming to see support for this suggestion. 'May I ask how you're getting on?'

'Impossible to say at the moment,' said Sir Richard. 'We progress, but in what direction – there's been no landmark of sufficient size yet to enable us to tell.'

'Do you still adhere to this absurd suicide theory?'

'You disagree then?' By lowering his voice at the end of the sentence the Inspector converted it from a question to a statement, which he contemplated resignedly.

'The idea is perfectly ridiculous. Yseut was rich, and had moreover just succeeded in creating a situation full of the most uncomfortable possibilities – a wide, fecund horizon of mischief-making. To abandon that would be to abandon every principle she ever possessed. Anything to give pain, as Hamlet might have said.' He considered the paraphrase critically for a moment, prior to casting it before lesser intelligences. 'Certainly she wouldn't have exchanged all that potential unpleasantness for being blown with restless violence round about the pendent world. Rachel, Jean, Donald and Robert were all tied to her apron-strings – more exactly I should say to her shoulder-straps – in an undignified huddle. I fear it was murder – motive either money or sex.'

'Fen,' said Sir Richard, 'has just been derogating sex as a murder motive.'

' "Murder's as near to lust as flame to smoke," ' answered Nicholas urbanely, and added: 'A trite comparison.'

'I beg your pardon, sir?'

'A quotation from *Pericles*, Inspector: a dirty play about brothels, by Shakespeare – of whom no doubt you have heard.'

Sir Richard interrupted in some haste. 'And money? The girl was rich?'

'Quite tediously so. About two thousand a year, I take it. Her sister Helen inherits. And while I'm on the subject I ought perhaps to mention that Yseut told Helen at the party the other night that she proposed visiting town shortly to alter her will.'

Nigel said: 'What the hell are you suggesting?'

Nicholas waved him aside. 'These mistaken impulses of chivalry, Nigel – originally, as the Inspector no doubt is aware, denoting an affection for horses – are wildly out of place.'

The Inspector gazed at him with distaste. 'You're prepared to swear to that, sir?' It was, Nigel thought, a perfectly unreflecting action which could be brought about by any particularly outrageous statement, like the salivating of Pavlov's dogs at the sound of the dinner-bell.

'Unlike yourself, Inspector,' said Nicholas with mock severity, 'I make no distinction between ordinary truth and truth under oath. And besides, I have an agnostic's mind. There's nothing I could sincerely swear by.'

'No primary philosophical principle?' put in Nigel sarcastically.

'Apart from the primary philosophical principle that there is no primary philosophical principle,' replied Nicholas unruffled, 'no. However: we're confusing the good inspector. You may take it, Inspector, that I did in fact overhear this conversation.'

'Was anyone else present, sir?'

'Innumerable other people were *present*, Inspector. Whether any of them heard what I heard I'm sure I couldn't say.'

At this point, Fen, who had been gazing critically at his features in a mirror at the other end of the room, turned and strode purposefully towards them. 'You are being imbecile and jejune,' he said offensively to Nicholas. 'Answer me a question: what were you and Fellowes doing this evening in a room not belonging to either of you?'

Nicholas' bland command of the situation vanished abruptly. 'We were listening to the wireless,' he replied lamely. 'Donald has none, and the owner of the room was out, so we took possession.'

'Did either of you leave the room at any time?' Fen's manner had become thunderously official, a forbidding parody of the Inspector's.

Nicholas scratched his nose apologetically. 'No,' he said with surprising brevity.

'Did you hear the shot?'

'Dimly. *Heldenleben* was going on at the time. Even though the windows were open it wasn't startling.'

'Good heavens, boy. Do you mean to say that you were playing that thing with all the windows open?'

'Well,' said Nicholas ruefully, 'it was hot.'

'You were playing the wireless with the windows open,' said Fen. 'Oh my ears and whiskers!' he added, abandoning the official manner. The Inspector gazed at him with polite astonishment. 'We have it at last. And what was on before *Heldenleben*, may I ask?' he inquired, adopting a tone of oily courtesy.

Nicholas looked surprised. 'The *Meistersinger* overture, I think.'

'The *Meistersinger* overture. Splendid, splendid!' Fen rubbed his hands, looking suddenly pedagogic. 'An admirable work, admirable, admirable.'

'Really, sir, I hardly think – ' began the Inspector, but Fen interrupted him.

'I suspected it all along,' he said. 'No, no, my dear man, not your powers of reasoning. The method, the method! We have it at last!' He collapsed into a chair in a state of subdued ecstasy and appeared to go to sleep.

'I think,' said the Inspector, 'that if Mr Fellowes has recovered – ' Nicholas moved obediently to the door.

'Just a minute!' Fen twisted uncomfortably round in his chair and meditated for a moment. 'What time did you do the blackout?'

'Shortly before we heard the shot, I think.'

'Did you do it, or did Fellowes?'

'I did the windows on this side, and Donald did those on the courtyard side.'

'Did you notice anything unusual at the time?'

'No. It was getting pretty dark by then.'

'Where did you sit?'

'In a couple of armchairs by the fireplace.'

Fen grunted. The information appeared to give him some obscure satisfaction. 'Who do you think is the murderer?' he asked.

Nicholas was taken aback. 'Robert or Rachel or Jean, I imagine; or Sheila McGaw or – '

'Or *who*?'

'Sheila McGaw.'

'This is a new one, Inspector,' said Fen with ill-concealed glee. 'Tell us about her,' he added to Nicholas.

'She's a young woman of arty proclivities who regularly produces at the repertory.' He pronounced the word deliberately, preciously avoiding the abbreviation. 'At the time of Yseut's short-lived excursus on the West End stage, she was to be offered the job of producing the play in which Yseut was to appear. That amiable young woman used her influence to lose Sheila the job, chiefly by publishing the fact that the woman's sexual reactions were not entirely normal.' Here the Watch Committee assumed a shocked, slightly cross-eyed stare. 'Sheila discovered about this, and not unnaturally took offence. You see, Professor' – he threw Fen a tentative offer of reconciliation – 'I know all the scandal, am in fact a latterday Aubrey. What more could the police want?'

'Apart from the fact that Aubrey could write,' said Fen frigidly, 'that he got tight when he drank a lot, and that he had a spontaneous and delightful sense of humour, no doubt there may be something in the comparison. Probably your information is quite as inaccurate as his. If I remember rightly, he went so far as to insist that it was Ben Jonson who killed Marlowe.' From the expression on his face it was apparent that he regarded the imputation as in the highest degree offensive.

Donald Fellowes, when he appeared, proved to be only partially recovered from the evening's carouse. The process of being sick had relieved the anaesthesia of his nerves, but the alcohol still crawled and sang and buzzed in his veins, and as a consequence he was feeling not only depressed but actively ill.

'Now, you sheepshead,' said Fen, who had completely taken

charge of the situation, 'what have you got to say for yourself?'

This unorthodox question had the effect of rattling Donald. He mumbled to himself.

'Are you sorry Yseut is dead?' Fen continued, and added in a painfully audible aside to Nigel: 'This is the psychological method of detection.'

Donald was roused. 'Psychological nonsense,' he said. 'If you want to know, I feel only relieved, not sorry. You needn't suppose I killed her because of that. I have an alibi,' he concluded, with something of the pride of a small child showing a favourite picture-book to a recalcitrant adult visitor.

'You *think* you have an alibi,' said Fen cautiously. 'But if one supposes collusion between yourself and Nicholas Barclay, you have nothing of the sort.'

'You can't prove collusion,' said Donald indignantly.

Fen abruptly abandoned this unprofitable topic. 'Did you practise the organ yesterday morning?' he inquired. 'And did you have a drink in the "Mace and Sceptre" beforehand?'

'Yes to both questions,' said Donald, who was recovering slightly. 'I'm playing a very difficult Respighi Prelude as a voluntary on Sunday.'

'And you took your music to the bar with you?' Nigel was puzzled at the turn the questioning had taken.

'As it happens, I did.'

'Lots of it?'

'A small pile,' Donald answered with dignity.

'Ah,' said Fen. 'Your witness, Inspector. My interest in the proceedings is at an end.'

And apparently it was. The Inspector asked a number of questions about Donald's movements that evening, about the episode of the gun, and about his relationship with Yseut, but they learned nothing new. Nigel had the impression that the Inspector was battering dutifully but ineffectually against a brick wall, that he was asking questions at random simply in the hope that something would emerge, and that having for the moment abandoned the idea of suicide he had been able to evolve no concrete line of inquiry to set in its place. With this state of mind Nigel profoundly sympathized. He himself was beginning to feel very tired, and, like Fen, inclined to lose interest in the proceedings altogether. His earlier reaction to the murder he felt had been sentimental, and he was now inclined to believe that Yseut's death might from many points of view not have been at all a bad thing; if she had been run over by a bus, the effect would have been the same, so why be disturbed by moral considerations? The Fiji Islanders, he reflected, murder their old men and women from the most admirable motives of social evolution. This was in his conscious mind; in the unconscious there lived and grew still a superstitious terror of death by violence, impervious to the niceties of rational calculation, and which the consciousness was attempting to suppress by refusing further speculation on the problem. The superstitious fear was there, no doubt, because the agency was mysterious – an atavistic throw-back to a belief in the powers of the spirits of earth and air. If he had seen Yseut struck down, if he had known the murderer, it would never have come into being.

Towards the end of the interview, Fen's interest, apparently a very volatile affair, was roused again.

'What do you think of Jean Whitelegge?' he asked, with an elaborate simulation of disinterested scientific curiosity.

'She's in love with me, I believe.'

'My dear man, we know that. Don't be so complacent about it. Do you think she can have killed Yseut?'

'Jean?' There was a fractional pause. Then Donald looked shocked. 'No: I certainly don't think so.'

'Ah,' said Fen. 'What service are we having at Evensong on Sunday?'

'Dyson in D.'

'Nice,' commented Fen, 'theatrical, but nice. You must come, Nigel. Musically, it's a battle of religion and romance, of Eros and Agape.' Nigel nodded bewildered at these gnomic utterances. Donald Fellowes departed to bed in one of the guest chambers, first procuring some things from his bedroom under the eye of a policeman.

A soporific atmosphere descended on Fen, Nigel, Sir Richard and the Inspector. Even the two latter appeared now to be sustaining their interest with difficulty. And besides that, it was by now close on midnight. The Inspector, returning with an heroic effort to the matter in hand, made a short attempt at condensation and summary.

'Certain specific things remain to be investigated,' he concluded. 'The alibis of the other people concerned; the question of whether the bullet came from the gun we found (though I've no doubt myself that it did); the question of the young lady's will; the ownership of the ring; and one or two other lesser matters.'

Sir Richard hurled a match, which for some moments he had been applying without noticeable effect to the bowl of his pipe, inaccurately at the fireplace. 'It remains a mystery to me,' he said, his face expressing suitable if momentary mystification, '*how* the girl was murdered. Could she have been shot from outside, do you suppose, and the window – ?' He indicated his lack of confidence in the suggestion by resorting to aposiopesis.

'Even apart from the fact of the powder burns,' said the Inspector, 'I can't see how it could have been done. If anyone had shot her from the passageway, Williams would have seen them. If Mr Fellowes and Mr Barclay are telling the truth, she wasn't shot from the room opposite. With due deference sir,' – he gazed at Fen without so much as a hint of deference in his manner – 'I don't see how it can have been anything but suicide. Of course I shall keep an open mind on the subject' – he nodded, apparently in approval of this generous and eclectic disposition – 'but it seems to me there's really very little doubt about it.'

'I'm sure we can leave matters safely in your hands, Inspector,' said Sir Richard, with something of an effort. 'And now perhaps – bed?'

The sense of relief caused by this suggestion engendered surprisingly a tendency to linger in amiable chatter. Eventually Sir Richard and the Inspector departed, Nigel remaining behind a few moments. Fen had abandoned equally his theatrical gloom and his unnatural exuberance, and was looking impressively grave. 'Talk to me,' he said, 'about abstract justice.'

'Abstract justice?' murmured Nigel.

'Pascal says that human justice is entirely relative,' said Fen, 'and that there is no crime which has not at one time or another been considered as a virtuous action. He confuses, of course, universal moral law with actions valuable through temporary expediency. Even so, I believe incest belies him; it has been universally condemned.' He sighed. 'The question is: is it worth while for anyone to hang for murder of that young woman? It seems she used her sex in the most debased manner possible – as a means to power, like Merteuil.'

'She was to some extent a sensualist,' said Nigel.

Gervase Fen contemplated the apolaustic proclivities of Yseut without satisfaction; a Cornelian struggle appeared to be going on within him. 'I don't like it,' he said. 'I don't like it at all.'

'You think you know who killed her?'

'Oh, yes. Perhaps I should have said that the conditions are such that they can only be fulfilled by one person, and that it will be easy enough to find out who that one person is. There are admittedly complications which will have to be looked into. It's possible I'm wrong.' His voice betrayed a certain lack of conviction on this last point. 'This McGaw woman –' He interrupted himself to say: 'Are you in love with Helen?'

Nigel pondered on the possibly unpleasant implications of the question. 'I hardly know her,' he said, hoping by evasion to draw Fen further. But Fen merely shook his head. 'I'll walk with you to the gate,' he said.

A half-moon hung lopsidedly over the great tower. The air was warm with a warmth that at once sapped physical energy and presaged a tremendous imminent change. They trudged across the quadrangle beneath the delicate finical gaiety of Inigo Jones, transformed by the darkness to a rather sinister, empty lecherousness. Nigel was reminded of Wilkes' ghost story.

'An interesting addition to the college legends,' he said.

'Tell me, Nigel,' said Fen, whose mind was on other things, 'were you here for the celebration on All Hallow E'en three or four years ago?'

'When the college danced naked on the lawn in the moonlight? Yes, I was involved – in fact suffered disciplinary penal-

117

ties which must have paid for the S.C.R. port for several weeks.'

'Those were the days. Were any fairies in evidence?'

'We counted at one stage of the evening and deduced the presence of an unknown among us. But whether it was a fairy or just one of the dons we never knew.'

'I shouldn't have thought it would have been so difficult to distinguish.' Fen sighed. 'We are all becoming standardized and normal, Nigel. The divine gift of purely nonsensical speech and action is in atrophy. Would you believe it, a pupil of mine had the impertinence the other day to tick me off for reading him passages regarding the Fimble Fowl and the Quangle-Wangle as an illustration of pure poetic inventiveness; I put him in his place all right.' In the semi-darkness his eye became momentarily lambent with remembered satisfaction. 'But there's no eccentricity nowadays – none at all. Except, of course' – he stopped and pointed – 'this.'

They had reached a part of the college which Nigel remembered as a small enclosed green. He saw that there had been erected on it a sort of enclosed pen, inside which he could dimly discern twelve typewriters on a table, and twelve monkeys, who sat about in attitudes of bored reverie or copulated in an uninteresting manner. This sinister and unexpected apparition took him momentarily aback. 'What is it?' he said.

'Either the Junior Common Room,' answered Fen gloomily, 'or Wilkes' Enclosure. The latter, I suspect. Of course it's since your time. Wilkes, who has a practical mind, has hired it from the college for a very great number of years to come. But so far not a single Shakespeare sonnet, not a line of a sonnet, not a word of a line, or even two consecutive letters, has been produced. The monkeys have to be replaced as they die off, of course – possibly that is prejudicial to the success of the experiment.' He sighed. 'In the meantime, they show little inclination to approach the typewriters, and content themselves with behaving in a normal though acutely embarrassing way.' He shook his head over the transitoriness of human effort. They went on and approached the lodge. 'By the way, remind me some time to give you my opinion of Wilkes' story; it interested me in more ways than one. And the problems of the dead are so much more satisfactory to solve than the problems of the living; they require no effective action.

'I suppose,' he added as they were saying good night, 'you wouldn't care to come with me on my rounds tomorrow? An internal itch compels me to get this thing cleared up, though if the police persist in their asinine suicide theory I rather doubt if I shall contradict them.'

Nigel gave his half-hearted assent to this proposal.

'I shall see you sometime,' said Fen with the determined vagueness of one who declines to be badgered into making definite arrangements. 'How tired I feel. I must go and set some collection papers for the bookish crew who return tomorrow.' He vanished incontinently; on the raven down of darkness the single word 'Cretins!' floated faintly back to Nigel's ear.

Nigel, now that he had arrived in the open air, felt disinclined for sleep, and he walked down past Christ Church to the tow-path by the canal, and stood gazing down into the water, in which patches of luminous white and jet-black performed silent, bewildering manoeuvres. The gas-works, the factory chimneys and the railway siding – from which the distant clatter of shunting goods trains could be heard from time to time – stood silhouetted against the moon like a Muirhead Bone etching. Somewhere far away an air-raid siren began its dismal portamento progression of minor thirds.

Little by little the events of the evening seeped back, rearranged themselves in fantastic patterns, clamoured for explanation, for scrutiny, even for dismissal. The figures of the participants inconsequently mingled in strange relationships. Broken phrases returned, and became perverted to extra-ordinary senses. The rational element, sated and wearied, stood back to regard with impotent disapproval this grotesque panorama. Was there, for a moment, a fleeting glimpse of the true pattern? Nigel never knew. Hunching his shoulders, despite the warmth of the evening, he returned to the hotel.

That night he dreamed he was again naked on the lawn of St Christopher's. Only it seemed somehow different, and the college receded to an infinite distance even as he looked at it. He was vaguely aware that Helen was clinging to the lower boughs of a tree and shouting something at him. It was only after a time that he realized she had taken refuge. Looking about him, he saw something on hands and knees crawling towards him through the bushes. The features, which were terribly distorted, were those of someone he knew; but when he woke up, and, shaking himself irritably free of the nightmare, lit a cigarette, he could not remember whose they had been.

9. Last Will and Testament

How! A woman ask questions out of bed?
Otway

The next day the weather broke. Early in the morning, before the first rays of light had touched the towers and pinnacles of the city, the rain began to fall from a leaden sky. When Nigel woke from a disturbed sleep the streets were already soaking, the elaborate and inefficient drainage systems of Gothic, Mock-Gothic, Palladian and Venetian architecture were already emitting accumulated jets of water on unwary passers-by. From Carfax the gutters streamed down the gentle slope of the High, past the 'Mitre', past Great St Mary's, past the Queen's, and so down to where the tower of Magdalen stood in solitary austerity above the traffic which ran towards Headington or Iffley or Cowley. Outside St John's, the trees began to creak and whisper, and the drops rattled with dull monotony from their branches, while a few solitary beams of pale sunlight rested on an architrave of the Taylorian, glanced off southwards down the Cornmarket, and were rapidly engulfed somewhere in the precincts of Brasenose. The cinereous sky echoed the grey of innumerable walls; water ran in streams down the ivy which more or less shields Keble from offensive comment; paused and momentarily glistened on the wrought-iron gates of Trinity; gathered in innumerable runnels and rivulets among the cobbles which surround the Radcliffe Camera, standing like a mustard-pot among various other cruets. The eloquent décor of Oxford is bright sunlight or moonlight; rain makes of it a prison city, profoundly depressing.

Tomorrow would be the first day of full term. Those under-graduates who had not already arrived moved towards the city. In the hubbub of greater England their thin, purposeful, converging trickles were still discernible. In the Clarendon Building, two new proctors contemplated resignedly a list of pubs to be visited that evening, while junior members of the University *in statu pupillari* calculated the chances of their remaining decently over their port until a late hour. Notices concerning club activities, many offensively designed, began to appear in college lodges; taxis appeared, piled high with luggage; a week or so later more luggage would arrive, under the system ironically described by the railway companies as luggage in advance; collection papers were set and distributed; tutors heaved regretful sighs, freshmen arrived in a state of crescent bewilderment and anguished self-consciousness, and college cooks meditated enormities.

It was a gloomy day; but Nigel, as he peered out of the window of his Baptistery, felt more than usually cheerful. This is the stage, he told himself, at which the stark, terrible realization of the thing envelops you with a sudden rush; fortunately it is doing nothing of the sort; on the contrary, its supreme unimportance is most impressive and is resulting in a perceptible lightening of spirit. He watched attentively a small rivulet of water as it dropped with gathering momentum from level to level down the front of the building and observed it precipitate itself on to the umbrella of the Regius Professor of Mathematics, who happened to be passing below. Then, fortified in spirit by this heartening sight, he withdrew his head, washed, shaved, dressed, and went down to breakfast.

'Murder,' said Nicholas Barclay didactically to Sheila McGaw, with whom he was having breakfast. 'Effective, no doubt – immediately effective – but basically unsatisfactory.' He made an expressive gesture, thereby projecting a globule of marmalade into the salt. 'Now, consider how incomparably better whipping and dragging at the cart-tail would have been. Murder is so *abrupt* – that it leaves nothing to be enjoyed afterwards; like drinking good wine at a gulp instead of lingering over it. Then again, think of the question of appropriateness. How admirable the Middle Ages were in that respect! – scold's girdles, ducking-stools, drunkards' cloaks, chastity-belts, stocks; all designed in the most rough-and-ready standards of retribution for particular failings of human nature. I tremble with joy, as Ruysbroek said, when I think for how many of those Yseut must have qualified. Murder is so abstract and impartial,' he complained, 'it lacks utterly the poetic element of *choice*, in fact I'm not sure that it isn't at any time in dismally bad taste.' He bit off a piece of toast, and regarded the remainder ruminatively before replacing it on his plate.

'May I ask,' said Sheila, 'whether you've contrived this argument in order to convince the police that you didn't kill the girl? If so, I'm afraid it's doomed to failure.'

'My dear Sheila: I had no possible *motive* for killing Yseut. It's true I lied to the police last night about whether Donald or I left the room, and equally true that I think Fen noticed it – damn him. But even if that should come out I can't see what I have to fear. Now you –'

Sheila looked up quickly. 'What motive have I?'

'Vengeance, my dear,' said Nicholas histrionically. 'I told them about your little fracas. You don't mind, I hope?'

To his disappointment she accepted this revelation without resentment. 'No,' she said slowly after a pause, 'I don't mind. They would have found out soon enough anyway. Are they going to question me?'

'No doubt. But it's an innocuous process; they haven't the slightest idea what they're about.' There was another pause. 'I think,' added Nicholas meditatively, 'I shall come to rehearsal this morning: it will be interesting to see how people react.'

In the small, unsolidly modern bed-sitting-room which she inhabited in her college, Jean Whitelegge awoke, opening one eye cautiously to admit the impressions of a new day; gazed at the mantelpiece opposite, with its little china dogs and wooden animals of all kinds; at the window with the rain streaming down it, the tree-tops and the red brick wall beyond blurred to fantastic images; at the wardrobe which held her small collection of garments; at the portable gramophone with the albums of Beethoven Quartets strewn round it; at the shallow, messy Gauguin reproductions on the walls; at the bookcase with its tall, thin-spined volumes of modern verse, its books on ballet and the theatre, its plays by Strindberg, Auden, Eliot, Bridie, Cocteau, and, in a place of honour on the top shelf, a uniform edition, well-thumbed and bound in austere uncompromising black, of the works of Robert Warner. Her eye rested long on this, reflectively, doubtfully; phrases from his plays leaped into her mind, characters reasserted themselves unbidden, a multitude of subtle, surprising, apparently inconsequent curtain-lines came to memory. She sat up in bed, deliberately readjusted a shoulder-strap which had fallen over her arm, looked at her watch and discovered that it was long since too late for breakfast, threw her shapely legs out of bed, stood up, and regarded herself contemplatively in the full-length mirror set in the door of the wardrobe: plain, she thought, but undeniably well-made; a good deal more attractive in that way than Yseut ... Her thoughts were suddenly checked, and she made an attempt to summon up dim and inaccurate recollections of criminal law.

There was a tap on the door; that it was a purely conventional signal of approach was proved by the rapidity with which its author followed it into the room. Estelle Bryant was one of the richer women undergraduates, painted and scented by Chanel, silk-stockinged and exquisitely tailored, as opposed to the brogues and indeterminate tweeds and blouses affected by the majority of her tribe. She flung herself down on the end of the bed in a state of high excitement.

'Darling!' she said. 'Have you heard about Yseut?'

Jean looked at her in silence for a moment. Then she said: 'Yseut? Well?'

'Murdered, my child: shuffled off unhousel'd, disappointed, unanneal'd, with a bullet-hole in the middle of her forehead. Your gang at the theatre will have to find a new juvenile lead. If it weren't for the allurements of Middle English I think I should apply for the job myself.' Lying on one elbow, she succeeded with difficulty in lighting a cigarette.

Jean said: 'Where, Estelle? And when?' Her voice sounded oddly incurious.

'In Kit's, of all places, in your precious Donald's bedroom. Oh Lord, I shouldn't have said that, should I? Sounds bad.'

Jean smiled faintly. 'Don't mind me. I happen to know Donald wasn't there at the time, anyway. Who do they think did it?'

'Can't imagine what you see in that youth, darling,' said Estelle inconsequently. She made a manifest effort to recall the question. 'Oh, as to who did it. I imagine they don't know; or if they do they're keeping it to themselves. Anyway, they haven't arrested anyone yet.'

'Thank God for that.'

'Yes, I see what you mean, child. A nasty piece of work, if all I hear is true. But I shouldn't like to be the murderer now Fen's on the job; even the way he tears my essays to pieces is blood-curdling enough.' She became momentarily wistful. 'God, how clever that man is! I mobilize all the resources of Hartnell for tutorials, but it's no good; he flirts violently, but quite insincerely. Ah me!' She sighed.

'They don't think it's Donald, do they?' asked Jean.

'My love, I am not privy to their secrets. Lord Almighty, child, what heavenly undies! Where from?'

From the discussion of underclothes they passed by a natural transition to the sempiternal feminine discussion of sex.

Donald Fellowes opened his eyes to the spectacle of an untidy heap of clothes piled on a chair by his bed. In the unfamiliar surroundings of the guest-room, it took him some moments to realize where he was, and why. A Breughel, of Flemish oafs all compact, stared at him from over the fireplace; a very bad Haden etching was suspended beyond it; otherwise, the room was characterless. He had a splitting headache and a bad mouth. He sat up and put his head in his hands, muttering 'God! Oh, God!' A scout poked his head in at the door and reminded him that breakfast was in five minutes. Pulling himself reluctantly out of bed, he thought, distantly and indifferently, of Yseut – and of something else. 'Lord, oh Lord!' he said to himself. 'Who in God's name would have thought . . . Women are inexplicable.' He ruminated this unoriginal conclusion at length as he put on his slippers and dressing-gown, and marched out to the baths under the protection of an umbrella.

Rachel West pulled back the corner of the negligée which had slipped away from her thigh and poured out another cup of tea. Robert, watching her from a chair opposite, reflected that she had lost none of her beauty in the years he had known her.

What was she now? Twenty-seven? Twenty-eight? Yet her figure was still firm, delicately-moulded, slightly boyish, and she had never allowed her long familiarity with him to make her neglect her appearance in the early mornings, the time when wives, official and unofficial, invariably look their worst; an unspoken convention and routine had in fact grown up to prevent this. He had been relating to her the events of the night before. There was a pause when he had finished. Rachel spoke at last.

'I feel I'm somehow to blame,' she said, 'for making such a damned fool of myself over you and the girl. It was a sort of madness.'

'I did nothing to ease the situation, I fear. And apparently the business of her coming to my room did look bad; even the police wanted to insist that I'd been sleeping with her.'

'If I'd been in my senses –'

'Oh, be damned to it now, darling. It's over.'

Rachel was grave. 'Over – yes. Have they any idea who did it?'

'As far as I could gather, very little. Fen may have an idea; but he does a lot of play-acting and it's difficult to tell. Anyway, for heaven's sake let's forget about it. I fear the police will visit you today.'

'Is there – anything – ?'

'Good Lord, no, I've got nothing to conceal. Tell them the truth.'

'The truth as far as I'm concerned is – well, darling, the fact is I didn't go to North Oxford last night; that was a blind. After we quarrelled, I – I – well, I just couldn't bear it, that's all. I had to go away somewhere by myself.'

'Tactless devil that I am.'

'No, darling, of course it wasn't your fault. But that made no difference to the way I felt. I – I went to the cinema and saw an awful film.'

'Well?'

'Don't you see? It means I've got no alibi. They'll say –'

'My dear, they're not going to arrest everyone in Oxford who hasn't got an alibi. You must simply tell them, that's all. Believe me,' Robert added grimly, 'if they start anything where you're

126

concerned, I'll have every forensic jackal in London on their tails.'

She looked so worried that he went over and kissed her gently on the lips. 'Bless your heart,' he said, 'don't worry. Personally, I shan't attempt to conceal the fact that I shall be more than delighted if they never find out who did it.'

He returned and sat down again. 'Thank heaven *Metromania* is going well: it will go better now, though I says it as shouldn't. You know I have an idea for a successor? Male chief character this time. Shotover or Giles Overreach stature – though again I says it as shouldn't.'

'I suppose,' said Rachel, 'that means you're going to shut yourself up again as soon as this is over? Really, I think you're outrageous.'

Robert chuckled. 'I know – aren't I? And it's not as if I enjoyed it.' He regarded her quizzically. 'I don't know whether it affects other people that way, but I find I get so bored with my own mind. Writing a new play is like having a baby or going swimming: it's only pleasant when it's over.'

Nigel ate his breakfast alone, the meantime carrying on what he imagined to be a sane and objective survey of the facts. Sanity and objectivity, however, were impotent; no spark of enlightenment entered his head. What primarily puzzled him was the business of the ring: what possible reason could a murderer have had for putting it on Yseut's finger after she was dead? His mind wandering, a number of Heath Robinson contraptions based on this fact peered over the mental threshold, and were hastily dismissed. Was Robert telling the truth when he said he had not been with Yseut on Wednesday night? Nigel thought not, but then it was really impossible to say. Why had Donald seemed so little surprised to hear of Yseut's death? What was the significance of the radio? Of the fact that Yseut had been killed in Donald's room? What had she been looking for there? Had Jean taken the gun, and if so, did that prove she was a murderer? Nigel realized that this internal catechism, faintly reminiscent of the dialogues between body and soul so popular in the seventeenth and eighteenth centuries, was totally valueless, and abandoned it in order to contemplate what possibilities there might be in Fen's professed intuitive method. He concentrated on intuiting, allowing desultory impressions to invade his mind without order or sequence, and as a consequence felt more confused than ever. For a moment, indeed, he did think he had hit on some obvious single element which bound the whole business into a plausible pattern; but he was evidently intuiting so hard that it failed to penetrate his consciousness, and he was quite unable to recapture it. Sighing, he abandoned the attempt.

The first thing, in any case, was to go and see Helen. Rehearsal was not until eleven that morning, and she ought still to be at her rooms. He collected a mackintosh and set off through the rain towards Beaumont Street.

As he approached No. 265 he observed two vaguely familiar figures coming towards him. The mists of distance dissipating, they were revealed as Inspector Cordery and Sergeant Spencer, evidently bound on the same errand as himself. He met them, in fact, at the door.

The Inspector was in high good humour. He greeted Nigel with the patronizing benevolence of St Peter admitting one of the minor evangelists to eternal bliss. 'Well, well, Mr Blake, it's a small world!' he opined tediously. 'I dare say you're on your way to see Miss Haskell, as we are?'

'Of course, if I shall be in the way – ' mumbled Nigel, unwilling to abandon the precedence which he felt a short head over the police had gained him.

'Well, sir, come up with us if you feel inclined. Only I must ask you to let us handle this our own way, and not to do any interrupting, while we're there.'

Nigel solemnly expressed his approval of this arrangement, and they went in and upstairs, Nigel and the Inspector jostling uneasily for first place on the narrow staircase.

Helen was in her room, writing letters. It was a large room, light, airy, and meticulously clean and tidy, and although most of the furniture and ornaments were not hers, she had succeeded, as women always can, in impressing on them the stamp of her own individuality without any striving after effect. Beyond that, Nigel noted, there was also the generic aspect: it was unmistakably a woman's room, the reason being – thought Nigel, succumbing to the masculine habit of analysis – the number of *small* objects which it contained. Unmistakably feminine – he thought of Chaucer's description of Cressida –

> But alle her limes so well answeringe
> Weren to wommanhode, that creature
> N'as nevere lasse mannissh in seminge.

As Chaucer rejoiced in the transcendental, the surpassing womanliness of Cressida, so he rejoiced in that of Helen. He looked at her grave, child-like face, the soft waved silk of her hair, and was lost. He made noises of greeting in the back of his throat, to which she replied solemnly.

Even the Inspector, Nigel noticed with ridiculous pride, was manifestly taken with Helen. His manner became as soothing as his rather bird-like physiognomy permitted. To Nigel's surprise, it was with a charming natural courtesy that he expressed his regret for what had happened, and his apologies for troubling Helen so early.

'I knew you'd be wanting to get off to rehearsal, miss,' he said, 'so I thought we'd get this troublesome business over with as soon as possible. A good deal of it's routine, you'll understand.'

Helen nodded and motioned them to sit down. 'I'm afraid you'll think me a little callous, Inspector,' she said. 'But Yseut and I never got on well – never knew each other well, in fact – and she was after all only my half-sister. So although naturally this appalling business has been a shock, I can't honestly pretend I feel it as a very personal loss.'

The Inspector, after a moment's consideration, appeared to find this view comprehensible; doubtless standards acquired in childhood by the reading of fairy tales, in which half-sisters are invariably flies in the ointment, still remotely affected his outlook. 'Well, that's none of our business, miss,' he said, and added illogically: 'though naturally we shall have to ask one or two questions about it. I wonder, now, if you'd mind giving your fingerprints to Spencer here?'

'Again a matter of routine, Inspector?' asked Helen mischievously. The Inspector ventured a responsible-looking smile. 'That's right, miss,' he said.

Spencer, who had on entering cast a desperate glance at the formidable battery of cosmetics laid out on the dressing-table, became apologetic. 'I'm afraid this is going to make a bit of a mess on your fingers, miss,' he said.

'Go ahead, Sergeant,' said Helen. 'As an actress I'm used to having horrible things painted on all over me.' The remainder of the proceedings went through in silence.

'Now, miss,' said the Inspector, 'we shall have to have a look at your sister's room.'

'Oh, yes. Next door to here, on the left. She always kept everything unlocked, so you shouldn't have any difficulty. Shall I come?' She half rose.

'Er – thank you, no, miss. In point of fact, Spencer was sent round here last night to lock it up until we could have a proper look at it. You didn't, I suppose, try to enter your sister's room at any time last night or this morning?'

'No, Inspector, I didn't, so you won't find any of my finger-prints on the knob.'

'Ah – exactly. Spencer, go and take a look round. You know what we hope to find, don't you?' he added sinisterly.

Spencer, who had not the least idea, grinned affably and went out. The Inspector said casually:

'So your sister was going to alter her will?'

Nigel looked quickly at Helen, but she replied with perfect calm: 'So she told me at the party the other night. She was to have gone up to see her solicitor today. I believe Nick Barclay was eavesdropping at the time, and I guessed he'd tell you.' The Inspector looked so crestfallen that she hastened to add: 'Not that I wouldn't have done in any case.'

'In the circumstances, miss, it looks a bit queer.'

'I quite agree,' said Helen tranquilly. Nigel, mindful of his vows of silence, projected a burst of telepathic applause in her direction.

The Inspector, a little taken aback, tried a new tack. 'Do you know who was to be the new legatee?'

'I really haven't the faintest idea. She had no close relations besides myself, and very few friends. What always astonished me was that she didn't alter it before, considering how little love there was between us. Not that it mattered as far as I was concerned: I've no particular desire for more money than I can earn, and I'd no reason to expect that she'd die before I would, anyway. She only told me about it out of sheer malice – which somewhat misfired for the reasons aforesaid.'

'The question of the will will have to be confirmed, of course. But I'm right in saying you are now a comparatively rich gi – woman, Miss Haskell?'

'I suppose so.'

'Ah. Do you know the name of your sister's solicitors?'

'Not the faintest idea. We never talked about money. She never offered me any, and I never tried to borrow any.'

'Doesn't it strike you as curious,' said the Inspector, 'that your sister didn't live – well, a little more up to her means? That she didn't take a house here, for example, or live in an hotel?'

'I don't think even Yseut would have had the cheek to do that with me about the place,' said Helen drily. 'She made herself pretty comfortable here, of course; but I think she must have enjoyed hoarding money, considering she spent most of her time industriously milking young men with incomes about twenty times smaller than her own.'

'Come, come, Miss Haskell!' said the Inspector. But he said it absently; it was obvious that his mind was on other things. After a while he took from an envelope the ring that had been on Yseut's finger and showed it to Helen. 'Did this belong to your sister?'

'That? Heavens, no. It be— What has that got to do with Yseut's death?'

'To whom does it belong?'

Helen was reluctant. 'If you must know,' she said, 'it belongs to Sheila McGaw, our producer. It's always been a standing joke in the theatre, it's such a grotesque and appalling thing. But—'

The Inspector nodded sagely. 'Just wanted confirmation on the point, miss. Miss McGaw has already admitted to ownership of the ring. Says she left it two days ago in one of the dressing-rooms. It seems,' he added heavily, as though the assertion required some peculiar extension of the powers of belief, 'that anyone, inside the theatre or out of it, could have walked in and made off with it.'

'I suppose so,' said Helen. 'There's no stage-door keeper, you know.'

'Just so. If Miss McGaw is telling the truth,' the Inspector added kindly to Nigel by way of exegesis, 'that means we're exactly where we were before.'

'For heaven's sake!' said Helen. 'What's the ring got to do with it?'

'It was found on your sister's finger, miss. And the evidence suggests that it may have been put on after death.'

'Oh!' Helen was suddenly and unaccountably silent.

'And now, Miss Haskell, can I have a brief account of your movements between six and nine last night?'

'Movements. Well, there weren't many. I left here to go to the theatre about half-past six, made up, went on at the beginning of the play – that's at a quarter to eight – was off again about ten minutes later, sat in my dressing-room and read, went on again about a quarter to nine—'

'Just a minute, Miss Haskell: do I understand you to say that you weren't on the stage between 7.55 and 8.45?'

For the first time Helen looked frightened. Nigel had a sinking feeling in the pit of his stomach; there was every reason – psychological, factual, evidential – why Helen should not have committed the murder – in his wildest dreams the thing would have been inconceivable – and yet he could not repress it.

'Yes; that's right,' said Helen.

'And do you share your dressing-room with anyone?'

'Yes, in the normal way; but not this week; the girl I share with isn't in the play. You mean I could have – slipped out without anyone knowing? I suppose I could. I can only say I didn't.' She recovered a little of her self-confidence. 'Certainly it would need a motive at least as strong as murder to make anyone take off make-up and put it on again half-an-hour later.'

It was at this point that Spencer returned, but his information was meagre; he had found no papers except a few personal letters of no importance and an address-book containing the address of Yseut's solicitor (which the Inspector pocketed).

'Apart from that,' he said, 'only the usual feminine artillery – begging your pardon, miss.' Helen gave him a smile in which humorous appreciation and mild flirtatiousness were mingled in exactly the right proportions.

The Inspector got to his feet. 'Well, I think that's all, Miss Haskell, thank you very much,' he said. 'Will you be wanting to see your sister at all?' Helen shook her head. 'Ah. Well, in the circumstances I think you're wise. You'll be required to identify the – her at the inquest, I'm afraid. That will be next Tuesday; we can't have it before because the coroner *and* the deputy-coroner have succeeded in being away at the same time.' He smiled sweetly at these happy evidences of incompetence in high places. Then, turning to Nigel, said in a lower voice: 'I don't mind telling you, sir, that the bullet which killed the young lady has been identified as coming from the gun we found.' Nigel contrived to look suitably impressed at this useless piece of information; if Yseut had been murdered, then the murder seemed equally impossible from whatever gun the bullet had been fired.

'Well,' continued the Inspector, 'I'll just take a look round the other room, and then I'll be off. And I don't mind telling you,' he added kindly, 'that *my* view, despite certain troublesome points, is that the thing was suicide. That,' he emphasized, 'is the official view.' He appeared to be hinting darkly at the per-niciousness of unofficial goings-on. Then, with a final affable nod, he left, Spencer and his apparatus trailing in his wake.

Nigel turned to Helen. She was a little pale. They looked at one another in silence for a moment; then Helen said 'Darling' and put her mouth to his.

10. Blooming Hopes Forfeited

What could possess you, in a critic age,
Such blooming hopes to forfeit on a stage?
And was it worth this wondrous waste of pains
To publish to the world your lack of brains?

Churchill

It must have been at least ten minutes later that they heard the rattle at the window. Nigel went over, opened it, and looked out. Gervase Fen, Professor of English Language and Literature in the University of Oxford, stood below, gazing mournfully at a grating through which the pencil he had thrown at the window had vanished beyond recovery. When he looked up, however, he appeared to be in his customary high spirits. He was muffled in an enormous raincoat and had on an extraordinary hat.

'Can I come up?' he shouted. 'Praise be to God, I've missed the Inspector and his minions. I must see Helen. I don't particularly want to see you,' he added as an afterthought.

Nigel waved an invitation, banging his head on the window-frame, and withdrew, swearing frightfully. Fen disposed of the stairs four at a time, and was in the room by the time he turned round again.

'You are old, Father William,' said Nigel, put out of countenance at this athletic display.

'All morning,' said Fen without preliminary, 'I've been going about in the wake of the good Inspector, comforting those he has affrighted, soothing those he has annoyed, and generally collecting a great deal of valueless and irrelevant facts.' He paused, resigning himself to the exercise of politeness, and beamed at Helen. 'Well, how are you, my dear? I'll spare you the condolences, because I know they aren't necessary.'

'Bless you, Gervase,' said Helen lightly.

'How long have you two known one another?' said Nigel suspiciously. 'And do you want to be left alone?'

'It's a *Wahlverwandtschaft*,' said Fen. 'Isn't it, Helen?'

'Stop this abominable flirting,' said Nigel with asperity, 'and tell us how the patient is this morning.'

'Oh, much the same as last night.' Fen collapsed heavily into a chair. 'One or two new things have come to light, though. It's a very complicated affair: wheels within wheels.' He nodded mysteriously.

'I suppose you realize,' said Helen, 'that I don't know the first thing about how my sister was murdered? Suppose one of you tells me the details, here and now.'

Fen suddenly became grave. 'You do it, Nigel,' he said. 'It may help me to get things a little clearer in my own mind.'

So Nigel went over those puzzling, delusive, improbable facts once again. No light came to him in the telling; and when he had finished he asked Fen for additions and comments. Fen paused for a moment and lit a cigarette; holding it between nicotine-stained fingers, he gestured vaguely.

'You know, of course,' he said, 'that the bullet did come from the gun we found? And that the ring is the property of Miss Sheila McGaw, who very carelessly left it lying about in a dressing-room?'

'Yes, yes,' said Nigel impatiently. 'We know all that.'

' "Mr Puff, as he knows all this, why does Sir Walter go on telling him?" ' Fen quoted irrepressibly. 'However: the point,' he reminded himself sternly. 'One or two other things may and should come up during the course of the day. You want comments. As regards the general set-up, contemplate this: suppose that each of the suspects in turn has committed the murder, and then consider which of the others, having seen that person commit the murder, would be inclined to protect him – or her.'

'Do you mean two people are in it?' asked Nigel.

'Oh Lord, no: nothing so dismal; all the unaided work of one person. But do as I say: think.'

'Well,' said Nigel slowly, 'I suppose Rachel would protect Robert, and *vice versa*; Jean would protect Donald – I don't know about the other way round, but I'm inclined to think he would protect her as well; Nicholas might protect anyone, for the sheer devilment of the thing, but most likely Donald; and this McGaw woman – I don't know about her.'

'Ah!' Fen seemed highly pleased. 'And now, the crime itself. Concentrate on the following points:

'(1) the fact that the wireless was playing the *Meistersinger* overture, followed by *Heldenleben* – a rich Teutonic concoction;

'(2) the fact that there was a smell of gunpowder smoke in the room when we entered it;

'(3) the fact that nothing was touched for at least a quarter of an hour after we came in.

'If that doesn't give it you,' he concluded, comfortable in the assurance that it would do nothing of the sort, 'then you're an imbecile.'

Nigel rapidly suppressed several unworthy desires, and contented himself with asking: 'You really know who did it?'

'I know,' said Fen sombrely. 'One way and another I've interviewed all the possibles now. But there's still a lot that wants confirming, fixing, strengthening. It was an ill-contrived crime – a rotten piece of work.' He turned suddenly to Helen. 'What would your reaction be if I were to let the person who killed your sister get away with it? It's a real problem, remember, not an argumentation; as far as I can see, the police don't seem likely to tumble to the real facts – not the way they're going about it now, anyway.'

Helen thought for a moment. Then she said frankly: 'It would depend who it was. If it were Robert or – yes, or Rachel, or even Sheila or Jean, I don't think I should mind. If it were Donald or Nick – it sounds beastly, I know, but – well, yes, I would.'

Fen nodded his head gravely. 'Very sensible,' he said. 'Personally, I should be in favour of giving a flimsy chance all round – a warning to get out, say. In this wilderness of ration-books and registration and identity cards, if anyone could get away, they'd really deserve it. All this is highly immoral, you know,' he said quizzically, unjustly involving Helen and Nigel in the accusation, 'and I'm not sure that I shouldn't in law be an accessory after the fact. But your sister, Helen – forgive me – was, it appears, rather a pest in a number of ways.'

They sat in silence for a few moments. Then Nigel said: 'But what about the ring, Gervase? The Gilded Fly?'

'Gilded Fly, indeed: you old poetizer,' said Fen. 'That, I

admit, puzzles me still. We shall have to dig that up with hard labour. And now' – he looked at his watch – 'we – and you, Helen – had better get off to this rehearsal, if we're not going to be late. In the doubtless immortal words of Mr Herbert Morrison, we must go to it. We should be able – Oh my dear paws! Oh my fur and whiskers!' He broke off, staring blankly in front of him. 'Lord, *Lord*, what a fool I've been! And yes – it fits – absolutely characteristic. Heaven grant Gideon Fell never becomes privy to my lunacy; I should never hear the end of it.' He gaped.

Nigel regarded him coldly. 'Stop this exhibition,' he said, 'which you know perfectly well is unintelligible to everyone but yourself, and let's go. It's five minutes to eleven. We shall have to run all the way as it is.'

With some difficulty they removed him from the room.

On the way to the theatre he recovered something of his high spirits, which manifested themselves in the normal way by an incessant stream of complaint. He complained impartially and at length about the weather, the progress of the war, food, and the University in general. On this latter subject he subsequently particularized to a libellous extent. As he talked he strode along at a rate which by the time they had reached the theatre had reduced Helen and Nigel to a state of mild exhaustion.

The reaction of the company at large to the news of Yseut's death appeared to be salutory; a sense of relief was plainly discernible, and no one seemed to be at all concerned at the reflection that a murderer might be in their midst. The general feeling was, in fact, that this could hardly be considered as murder, and was on a par with such actions as the drowning of superfluous kittens, the painless putting-away of aged dogs, and the necessary destruction of vermin. The rehearsal began well and went on well. Nigel sat and watched it from the front, while Fen prowled about getting in everyone's way, exhibiting an exaggerated interest in the proceedings, and asking idiotic questions.

Shortly after twelve Robert called a halt, and the majority of the company retreated to the 'Aston Arms', Fen and Nigel following with Helen. The 'Aston Arms' was none of your brightly-painted, up-and-coming hostelries. It exuded so strongly an atmosphere of the past that drinkers living were spiritually cowed and jostled by the shades of drinkers long dead and gone. Every suggestion of improvement or modernization was grimly resisted by the management, which consisted of a large, ancient man manifestly disintegrating at a great rate into his component chemical elements. An elaborate ritual, the abandonment of which was anathema, presided over the ordering and consumption of drinks; a strict social hierarchy was maintained; irregular visitors were unwelcome, and regular customers, particularly the acting profession, were treated with a mild pervasive contempt. The only salient feature of the small, rather shabby public bar was an enormous nude parrot, which had early contracted the habit of pecking out all its feathers, and which now, with the exception of the ruff and head, which it could not reach, presented a dismal and ludicrous grey, scraggy body to the gaze. It had been given to the proprietor of the 'Aston Arms' in a fit of lachrymose gratitude by a visiting German professor, and was in the habit of reciting a lyric of Heine, which feat, however, it could only be induced to perform by the careful repetition of two lines from the beginning of Mallarmé's *L'Apres-midi d'un Faune,* this appearing to start some appropriate train of suggestion in its mind. This aptitude aroused the deepest suspicions in such soldiery as frequented the 'Aston Arms', equalled only by their suspicion of those of their countrymen who were capable of similar or greater achievements in the same direction; it was employed by the proprietor to warn customers of the imminence of closing-time, and the raucous tones of *Ich weiss nicht, was soll es bedeuten, dass ich so traurig bin* were the normal prelude to more forcible means of ejection.

In the small room Fen's entrance was overwhelming; even the sibyl behind the bar appeared to be cowed by his exuberant presence. He ordered drinks in a profane and iconoclastic manner.

'When I was a proctor,' he said, 'I used to have great difficulties – about pubs, I mean. The people I found in pubs were invariably my most brilliant pupils, and I wanted nothing better than to stop and drink and talk books with them. So I used only to come when I simply had to, and then march through, with a stern expression, taking no notice of anyone. When the junior proctor was going out, I discovered his itinerary and rang up my best friends and warned them. All very illegal, I fear.' He sighed.

'Dear me,' said Nigel mockingly. 'What a *picaro* character you are, to be sure!' Fen gazed at him reproachfully.

Sheila McGaw and Nicholas were standing in a corner together, Nicholas making uncertain attempts to ruffle the parrot's poll.

'If it tries to bite you,' said Sheila helpfully, 'don't take your hand away; that only encourages it.' Nicholas suffered some moments of acute agony, then pulled his finger away and regarded it ruefully. 'That,' he remarked briefly, 'is a fallacy.'

Fen went across to them. 'Ah, Barclay,' he said. 'A brief moment of conversation, if I may.' He smiled affably at Sheila, who drifted away to join Robert and Rachel at the bar. An uneasy silence fell, through which Donald Fellowes, in another part of the room, could clearly be heard discoursing on the technique of orchestration. 'Dear me,' said Fen. 'How quiet everything is. I don't want our conversation to be as public as all this.' He apostrophized the parrot in French: it became launched on *Die Lorelei*; general conversation hurriedly reasserted itself in self-defence. Through the hubbub Fen said:

'Has the Inspector been to visit you this morning?'

'No,' said Nicholas. 'Thanks be to God. No doubt he found my evidence so lucid last night that he had nothing further to ask. How are things going?'

Fen looked at him curiously for a moment. 'As well as can be expected,' he said. 'You're perfectly certain that neither you nor Donald left that room at any time last night?'

' – *Die schönste Jungfrau sitzet dort oben wunderbar*,' the parrot was saying in heartfelt tones; it paused and breathed stertorously before proceeding with the next couplet.

Nicholas threw up his arms in mock surrender. 'Maestro, I am discovered,' he said. 'How did you guess?'

'I guessed,' answered Fen uncommunicatively. 'It was, I suppose, Donald who went out – immediately after doing the black-out?'

Nicholas sat up sharply. 'How do you know that?'

'A conjecture merely. I believe that when he went to the windows he saw someone he knew, and went out to speak to them. There are certain things which can't be explained in any other way.'

'As it happens, you're right. He and the other person chattered just round the bend in the passage which leads through to the courtyard. I don't suppose that fool of a workman noticed anything. Anyway, Donald was back in under two minutes. There's no reason to suppose either of them had anything to do with the murder.'

'Then you know who the other person was?' said Fen softly.

Nicholas set his lips. 'No,' he answered.

'I suggest that even if you didn't know at the time, Fellowes would have told you when he returned.'

'Why should he?'

'It would have been natural. Unless' – Fen paused – 'unless of course he already knew that a murder had been committed, and was anxious to cover up.'

Nicholas went white. 'I don't know who the other person was,' he repeated slowly and emphatically.

Fen grunted and got up. 'You're being very unhelpful,' he said, 'though fortunately it's of no importance. There's already sufficient evidence to hang someone – perhaps you know whom. I assure you, it's only for my own satisfaction that I want things nicely ticketed and catalogued, and I suppose I can't expect you to subscribe to that.' Nicholas glanced across at Donald. 'It's all right,' added Fen ironically, 'I'll give you plenty of time to fix your story with Fellowes before I question him. Fools are too easy prey without courtesies of that kind.' His eyes were hard.

' – *Und das hat mit ihrem Singen die Lore-Ley getan,*' the parrot concluded with hoarse triumph, and fell abruptly silent.

Fen turned back again to Nicholas. 'Tell me,' he said, 'your opinion on the ethics of murder.'

Nicholas looked at him in silence for a moment. 'Very well,' he said at last. 'I believe killing to be an inescapable necessity of the world in which we live, the abominable, sentimental, mob-ruled world of cheap newspapers and cheaper minds, where every imbecile is articulate and every folly tolerated, where the arts are dying out and the intellect is scorned, where every little cheap-jack knows what he likes and what he thinks. Our mora-lities, our democracy, have taught us to suffer fools gladly, and now we suffer from an overplus of fools. Every fool dead is an advance, and be damned to humanity and virtue and charity and Christian tolerance.'

Fen nodded. 'Quite the little fascist,' he said. 'Julius Vander, in *The Professor*, would appeal to you very much. The facts, allowing for a certain wildness, may be correct; the conclusion is fortunately false. What you need,' he said benevolently, 'is a little elementary education; I think you would find it helpful.' He smiled sweetly and was gone.

Fen studied Sheila McGaw curiously as he put his drink on the table and settled down opposite her. The immediate im-pression was that she was somewhere in her thirties. Her sharp-ly-cut features were pale and lined; her voice was hoarse with overmuch smoking, and she coughed frequently. Only after a while did one realize that she was in fact much younger than this – hardly more than twenty-two or twenty-three. Small ges-tures, a sort of underlying softness in the features, and little mannerisms of speech and expression betrayed this. Less tough than she looks, thought Fen, who was prone to slightly out-of-date Americanisms.

She offered him a cigarette saying: 'Well? More about the murder?'

Fen nodded. 'In a way. All I really wanted was to confirm the business about the ring.'

'Oh, that. I gather it puts me in the front line of suspects. And the fact that I had a motive. And the fact that I haven't got an alibi.' She blew smoke in two tapering jets from her rather prominent narrow nostrils.

'No alibi?'

'I was in my room reading all last evening. The police have made the brilliant deduction that I might have slipped out and back again at any time without anyone knowing.'

Fen sighed. 'There's an almost total lack of alibis in this case. Lots of motives, no alibis, and, in the Inspector's opinion, an impossible crime.'

'You mean it was suicide?'

'I'm certain it was nothing of the sort. It would be too perfect an example of dramatic irony to be real.'

She nodded, and then said: 'If the police think it's suicide, must you disabuse them? Suicide or murder, it was really an awfully good thing.'

'This young woman must have been very much disliked,' Fen murmured. 'I sometimes wonder if you haven't all lost your sense of proportion over her.'

'If you'd worked with her for a couple of years you wouldn't say that.'

'Tell me: this ring of yours; has anyone ever particularly remarked on it?'

'I should think it's provoked a witticism of some sort from everyone in the theatre.'

Fen grunted, gazed at his beer with distaste, and swallowed half of it at a gulp. Just such an expression must Brother Barbaro have had when, at Francis' behest, he swallowed the ass's dung. Whisky was unobtainable at the 'Aston Arms'.

'Has there been any comment on it just recently?' he asked. 'Within the last week?'

'There was some talk about it in the green room after rehearsal on Wednesday, in which more or less everyone joined. Afterwards I went into one of the dressing-rooms to wash some paint off my hands, took it off and left it on the wash-basin. When I went back for it half-an-hour later it was gone.'

'Whose dressing-room?'

'Well, they're swapped about a good deal; it's the one Rachel will have next week. It happens to be the first you come to.'

'And who was present when there was this talk about the ring?'

'Almost everyone, I think, including the hangers-on.'

'Including – ?' Fen named a name which made Sheila sit up abruptly and stare at him for a moment or two before replying.

'Yes,' she said slowly, 'but surely – '

'Don't misinterpret me,' said Fen. 'It would be most unwise to jump to conclusions.' He relapsed into a moody silence. Then he said:

'Have you any objection to Warner's coming here and producing this play over your head, as it were?'

Sheila shrugged, and fell into a paroxysm of coughing. 'Damn,' she said, wiping her eyes with a handkerchief. 'I'm sorry. What were you saying? Oh yes, about Robert's producing this play. Well, I suppose it would have been good publicity if I could have done it. But he's an infinitely better producer than I am, and it's only reasonable that he should have wanted to produce his own play. No, I don't mind. I could have prevented it being put on here if I'd chosen, but I didn't choose.'

'You admire his work, then?'

Sheila grinned. ' "Admire": hardly the appropriate word, I think. Does one venture to "admire" Shakespeare?'

Fen raised his eyebrows. 'All that, eh? Of course,' he added hastily, 'I'm no judge of contemporary literature, but I think I agree. Yes, I think I agree. And *Metromania* is –'

'The best thing he's ever done.'

Donald Fellowes joined them, clutching a half-pint. 'Nicholas tells me,' he said stiffly to Fen, 'that I am now under suspicion.'

'Fellowes,' said Fen kindly, 'you are every sort of imbecile. You don't, alas, realize that withheld information always comes out in the end. Then why do you withhold it? It makes you look so silly to go on like that when everyone knows exactly what you're hiding.'

Donald muttered: 'Well, go on then. Tell me what I'm hiding.'

'My good young man,' said Fen with some asperity, 'I'm not here to do what you think fit. I shall tell you when I'm ready. In the meantime – '

'In the meantime,' Donald put in with sudden violence, 'what the hell's it got to do with you, anyway? You're not the police.'

Fen got to his feet; he towered over Donald as a liner towers over a tug. 'You are,' he said, 'without exception the most imbecile ignominious cretinous poltroon it has ever been my evil fortune to meet. What is worse, you become more imbecile, ignominious, cretinous and poltroonish with every hour that passes. You are, one must grudgingly admit, a very good organist and choirmaster. Otherwise it's extremely unlikely that the college would have tolerated you for so long. Several times I've had to use my influence to prevent you being sent down for idleness. And now you have the impertinence to come to me and question my right to discover what I can about this case. I'd better warn you here and now that if you continue this idiotic policy of concealment you'll quite justly get yourself landed in gaol; and this time I shall not get you out of it.'

Donald was pale. 'Damn you!' he said. 'What right have you got to talk to me like that? Oh my God, I shall be glad to get out of this place – with its lousy traditions and cheap minds and jacks-in-office. If you imagine I care twopence about your threats, I can assure you you're quite mistaken.' He glared at Fen for a moment, then turned and went out.

Nigel, who had come in on the tail-end of this unexpected and disgraceful scene, whistled softly. 'Well, well!' he said. 'Invective with a vengeance!'

Fen grinned cheerfully. 'A calculated performance on my part, I fear, designed to a perfectly dispassionate end. Maybe I shouldn't have done it.' He looked dubious. 'Still, it might have helped.' He rubbed his nose thoughtfully.

Sheila chuckled. 'Donald on his dignity is always slightly ludicrous,' she said. 'He'll have got over it in half-an-hour or so.' She yawned and stretched.

'And now,' said Fen, looking anxiously about him, 'I must see Miss West, before this rehearsal gets on the move again.' He pointed at his tankard. 'Nigel, be a dear boy and get me some more of this odious concoction.' He moved off purposefully in the direction of Rachel, who was talking to Robert.

Robert said: 'I hope you're not too bored with the rehearsal.' His eyes twinkled behind his glasses.

'On the contrary, I find it fascinating,' said Fen, 'and inconceivable.'

'Inconceivable?'

'In this, as in a very few other works of literature, there are things which one can only put down to divine inspiration. Normally one can easily follow the rather laborious and mechanical processes of an author's thought. It's the unexpected, inconceivable things which don't fit into that process, and which yet are absolutely *right*, that I mean.'

Robert chuckled. 'Tricks! A bag of tricks solely, I assure you. I'm going to begin on another shortly which I hope will be better – or less bad.'

Fen was pensive. 'Another?'

'As soon as I get finished here. And next time it will go on in town, with all the bunting and flags out. I hope and think this will, too. In fact I'm certain of it, now we've got this far. Even after years of experience one never quite knows when one's writing a thing how it will turn out in practice.' Under the sober indifference of his tone there was a strain of fanaticism which led Fen to ask:

'Why, chiefly, do you write?'

Robert smiled. 'For money – and for the sake of showing off; I think that's why most men, even the very greatest, have written. The Creation of Art' – he succeeded in making the capitals articulate – 'is an object which seldom enters into their calculations. Necessarily. Most original artists don't know what art is, or beauty. They're almost invariably hopeless critics; writers never know the first thing about music, or musicians about writing, or painters about either, so it can't be beauty they're all intent on. That presumably is a sort of incidental occurrence, like the pearl in an oyster.'

There was a fractional pause. Then Fen nodded vigorously. 'I look forward,' he said, 'to Monday night. Are you getting on all right without Yseut?'

Robert looked uncomfortable. 'Callous as it seems, we're getting on like wildfire without Yseut. Her habit of unintelligent but persistent criticism was becoming very wearing. I've no objection to having my plays criticized, providing it's along the right lines. But she, dear child, never knew the first thing about plays, and simply slanged anything that offended her commercial-bred prejudices. Slanged publicly and offensively, what's more. I may say it was getting to be something of a serious problem.'

'Granted that,' said Rachel, 'I think everyone has been making too much of her nuisance-value, particularly since they've heard she's dead. After all, she wasn't more than one of many tiresome people Providence has seen fit to inflict on the world.'

'I quite agree,' said Fen. 'The forked tail has been overmuch in evidence. It's been very harassing.' He sighed. 'Everyone has been so anxious to tell the police how much they disliked her – to divert suspicion from themselves, I suppose, by a sort of sophisticated double-bluff – that it's been impossible to sort out any finer and more significant shades of opinion.'

'Is it usual,' asked Robert mildly, 'for the detective to discuss the crime with his suspects in this impartial and informative fashion?'

'A *sine qua non*,' said Fen cheerfully. 'In the course of the discussion they are supposed to give away their inmost feelings. But do you regard yourself as a suspect?'

'Well,' said Robert a trifle vaguely, 'I suppose I could have rushed out of the lavatory, shot the girl, rushed back again, and re-appeared at the appropriate moment.'

'I'm sorry to say,' said Fen, 'that for reasons which have been discussed, you could have done nothing of the sort. You're quite cleared from that imputation.'

'I won't say I'm relieved, because I never really considered it seriously. But it's nice to have things cleared up.' Robert appeared to be filing the matter away in some remote corner of his mind. Rachel said:

'And what about me? Am I above suspicion too?'

'That depends,' Fen replied affably. 'What were you doing at the time of the crime?' he apostrophized her sternly.

'Please, sir, I was at a cinema, brooding over the failings of the male sex.'

'Oh?' Fen was surprised. 'But I expected you to be impeccably vouched for by someone in North Oxford.'

'My fault,' said Robert. 'What with my literal mind and my personal vanity, I couldn't believe that was only an excuse to get away from me.'

'The Inspector,' pursued Rachel, 'was furiously suspicious about that. What was worse, I couldn't for the life of me remember what cinema it was – I just went into the first one I came to – or what film was on. I didn't pay the least attention to it in any case, and I'm not sure I could even say what it was about. The Inspector is obviously one of those people who set out to see a particular film, arrive punctually at the beginning, and pay the closest attention throughout.'

Fen nodded. 'Personally,' he said a little absently, 'I never go to the cinema except to sleep; I find the atmosphere very soporific.' He gazed about him, seeming to seek admiration and approval for this eccentricity. Then his face clouded slightly, and he added: 'But I shouldn't treat your lack of alibi too lightly, if I were you. We know it's all very human and natural, but the fact remains that you still haven't got an alibi for the time when murder was committed.'

'Rebuked,' said Rachel soberly. 'Of course you're right. But is it quite certain that Yseut didn't commit suicide? I know it seems improbable, but – '

'Nothing is certain,' said Fen, 'until the police make up their minds. They'll more or less instruct the coroner, he'll more or less instruct the jury, and unless fresh evidence turns up – there, one way or another, the matter will rest.'

'But you're working with the police,' Rachel insisted. 'What do you – you personally – think?'

'I think it was murder,' said Fen slowly, 'and I have known for some time who the murderer is.'

Robert contrived to look suitably outraged. 'Then why on earth,' he asked, 'don't you tell the police and get it over with? Not enough proof?'

'Not enough incidental proofs, of course. The main fact stands out as plain as daylight. Only one person in this whole wide world could have killed Yseut Haskell. I admit that it depends on the reliability of one witness, but I've no reason to suppose that witness anything but reliable on that point.' His face was grave.

'Then there's to be an arrest?' asked Robert. 'Why not straight away?'

Fen gestured vaguely. 'The murderer is a human being, not a cipher, an x, though he's that till he's discovered. On the discovery the hunt inevitably slows down. One has been pursuing an electric hare, and on cornering it, one finds it to be a real one. I confess I'm very reluctant – ' He fell silent.

Robert nodded briskly. 'Understandable,' he said, 'if a trifle sentimental. The crime is a sudden, final, unanticipated blow, the detection of the criminal has all the cumulative cruelty of the hunt. Still, murder's murder.' He appeared to find comfort in this simple reflection.

Nigel approached with a pint of beer, which Fen regarded with some dismay. He put it down on the counter and turned his back on it, apparently hoping that by ignoring it he could induce it to disappear. 'I remember,' he said vaguely to Robert, 'something about your going to South America before the war. Was it pleasant?'

Robert seemed a little taken aback. 'You seem to take a passionate interest in my travels,' he said drily. 'Last night it was Egypt. Yes, I've been to South America several times – Buenos Aires and Rio mostly.'

'And with what' – Fen addressed Nigel sternly – 'do you associate South America?'

'Nuts, pampas grass, and Carmen Miranda,' replied Nigel promptly.

Fen made remote noises indicative of pleasure. 'Excellent well, i' faith,' he said, 'a splendid index to the journalistic mind. Free association has its uses.'

'We must be moving,' said Robert, glancing at his watch. Fen turned his attention reluctantly to his beer, and contrived to swallow it in one gulp, amid a good deal of admiration. 'I think,' he said thoughtfully as he put the tankard down, 'I shouldn't have done that.'

'*Revenons à nos moutons,* dear hearts,' said Robert, 'we must press on, press on.' In twos and threes they moved towards the door. The parrot gazed sedately after them.

11. The Questing Beast

And aloof in the roof, beyond the feast,
I heard the squeak of the questing beast,
where it scratched itself in the blank between
the queen's substance and the queen.

Charles Williams

Jane met them as they trooped in at the stage door. 'I was just coming to fetch you,' she said to Fen. 'There's a call for you on the phone outside the green room, from a Sir Richard Freeman. He says it's important and he's been trying to get you everywhere.' Fen nodded and bustled away. Nigel went and settled down in the auditorium to watch the remainder of the rehearsal. He was impressed by the business-like air which had come over the production since Tuesday; props were available, the stage was accurately set, the prompter sat in his corner, people were no longer carrying books; moves were contrived with apparent ease, and there were comparatively few interruptions. Nigel regretted that he had not seen the intervening rehearsals and observed the step by step elevation from open play-acting to conviction and realism, the gradual disintegration of the barrier between the actors and the play, the progressive convergence and eventual fusion of real people and fictional people. Certainly the process made one realize the cumulative nervous strain through which actors and actresses have to go up to the first night.

Fen returned and dumped himself down in the next seat. 'That was Sir Richard,' he whispered unnecessarily, 'giving the official view. Apparently they've more or less finally plumped for suicide. I was non-committal, but it does give me a rather tiresome responsibility.'

'By the way,' said Nigel, 'what was the result of the autopsy?'

'Exactly as we expected. Nothing new.'

'H'm,' said Nigel. 'Then where do we go from here?'

'We carry on as we were, and get things cleared up as far as possible. After that, God knows. I think I shall have to closet myself with the Professor of Ethical Philosophy in an endeavour to work out the best course of action. – Nigel, what character is that who is walking across the back of the stage?'

'That's one of the stage hands.'

'Oh. – Now, what was I saying? Oh, yes, about the Professor of Ethical Philosophy. How in heaven's name did I come to be talking about him? The man has no sense of responsibility whatever. It's my belief he's a bigamist.'

Nigel sighed. 'You've lost the point again, Gervase,' he said. 'I asked originally what you were going to do next.'

'Oh, yes. Well, first I must see this Whitelegge girl, then I must put through a phone call to a friend of mine who used to be on the Secretariat of the League of Nations, and then I must go and talk to the porter at the "Mace and Sceptre". Did I tell you, by the way, that the police have investigated Yseut's movements during the hours before she came to the college? Very little of importance. She wrote some letters during the afternoon, had tea in her rooms, went and visited a young man in B.N.C., returned, put through an unidentified phone-call from the "Mace and Sceptre" – procuring a London directory from the porter, by the way, which is why I want to see him – and then apparently went straight to the college.'

'Is that helpful?'

'Not particularly. Actually, there's an outstanding blank in the whole business which I should like to be able to fill in, though I don't see how I can. If only you hadn't gone gallivanting up to town,' he added with mild indignation, 'you might have been able to help.'

'I didn't know there was going to be a murder.'

'I thought you had intimations – intimations of mortality. But never mind. Is the man who has just fallen down a flight of steps part of the play?'

Nigel listened carefully for a moment, and then said: 'No.'

The door to the left of the auditorium opened, and Helen slipped out and joined them. 'A few minutes' respite,' she said. 'Lord, I don't know my lines in this act. Is this just recreation, or do you hope to find a clue by watching us all?'

'Idleness merely,' said Fen. 'Do you get nervous when it gets close to a first night?'

'I'm scared out of my wits,' said Helen. 'Ordinary first nights are bad enough, but this is something in the way of a national event. Half the London agents, managers and producers will be down, and everyone will be trying to catch their eye. If it wasn't that Robert has a sort of iron remote-control over the whole business, we should all overplay frightfully.'

'Would it help you,' said Fen, 'if I asked my friend — ' (he gave the name of an actor so celebrated that Helen's eyes widened) – 'to come down? He's looking for someone to play opposite in his next production, and I can see to it that he takes no notice of anyone but you. Besides, I have a hold over him. We were at school together, and he did awful things.'

'Could you?' said Helen with as much composure as was possible in the circumstances. 'I shall be terrified, but one must go through with these things.'

'He shall be summoned,' said Fen solemnly, 'and appear under threat of horrible revelations. And now tell me. Is this girl Jean Whitelegge anywhere about in the theatre?'

'She should have arrived by now, though I know she said she'd be late this morning. She'll probably be in the prop room; down the stairs to the left of the stage door.' Helen glanced momentarily at the stage. 'God, I'm off!' She hastily retreated the way she had come, reappearing a moment later on stage to say:

'I can't find him anywhere. I've looked all over the house, under the – under the – ' She flicked her fingers in the direction of the prompt corner. 'Yes?' she queried; no prompt was forthcoming.

Robert marched irritably down the gangway. 'Is there no one on the book?' he asked. 'Jane! Jane dear!'

There was a subdued scuffling and turning of pages in the prompt corner, into which those on the stage gazed with weary contempt. Eventually a voice announced:

'Under the floor, on the roof – '

'Yes, dear,' said Robert. 'Do *keep* on the book, otherwise we waste such a lot of time.'

Jane appeared momentarily. 'I'm sorry, darling,' she said, 'but Michael's on the book during this scene, because I have to look after the panatrope.' There ensued a sound of surly argument backstage.

'Well, I don't care who does it,' said Robert, 'provided somebody's there. All right, people. On we go.' The rehearsal proceeded on its way.

Fen stirred uneasily. 'I must seek out the Whitelegge dame,' he announced outrageously.

'Me too?' asked Nigel.

'No, thank you, Nigel. This will be delicate and confidential rapprochement. Quite unsuited to one of your frank, open, athletic temperament.' Nigel glared after him as he went.

Fen eventually ran Jean Whitelegge to earth in the green room, where she was sitting alone, reading a copy of *Metromania* without any particular attention. She was, Fen thought as he introduced himself, pretty obviously distrait. He regarded her with a curiosity befitting the final link in the little complex of motive and passion which had led up to the murder of Yseut, noted that she was plain but not unattractive, quiet but by no means characterless, competent, and, he suspected, a little fanatical about the arts. Her soft brown hair, gently glowing in the morning light, was curled behind her ears, her mouth was carefully rouged, and she wore a plain blue frock designed to fit the needs of one easily conscious that her figure needs no disguising. Fen took a moment to admire her natural, stealthy grace, and to wish that she could order her life more usefully than in performing mechanical jobs in the theatre.

'You must forgive my bothering you,' he said, 'particularly as I believe the Inspector has been at you earlier on this morning.' He cautiously assumed a pose of intellectual superiority. 'But frankly, I don't think he much knows what he's about. And besides, I have an insatiable curiosity about these things. Like Webster, I am much possessed by death.' He introduced the allusion deliberately, and watched with interest to see what reaction it would provoke.

Jean smiled. 'The skull beneath the skin,' she said. 'I'm a little morbid myself.' Her voice became suddenly guarded. 'Do ask anything you like.'

'First of all, then: you took the gun away from Captain Graham's room?'

He thought he saw a momentary expression of relief in her

eyes. 'Yes,' she said. 'I went back to borrow it, found he'd gone to bed, and – well, I'm afraid I just took it. I meant to let him know, but I've been hopelessly busy, and somehow or other I never got round to it.'

'And you took it, of course, because you wanted it as a property for *Metromania.*'

Jean nodded vigorously. 'That's right. It's used in the last act. We did have property guns, of course, but they went to the war effort, and we were told we could borrow any we wanted from the local police.'

'Why didn't you do that?'

'Well, it seems ridiculous, but – you see we did borrow one once before – and – well, we lost it.'

'Lost it?'

Jean made a helpless gesture. 'It just disappeared at the end of the week. Things do tend to do that in repertory. If people don't borrow them, they get covered with a mass of other stuff, and prove impossible to find. Anyway, the result is that the police don't regard us in the least favourably, and I simply hadn't the nerve to go to them. Actually,' she added in a burst of frankness, 'I didn't think Peter Graham would lend me the gun, so I just took it.'

Fen appeared to be making a rapid mental estimate of the morality of this proceeding. 'Rather a risk, wasn't it?' he said mildly.

'Well, Robert wanted it for Thursday morning – he told me so at the party – and I thought we could at least use it temporarily.'

'And then, of course, it disappeared. Where was it left?'

'In the prop room.'

'Can anyone get into it?'

'Yes, anyone. Some time late on Thursday it – it just went.'

'And with it, I suspect, something else.' Fen named it, and she stared incredulously at him. 'How did you know?' she said. There was a hint of sudden panic terror in her eyes.

'Why not from there?' said Fen softly. 'It was perfectly convenient. I presume you didn't take the cartridges? You wouldn't have needed them.' She shook her head.

'Were they there when you took the gun?' Fen pursued.

'I – I really don't remember.'

'They might have been removed some time during the party, then?'

'I suppose so.'

Fen nodded, apparently satisfied. 'So I thought,' he said. 'And of course, there's only Captain Graham's chance remark to suggest they were there at all.' He paused. 'And now, would you mind giving me a true account of your movements yesterday evening – as opposed to the account you gave the police?'

She was pale. 'I told the police the truth. I didn't kill Yseut. I was in my room at college all evening.'

'I think not,' said Fen.

Tears came into her eyes. 'Please, Mr Fen. That's the truth. I didn't kill Yseut.'

Fen was slightly embarrassed. 'I didn't exactly say you had. In any case, I'm so well acquainted with the truth about this business, that your assurances, one way or the other, don't particularly matter. It's simply that I like to get things straightened out.'

'You know who did it?' she leaned forward, and there was a catch in her voice.

Fen nodded, and awaited the inevitable request.

'Need you tell the police? That is – '

Fen sighed. 'Upon my soul,' he said, 'you are either the most charitable or the most immoral set of people I have ever come across in my life. Not one of you but wants the whole business passed over in silence. I find it very discouraging.'

Jean rose and began to pace about the room. 'Well?' she said.

'That,' Fen replied, 'I shall have to think about. You are, if you'll forgive my saying so, a poor liar, Miss Whitelegge. But then an adequate ability to dissemble seems completely lacking in this case. From beginning to end' – he looked at her intently – 'the whole thing has been an incompetent muddle, in which the hand of the author has been painfully obvious. I find it depressing. It hasn't been a battle of wits, it's been a walk-over, and like all walk-overs it's turned sour on me. Perhaps that's why I feel reluctant to give the poor fish away – an atavistic survival of the code of honour. It's too easy to triumph over a second-rate mind.'

She turned to him, her eyes blazing. 'Hasn't it occurred to you,' she cried, 'that whoever did this may simply not have cared about dissembling, about the niggling intellectual puzzles and cryptograms which seem to delight you?'

'It has occurred to me,' said Fen coolly, 'and I think that at first that was that person's attitude. A good deal of deliberate carelessness seems to suggest that. In actually committing the murder, however, that person decided, at the eleventh hour, to create a cryptogram; and like all *extempore* cryptograms, it was only too dismally easy to solve.' He rose. 'Thank you, Miss Whitelegge. You've been involuntarily informative to a high degree.'

She seemed suddenly helpless and bewildered. 'I – I – '

'I've no wish to play the heavy uncle with you,' said Fen kindly, 'and doubtless you're prepared to accept the responsibility for your actions. But I must warn you quite frankly that the game is up. I'm not suggesting that you should go to the police; but I give you until Monday morning to come to me.' She was silent. 'God knows, girl, I know how difficult it will be. Take a grip on yourself.' He turned to go, then added, as an afterthought:

'By the way, what are you reading up here?'

She stared at him blankly. 'Greats – Greek and Latin.' Fen nodded. 'I'll leave you now. Think over my peroration. If you don't do as I say, then I warn you: you may be putting another person's life in danger.' He turned and went out.

Nigel was beginning to feel hungry. His attention wandered frequently from what was going on on the stage to the contemplation of lunch. This was the more so as it had suddenly occurred to him that by watching rehearsals he might be spoiling Monday night's performance for himself. This view was apparently shared by divine providence, which suddenly erected a barrier between him and *Metromania* in the shape of the safety curtain, a heavy contraption which was abruptly lowered, narrowly missing the head of the husbandly Clive, who leaped out of the way with a startled oath. Nigel had barely time to digest the information imprinted thereon, to the effect that in the event of fire the theatre could be cleared in three minutes, before there was a bellow of rage from Robert, who was sitting some way behind him. This minatory noise apparently had the desired effect, and the safety curtain went up again, to disclose a small, bewildered group on the stage, casting vague glances up at the electrician's gallery, whence the curtain was operated. A confused discussion about responsibility was still going on when Fen returned.

'*Allons*,' he said. 'We have no further business here.' They left the rehearsal in a state of mild chaos.

Once they were out in the street, and marching at a brisk pace towards the 'Mace and Sceptre', Fen drew a deep breath. 'I've been bullying,' he said, 'in the most ungentlemanly fashion.' And he gave Nigel a brief account of his interview with Jean. Nigel looked bewildered.

'Well,' he said, 'so what?'

'So my conjecture was right. We've very little more to do now. One thing, as a matter of routine, we must search Fellowes' room, though I've little hope of our finding anything.'

'You mean for whatever Yseut was looking for?'

'Nigel,' said Fen with heavy sarcasm, 'you are a brilliant pupil. We shall make a detective of you yet.'

'I've no wish to be a detective,' said Nigel huffily.

'I confess,' said Fen, 'that in a case like this it's a singularly unpleasant job. Be honest with me, Nigel; what ought I to do? I confess my instinct as a good citizen is to hand over my results to the police, as I've done on other occasions. But then there are other considerations: Robert's a great playwright, Rachel's a fine actress, Nicholas, when he pulls himself together, has a first-rate brain, Fellowes is a brilliant organist, Sheila McGaw is a good producer, and Jean Whitelegge is just an essentially nice person. Yseut wasn't any of those things, and I don't want to see any of them caught in the soulless grinding of the forensic machine on her account, or by my agency. If only the police would use their commonsense! It's their profession to catch and kill people, and such considerations wouldn't count with them. But they're going rampaging off on this suicide idea, and only my intervention will stop them.'

'It depends,' said Nigel slowly. 'Do you think the murderer is likely to act again?'

'Another murder? I doubt it, though I used that as a bait a few minutes ago.'

'Then I think,' said Nigel with sudden inspiration, 'that you should read Goethe's *Tasso*. More or less, it's a study of how far the artistic temperament can go in defiance of society.'

'My dear Nigel: it states the problem, but it never gets anywhere near solving it. I'm inclined, you know, to take the philistine view that there's a good deal of hooey about the artistic temperament. So many of the greatest artists have been without it, or rather they've had sufficient low cunning to satisfy their beyond-good-and-evil tendencies *sub rosa*, without arousing the wrath of society. The artistic temperament is too often only an alibi for lack of responsibility – *vide* the late lamented Yseut. A skirt,' he added solemnly, 'if ever there was one.'

'My dear Gervase, if you must use these vile Americanisms, for heaven's sake use them correctly. Read Mencken. "A skirt" is a vulgarism for any sort of woman.'

Fen appeared to be considering this; but when he spoke, it was to say: 'I think that what I suggested to Helen would be the best thing: a brief and succinct warning to get out. The trouble is, we're all so damnably intelligent at Oxford,' he said irritably. 'The fact of murder, which rouses an immediate instinct of self-preservation in the unsophisticated, has to penetrate to our animal souls through a thick barrier of sophisms; apparently in the present case it hasn't even done that – merely bounced off again. Yet murder remains murder, none the less' – (to lie in cold obstruction and to rot, thought Nigel) – 'and there's no way of getting round it. Prayer and meditation seem to be my only course; what it is to have a conscience! And to think that only a few days ago I was looking forward to some nice clean uncomplicated killing! You know what holds this business together, Nigel? Sex – the Questing Beast. That's the root and origin of the whole thing. Reduced to its essentials, it's the coupling of the monkeys in Wilkes' enclosure.'

'You mean,' said Nigel, 'that this has happened because people have been taking it too seriously?'

'No,' said Fen, 'ironically enough, it's happened because someone has not been taking it seriously enough.'

'I thought you didn't think sex was a motive for murder?'

'Nor do I. But it lies at the root of this thing just the same. I'll explain later, Nigel; whatever happens, you shall know. And God forbid,' he added more lightly, 'that we should wrap up this dismal tale in a heavy mantle of moralistic symbolism. The questing beast is a poetic convenience; in fact, it doesn't exist.'

They reached the hotel in silence, and Fen made straight for the porter's box. The porter, a thin, competent-looking elderly man, received him with a smile.

'Well, sir,' he said, 'and how goes the investigation, if I may make so bold as to ask?'

'Ah,' said Fen, 'I think you can probably help me a little, Ridley. How did you come to hear about it, by the way? I suppose your racketeers,' he said offensively to Nigel, 'have got hold of it at last.'

'All in the morning papers, sir,' said the porter, tapping a news-sheet which lay in front of him, 'which is to say, nothing at all beyond the bare facts. The local has a bit more, but only vapourings.' His voice was scornful. 'Terrible thing, though, with a young girl like that; not but what she wasn't a bit of a Jezebel, if you'll pardon the liberty.'

Fen appeared to be struck by the Biblical reference. He said: 'Tell me, Ridley: do you think that if a thoroughly objectionable person is murdered, the murderer deserves to get away with it?'

The porter considered. 'I don't think so, sir, no. There's other ways of dealing with objectionable persons than by murder.'

Fen turned to Nigel. 'You see?' he said.

'I take it then, sir, that it was murder, and not suicide?' asked the porter.

'That's what we're trying to find out,' said Fen, 'and that's where you can help me. The young lady came in here last night?'

'Yes, sir. About twenty-five or twenty to eight, it would have been. She asked for the London directory, put through a call

158

from one of the boxes over there, and left immediately afterwards.'

'Did you happen to notice if she was wearing any jewellery?'

'Well now, sir, it's funny you should ask that, because I was just thinking as she looked up the number how little jewellery young women wear nowadays as compared with thirty years ago. Not a ring, not a necklace, not a bracelet, not a brooch even.'

'You're sure about that?'

'Absolutely, sir. I noticed particular.'

'And that,' said Fen as they turned away, 'disposes finally of the possibility that Yseut took the ring herself. And, incidentally, completes my case.'

'All done by intuition.'

Fen looked uncomfortable. 'Well,' he said cautiously, 'no, not exactly. There was really no occasion for it. You've had all the facts that I've had; more, you've had a lot of them at first hand; they give you everything you want. Do you honestly mean to tell me you still don't know what this is all about?'

Nigel shook his head. 'Not an inkling,' he said. 'I look to the resurrection; until that, I'm in black darkness.'

Fen gazed at him severely. 'Your execrable profession,' he said, 'has had a numbing effect upon a whilom promising, if mediocre, brain. Anyway, enough for now. I leave you until Evensong tomorrow. I have a lot of beastly collection papers to correct, my notes to write up, and lecture to prepare on William Dunbar, *mort à Flodden*.' He marched to the door, turned, and waved cheerfully. 'Concentrate,' he said. 'It will come to you eventually.' In another moment he was gone.

12. Vignettes

'Non other lyfe,' said he, 'is worth a bene;
For wedlock is so esy and so clene.'

Chaucer

On Saturday evening, after the show, the theatre was given over to the technicians. While the company was still changing and removing make-up, the old set was already being demolished. Sunday morning saw the new one going up, by the united labours of scenic designer, scene painter, stage hands, stage manager and electricians, while actors and actresses gave themselves up to long, luxurious hours in bed, read or walked or drank according to their tastes, or in rare cases even ran over their lines for the dress rehearsal in the evening. It was an interlude of calm before the final effort, before the culmination of that effort on the Monday night, and before another culmination more serious and less pleasant.

Donald and Jean walked in the university parks. The previous day's rain had given place to a cold, invigorating autumnal sunlight. The bells were silent, but in the churches and chapels of Oxford the worship of God was being prepared in sundry different ways, ranging from the highly-polished brass of the Salvation Army to the incense and chasubles of the high church through a series of elaborate and faintly ludicrous doctrinal variations. Oxford retains some vestigial reminders of the fact that it was once one of the Christian centres of Europe. Choirboys unselfconsciously march the streets in gowns and mortar-boards; organists secretly meditate on the registration (supposed by their admirers to be spontaneous) which is to be used in accompanying the psalms; lay clerks put off their weekday occupations; scholars destined to read the lesson wander about inquiring as to the pronunciation of the more recondite Hebrew proper names; the clergy are pregnant with brief intellectual sermons; dons prepare to pay homage to the deity.

For some time Donald and Jean had walked in silence, a

silence on both sides of embarrassment, and a little of shame. Then Donald said:

'I seem to have been making a damned fool of myself. First over this girl; then by telling a lot of silly lies over what I was doing at the time of the murder. But you know why I told them, don't you?'

Jean's eyes were soft. 'Yes,' she said, 'I think I know. But really it wasn't necessary.'

'Jean,' he said. 'Then you didn't – ?'

'Darling, it's really intolerable of you to suspect that. Why should I?'

'I just jumped to conclusions, I suppose. Silly of me. You know I've been a bit mad these past few months.'

She said softly: 'Were you really in love with her, Donald?'

'No.' He hesitated. 'That is – I don't think so. I think I was just fascinated by her beastliness. Despite the Helens of this world, men will still run after shop-girls. You know – in the circumstances I've got a nerve to say it, but – I think I'm in love with you.'

'Oh, Donald. How nice you are.'

'I'm not. I've behaved perfectly abominably.'

'So have I. If I'd had a little more common sense, I'd have realized it was only an infatuation. Now' – her face clouded – 'it's too late.'

Donald looked uncomfortable; he poked idiotically at a fallen leaf with the ferrule of his stick. 'No,' he said slowly, 'I don't think it's too late. Don't you see the way her death has cleared everything up? It's brought us together again, and Rachel and Robert – the whole atmosphere's better, and there seems to be no one who hasn't gained by it.'

Jean said sombrely: 'Someone killed her. Who?'

'Whatever Fen says, I think it was suicide; and I hear that's what the police think too. I hope to God they're right. What a glorious relief it would be if it all ended that way.'

She answered: 'Fen knows what he's doing, I'm afraid. It's maddening that it should all rest with him; I don't want to see anyone hanged for this. He wanted me to give away – '

Donald looked at her quickly. 'Give away what?'

Her manner was guarded. 'You know.'

He nodded, then stopped and turned to face her, putting his hands on her arms. 'Jean,' he said, 'I've made up my mind. As soon as this term's over, I'm going to volunteer for the R.A.F. It seems to contain most of the organists in the country anyway. You'll have finished here by then, and – well, as soon as I get my commission, I should like you to marry me.'

She laughed – a small, happy laugh. 'Oh, Donald, how lovely that will be. I – I shall give up the theatre and keep house for you. I think that's really what I've wanted all along.' She looked at him for a moment with tears in her eyes. Then they kissed.

Somewhere, out of the mists of enchantment, a clock chimed. Donald jumped as though he had been shot. 'Lord,' he said. 'Mattins in a quarter of an hour.' He took her hand. 'Come on, darling. I shall sit and plan a full choral service for our wedding – "Let the Bright Seraphim" for the anthem, and I'll hire St Paul's Cathedral choir to sing it!'

'People appear to get married,' said Nicholas to the blonde, 'for no reason at all. The reasons adduced by Christ's church on earth have become, thanks to the march of science, grossly inadequate. I like to observe, though, the way the standards of the church have dropped. Originally, complete continence was the standard of virtue, and marriage a derogation of it. Now, marriage is the standard of virtue, and unmarried love the derogation. No one nowadays takes seriously the imputation of feebleness contained in the words "such persons as have not the gift of continency".' He sighed. 'It's a great pity no one has any regard for chastity nowadays; even the church has more or less abandoned it, along with Commination Service and other inconvenient and uncomfortable parts of its rites.' He smiled benevolently. 'Of course, there are advantages to marriage: it eliminates the tedious and anaphrodisiac process of wooing, for one thing.'

'Oh, don't try to be clever, Nick,' said the blonde disgustedly.

'On the contrary: I was trying to bring my conversation down to a level where it would be comprehensible to you. Have another drink?'

'No, thanks.' The blonde crossed her very attractive legs and adjusted her skirt over them with meticulous care. 'Tell me about the murder. I want to hear all about it.'

Nicholas emitted a snort of disgust. 'I'm fed up with the murder,' he said, 'I never want to hear another word about it to the end of my life.'

'Well, I do,' the blonde persisted. 'Do they know who did it?'

Nicholas was sullen. 'Fen *thinks* he knows,' he said. 'I know he's been right on other occasions, but I don't believe in the infallibility of detectives.'

The blonde was emphatic. 'If he says he knows, then believe me, he does. I've followed all his other cases, and he's never been wrong yet.'

'Well, if he does, I hope he keeps quiet about it, that's all.'

'Do you mean you don't want to see the murderer arrested? A nice thing,' said the blonde indignantly, 'if people can go about killing girls and getting away with it.'

'With some girls,' rejoined Nicholas severely, 'it appears to be the only way.'

'Who do you think did it?'

'Who do *I* think did it? Good heavens, girl, I don't know. I expect I did it myself, in a moment of mental aberration.'

The blonde looked suitably alarmed. 'No, really,' she said anxiously.

'Lots of people had reason to, and half the town seems to be incriminated one way or another. Jean Whitelegge took the gun, Sheila McGaw owned the ring that was found on the body, Donald and Robert Warner and I were all about when it happened, and Helen and Rachel have no alibis. I plump for Helen, myself. She had the only real motive – money. And Fen's been running about after her with his eyes goggling and his tongue hanging out. He's always particularly nice to his murderers – before he has them arrested. Yes, I think Helen's the obvious choice; she's just the sort of sentimental, ignorant little thing who'd do something primitive like that.'

'I suspect sour grapes,' said the blonde with unusual acumen. 'She's been going about with that good-looking young journalist recently, hasn't she?'

Nicholas sneered. 'Well, really,' he said, 'if that's your standard of male beauty – '

'All right, Mephistopheles,' the blonde interrupted with spirit, 'we know anything outside your infernal, Byronic charm is anathema. You can get me another drink now, if you like. I'm going to gold-dig you for all I'm worth this morning.'

Nicholas rose with reluctance. 'There are times,' he said, 'when I wish that Timon's comments on Phrynia and Timandra had been a little more subtle and a little less openly offensive. They'd come in so useful.'

Robert and Rachel progressed in circles round Addison's Walk, the soft, clean, effeminate beauty of Magdalen just beyond them.

'Are you nervous about tomorrow?' asked Rachel.

'Not exactly nervous; excited, though. I think it's going to be a good performance. The company's played up brilliantly, and you, my dear, are God's own gift to a producer.'

'Thank you, sir,' she said prettily.

'A first performance,' he said. 'Ridiculous effervescence of personal vanity. "Look at me, the brilliant Mr Warner, showing off with a gang of actors and actresses" – that's all it really amounts to. I remember the first play I ever had put on – at a little theatre club in London, when I was still a struggling, insignificant repertory actor of twenty-one. Lord, but wasn't that exciting! I went about pretending that it was the sort of thing that happened to me every day, and weaving fantastic daydreams about a year's West End run – which, I may say, never materialized.'

'And I remember,' said Rachel, 'my first part in London – a very tarty Helen in a production of *Troilus*. I imagined all the critics would give me flattering bit-part notices – "special attention should be given to Miss Rachel West, who makes a brilliant miniature of an unsympathetic part" – but in fact none of them said anything about me at all.'

Robert eyed her whimsically. 'You see?' he said. 'It's all vanity really. Costals, in Montherlant's novel, is the quintessential type of the artist – the self-sufficient, childish, ruthless egotist. Pulled to pieces, that's certainly all I amount to.'

She laughed. 'Oh, no, my Robert,' she said, taking his arm, 'no fishing for compliments. I'm not going to swell your vanity any further.'

He sighed. 'How well you know me, my dear.'

'After – what is it? – five years I ought to.'

'Rachel,' he said suddenly, 'would you consider marrying me?'

She stopped and looked at him in amazement. 'Robert, my sweet,' she said, 'what has come over you? Is this a belated consideration for my honour? I warn you, if you say that again, I shall take you at your word.'

It was his turn to look surprised. 'You mean you would?'

'Why the astonishment? My feminine instinct has always been to get married, only you don't want to, and anyone else would have been intolerable.'

'You realize it will involve a lot of rather tiresome gossip? About the imminence of little strangers and so on?'

'That can't be helped. If people want to gossip, let them.'

He made her sit down on a bench facing the river. 'For a long time now,' he said, 'I've been lusting after permanence. It's wearing to hold out against the conventions of society indefinitely.'

'That does a little take the edge off the compliment.'

He grinned. 'I'm sorry. I didn't mean it like that. I think it would be rather a good marriage, don't you? – one of those tranquil, permanent affairs. We know enough about one another to respect each other's madnesses and obsessions.' He mused. 'Perhaps, like Prospero, I'm developing an obsession about marriage.'

She took his hand. 'Has Yseut's murder got anything to do with this?'

'Oh, a little, perhaps. An object lesson in the awfulness of unregulated sex.'

'Robert' – her voice was serious – 'what is going to happen about that – the murder, I mean? Do you think this man Fen really knows who did it?'

He shrugged. 'I suppose so. I hope he keeps it under his hat till after tomorrow night, anyway.'

'Wouldn't it be better if it were cleared up – rather than have it hanging over us?'

'My dear, it might be one of the cast – you or me, for that matter. If it were Donald or Nick, I suppose it wouldn't matter. But if you asked me, he's not going to do anything about it at all.'

'Yes, what *are* you going to do about it, Gervase?' asked Mrs Fen.

Fen absently retrieved a ball hurled more or less in his direction by his small son, and threw it back again. 'Don't ask me,' he said. 'I'm sick to death of the whole business.'

'It's no good to keep on saying that,' said Mrs Fen reasonably, rescuing her knitting-wool from the attentions of the cat. 'You've got to make up your mind one way or the other.'

'Well, you advise me.'

'I can't possibly advise you unless I know who did it.'

Gervase Fen told her.

'Oh.' Mrs Fen paused in her knitting, and then added mildly: 'But how extraordinary.'

'Yes, isn't it? Not what one would have expected.'

'I won't question you as to why and wherefore,' said Mrs Fen. 'No doubt I shall hear all about it eventually. But I suggest you drop a gentle hint.'

'I thought of that. But don't you see, *whatever* I do, I shall have it on my conscience till I reach the grave.'

'Nonsense, Gervase, you're exaggerating. Either way you'll have forgotten completely about it in three months. Anyway, a detective with a conscience is ludicrous. If you're going to make all this fuss about it afterwards, you shouldn't interfere in these things at all.'

Fen reacted to this bit of feminine common sense in a characteristically masculine way. 'You're most unsympathetic,' he said. 'Everyone is. They advise me to read *Tasso*.' He evoked the image of a monstrous and far-reaching persecution. 'Here am I on the horns of a Cornelian dilemma – torn between duty and inclination – ' He wavered, forgot what he was talking about, and seized on the last thing he could remember. 'Why has a dilemma *horns*, by the way? Is it a sort of cattle?'

Mrs Fen ignored the digression. 'And to think,' she said, 'that I never even remotely suspected. Mr Warner was lecturing me on the murder, by the way, while you were downstairs. He said he thought the killer had come in by way of the West court-yard.'

'Did he?' said Fen vaguely. 'That was very lucid of him.'

'As far as I could see, that was impossible, and I told him so. He seemed very disappointed.'

'I imagine that was only politeness. He's quite genuinely not interested in the investigation. Not really surprising, when he's got a first night coming off on Monday.'

'Is it a good play?'

'Brilliant. Rather in the Jonsonian tradition of satire.'

Mrs Fen shuddered elaborately. 'I never did like *Volpone*. It's cruel and grotesque.'

Fen snorted. 'All good satire is cruel and grotesque,' he said. 'John,' he added to his offspring, 'you mustn't take the cat by the tail and dip it in and out of the pond like that. It's cruel.'

'Well, anyway,' said Mrs Fen, 'I shan't come and see it.'

'You can't come and see it,' Fen answered rudely, 'there's no room.' The phraseology of the more abominably offensive of creatures in *Alice* tended to insinuate itself into his conversation.

'Who are you going with, then?'

'Nigel and Sir Richard.'

'Nigel's a nice boy,' said Mrs Fen reflectively. 'Didn't you say he was going about with Helen?'

'No doubt he's gadding about somewhere with her now,' said Fen gloomily. 'Anyway, he borrowed my bicycle. I hope he looks after it. People are so careless.'

Fen's bicycle was a large, uncompromising affair apparently constructed out of pig-iron. Nigel, as he toiled down Walton Street on it with Helen at his side, regretted, not for the first time, Fen's monastic indifference to scientific progress. Once they reached the tow-path, however, the going was easier, and they bowled along merrily enough towards their destination, the 'Trout'.

'I wish,' said Nigel, panting heavily, 'that you didn't imagine you were in for a track-race.'

Helen grinned back at him over her shoulder. 'All right, slowcoach!' she shouted, and slowed down to allow him to catch up with her. 'Honestly, though,' she added, 'I have a conscience about this expedition. Yseut killed only the day before yesterday, and here am I cycling about Oxford in a pair of red corduroy slacks. Everyone who's passed has looked profoundly shocked.'

'That's the trousers,' said Nigel with some justice, 'not your unsisterly behaviour. I wonder if Fen ever oils this thing?' He appeared to be searching for traces of this activity.

'Look out!' said Helen. 'You'll be in the water in a minute.'

Nigel altered his direction with as much dignity as he could muster. 'I'm not going to talk,' he said, 'until we arrive. This is too exhausting. Then a drink – several drinks in fact – and we'll have our lunch somewhere in the meadows beyond. What time have you got to be back for your dress-rehearsal?'

'I ought to be in the theatre by half past five.'

'I've got Evensong at six, so that will fit nicely.' They rode on enjoying the clean tang of the air and watching the perilous manoeuvres of two undergraduates in a sailing-boat.

At the 'Trout' they found Sheila McGaw with a miscellaneous party. 'Hello,' she said, waving to them. 'Are you taking the opportunity of getting out of Oxford, too? What with policemen and one thing and another, it's getting to be unlivable in.'

'Don't talk to us about policemen,' said Nigel. 'Like the Foreign Legion, we've come out to forget.'

They had their lunch on the bank of a tiny tributary stream which meandered absurdly over a muddy bottom. There they ate sandwiches and tomatoes and apples. Helen, raising herself on one elbow, remarked:

'It's extraordinary how hard the ground can be.'

'Don't slide off the mackintosh, silly,' said Nigel. 'The ground's still damp from yesterday's rain. Is there another tomato?'

'You've had four already.'

'I asked for a tomato, not a lecture.'

'I gave you the lecture in default of the tomato. There aren't any more.'

'Oh.' Nigel silent for a moment. Then he said: 'Helen, will you marry me?'

'Darling, I was hoping you were going to say that. No, you can't kiss me now, my mouth's full.'

'You will, then?'

Helen considered. 'Will you make a good husband?' she asked.

'No,' said Nigel, 'abominable. I'm only asking you because you've just come into such a lot of money.'

She nodded gravely. 'Would you be likely to interfere with my career?'

'Horribly.'

'How soon do you want to get married?'

Nigel shifted uneasily. 'I wish you wouldn't scrutinize my proposal as if it were a length of bad cloth. The proper thing to do is to fall rapturously into my arms.'

'I can't,' Helen complained. 'All the food's in the way.'

'Well, we'll move the food, then,' shouted Nigel, exhibiting a sudden energy and hurling it wildly in all directions. *'Voici, ma chère.'* He took her in his arms.

'When can we get married, Nigel?' she asked after a while. 'Can it be soon?'

'As soon as you like, my very dearest.'

'Don't there have to be banns and licences and things?'

'You can get special licences,' said Nigel, 'in fact if you pay twenty-five pounds for an Archbishop's Special Licence you have powers of life and death over every clergyman in the country.'

'How nice.' She snuggled down comfortably in the crook of his arm. 'You do make love beautifully, Nigel.'

'Darling, you should never say that. Nothing goes to the head of the male species more disastrously. Of course,' he said, 'although you're now disgustingly rich, I shall insist on supporting you.'

Helen sat up indignantly. 'You'll do nothing of the sort. What, let all that money go to waste!'

Nigel sighed happily. 'I was hoping you'd say that,' he said, 'but I thought I'd better say the proper thing.'

She burst out laughing. 'You beast,' she said happily. Then, when he had kissed her: 'You know, I don't think the open air is a good place for making love.'

'Nonsense, it's the only place. Look at the eclogues.'

She said meditatively: 'I think Phyllida and Corydon must have ended up with a lot of bruises.'

'What is the best place to make love, then?'

'Bed.'

'Helen!' said Nigel in shocked tones.

'Darling, we are husband and wife in the sight of God,' she said solemnly, 'and these things are a fit subject of discussion between us.' Her tone changed suddenly to one of dismay. 'Oh, Nigel, *look* what a mess I'm in!'

'A sweet disorder in the dress,' said Nigel, 'kindles in clothes a wantonness – '

'No, Nigel, remember you promised – no Elizabethan verse. Oh dear, why do you literary young men always quote? Stop it, darling!' She put her arms round his neck, and Herrick was very appropriately smothered in a kiss. They lay back, laughing and exhausted, and gazed at the cream-soft clouds which hung motionless in the pale blue sky above their heads.

13. An Incident at Evensong

A dirty pillow in Death's bed.
Crashaw

Nigel reflected, as he turned into St Christopher's at twenty to six that evening, that there was something extraordinarily school-boyish about Gervase Fen. Cherubic, naïve, volatile, and entirely delightful, he wandered the earth taking a genuine interest in things and people unfamiliar, while maintaining a proper sense of authority in connection with his own subject. On literature his comments were acute, penetrating, and extremely sophisticated; on any other topic he invariably pretended complete ignorance and an anxious willingness to be instructed, though it generally came out eventually that he knew more about it than his interlocutor, for his reading, in the forty-two years since his first appearance on this planet, had been systematic and enormous. If this ingenuousness had been affectation, or merely arrested development, it would have been simply irritating; but it was perfectly sincere, and derived from the genuine intellectual humility of a man who has read much and in so doing has been able to contemplate the enormous spaces of knowledge which must inevitably always lie beyond his reach. In temperament he was incurably romantic, though he ordered his life in a rigidly reasonable way. To men and affairs, his attitude was neither cynical nor optimistic, but one of never-failing fascination. This resulted in a sort of unconscious amoralism, since he was always so interested in what people were doing, and why they were doing it, that it never occurred to him to assess the morality of their actions. This fuss about what he shall do in connection with Yseut's murder, thought Nigel, is entirely characteristic.

He was discovered in his room, putting the final touches to his notes on the case. 'The police have definitely decided it was suicide,' he said, 'so these' – he pointed to the small heap of papers – 'will have to be put in cold storage for a while. By the way,' he added, 'I've decided what I'm going to do.' He handed Nigel a small sheet of notepaper.

On it were three words, from one of the satires of Horace: *Deprendi miserum est.*

' "It is horrible to be found out," ' said Nigel. 'So – ?'

'So I put this in the post this evening, and hand over my notes to the police on Tuesday morning. That gives h – the murderer a remote chance to clear out. By the way, I rely on you not to let this go any further. I've discovered it's a criminal offence.' He grinned cheerfully.

'In that case,' murmured Nigel, 'do you think it's really wise – ?'

'Hopelessly unwise, my dear Nigel,' said Fen. 'But after all, I've got the whip-hand. I can always tell the police I've realized my idea was wrong, and that I'm as much at a loss as they are, and no one can prove anything to the contrary. Besides, if one wasn't a little adventurous sometimes, the world would be intolerable.' He appeared to be hoisting a symbolic skull and crossbones at the mast-head.

Nigel grunted, whether in agreement or disapproval it was impossible to tell. Fen wrote a name and address on an envelope, put the paper inside and sealed it up. 'This shall be delivered into the hands of the G.P.O. after chapel,' he said, putting it into his pocket.

'Has it occurred to you,' said Nigel, 'that you may be endangering the lives of a lot of totally innocent people by setting a murderer on the run?'

Fen looked suddenly worried. 'I know,' he said. 'It has occurred to me. But I don't think this person will kill again. Tell me,' he added, hurriedly dismissing the uncomfortable topic, 'have you still no idea of who did it?'

'I spent last night in the time-honoured stooge's task of getting out a time-table, and as I expected got no enlightenment from it whatever. Anyway, half the assertions in it are unproved or unprovable, so I needn't have expected anything.' He took out a sheet of paper and gave it to Fen. 'It's your business now, as the great detective, to glance at it, tap it with your finger, and say "This reveals all." '

172

'Well, so it does,' said Fen, 'and I can't help it if you're so dumb that you don't see why. I've got a similar table, with certain things underlined and a few comments added. Look at it again, dear boy. Doesn't it leap out at you like a wart on a bald head?'

'No, it doesn't,' said Nigel, staring at the list in a bemused way. It ran:

From 6.0. Robert, Rachel, Donald and Nicholas in bar of 'Mace and Sceptre'; Yseut at B.N.C.; Helen in her room; Sheila and Jean in theirs (last three unconfirmed).

6.25. Donald, Nicholas leave 'M. and S.', arriving in college at

6.30 approx., when Rachel also leaves to go to the cinema (destination unconfirmed).

6.45 approx. Helen arrives at theatre.

7.10 approx. Yseut leaves B.N.C.

7.35–40. Yseut arrives at 'M. and S.', puts through phone call.

7.45. Helen goes on at theatre. Donald and Nicholas cross to room opposite Donald's.

7.50 approx. Robert leaves 'M. and S.' for college (unconfirmed).

7.54. Yseut arrives at college.

7.55. Helen comes off stage.

8.5. Robert arrives at college.

8.21 approx. Robert goes down to lavatory.

8.24. Shot heard.

8.25. Yseut found dead.

8.45. Helen goes on again at theatre.

Jean and Sheila say they remained in their rooms all evening (unconfirmed).

Rachel says she remained in the cinema until 9.0 (unconfirmed).

Donald and Nicholas say they remained in room from 7.45 (unconfirmed).

'I don't see,' said Nigel, 'that it's any use at all. Half the statements may be false.'

'No doubt they are,' Fen replied equably. 'But how revealing all those "unconfirmeds" are! It does give the game away, Nigel,' he added, patting him benevolently on the back. 'Why did you include Helen, incidentally? You don't suspect her?'

'Of course not, but it filled it out a bit. It was rather thin otherwise. Look here, Fen: I don't want to know who did it, but I should like to know it wasn't Helen.'

Fen grinned. 'No, of course it wasn't Helen.'

'As a matter of fact, I've just asked her to marry me.'

Fen fell into a mild ecstasy. 'My dear fellow!' he shouted. 'I'm delighted! We must celebrate – but not now,' he added with a reluctant eye on the clock. 'Evensong awaits us.' He picked up a surplice which was lying over the back of a chair. 'This thing,' he said, putting it over his arm as they went out, 'puts me in mind of shrouds.'

As he entered the chapel, Nigel had the comfortable sense of one who returns to a remembered spot in the certainty that it will not have been altered. On the whole, he had always been inclined to agree with old Wilkes that the restorations had been well carried out. The place had a clean, finished look about it without being aggressively new, and it fortunately lacked the faint odour of corruption which is generally present in old churches. The glass, while not being of the sort to attract connoisseurs from all parts of the country, was pleasing enough, and the organ, a new instrument put in seven years previously and occupying the gallery on the north side of the chancel, had plain gold pipes charmingly arranged in a simple geometrical pattern. The organist – and his mode of exit, an iron ladder leading down to the vestry – was hidden from view by a large fretted wooden screen (his means of ascertaining what was going on below being a large mirror suspended above his head); and from the instrument there issued now one of those vague opiate improvisations which organists appear to consider the limit of their responsibilities before the service actually begins.

Fen departed to the seats reserved for the Fellows, Nigel settled himself close by the choir. There were few people in chapel that evening. The President glowered morosely from his box; there was a small number of undergraduates and visitors. Before long, the choir and the Chaplain came in, and the improvisation performed a rapid, pyrotechnical series of modulations into the key of the first hymn and stopped. Announcement. First line of 'Richmond'. Then Samuel Johnson's fine hymn:

> City of God, how broad and far
> Outspread thy walls sublime ...

For once Nigel was unmoved by what he considered one of the best pieces of religious verse in the English language. As he held the book up, making conventional noises in his throat and opening and shutting his mouth in a rhythmic but improbable way (to the alarm of one of the smaller Decani boys, who stared at him with mingled horror and fascination), his thoughts wandered to the events of the past few days. *Who had killed Yseut Haskell?* Robert Warner was the most likely candidate, but it was difficult to see how even he could have done it. Was the suicide perhaps faked before the girl was shot? But no, ridiculous; unless she was hypnotized, Yseut would never have allowed herself to be put through the necessary rigmarole. He wondered, as the Doctor in illustration of his thesis demonstrated the vanity of the surge's angry shock, whether she had ever known who killed her, and then realized that she must, for one terrible moment, have seen the murderer. Those powderburns – she had been shot point-blank in the middle of the forehead ...

'Dearly beloved brethren, the Scripture moveth us in sundry places ...' Nigel hastily kicked a kneeling-mat into position, and as he dropped down on to it, glanced across at Fen. But the Professor seemed preoccupied. The Fellows' stalls were cleverly designed so that no one outside could see whether they were kneeling or not, with the result that most of them had developed the lazy and irreverent habit of simply slumping forward on the desks in front of them during prayers. Old Wilkes, a short distance away, was apparently sunk in a deep coma. Nigel remembered his story, told on that fatal Friday evening (only two days ago? It seemed more like two years) and looked instinctively into the antechapel where John Kettenburgh, too-militant champion of the reformed faith, had been hunted to death by Richard Pegwell and his associates. *'Cave ne exeat* ...' 'Vex not his ghost ...' Nigel dismissed these unprofitable reflections to

admire the singing of the psalm, and the musicianship that had gone into it; just that touch of preciosity, that lengthening, shortening or corruption of vowels which is the prerogative of a good choir. The boys were good – even the head boy showed none of the all too common tendency to exert his authority by hooting. Here, Nigel felt, Donald was in his element; outside he was ineffectual, incompetent in his affairs, foolish in his relationships; here he had unchallenged mastery.

It was after the theatrical and triumphant strains of the Dyson Magnificat had reached their elaborate conclusion that a sense of unease first became discernible. For one thing, the boys seemed unusually fidgety; they scratched their ears and gaped about and whispered and dropped their books to such an extent that even the lay clerks, who had the prerogative of poking them ferociously from behind when they misbehaved, seemed unable to restore order. Then the senior scholar, who was reading the lessons, dropped the marker out of the book and seemed to take minutes finding the place again. Finally, it was discovered that the head boy had forgotten, for some reason which remains unknown to this day, to give the men their copies of the anthem. So at the beginning of the Nunc Dimittis, the second boy was sent out to the vestry by the Cantoris tenor to fetch them. He astonished the gathering by returning empty-handed during the Gloria and fainting before he got back to his place. There was some confusion. Two of the men took him out and left him in charge of the porter, returning hastily at the end of the Collects with the necessary copies.

For a while all was well. The anthem – Charles Wood's 'Expectans Expectavi' – passed without incident, as did the subsequent prayers which preceded the final hymn (there was to be no sermon that evening). Order appeared to be restored. '. . . *In Hymns Ancient and Modern No. 563, in Songs of Praise . . .*' The choir awaited the statement of the tune. There was no sound from the organ.

Eventually the Decani tenor, a fat authoritative man in full command, gave a note and a signal and the hymn went forward unaccompanied. The Chaplain, the President, and the Fellows were staring in a puzzled way at the organ loft. Out of the corner of his eye Nigel saw Fen leave his seat and slip out of the chapel. Stealthily he followed, catching him up as he entered the vestry by the outside door and switched on the light. On his face Nigel saw an expression of mingled anger and anxiety that was so unusual and so intense that it shocked and alarmed him.

There was no one in the vestry, and Fen made straight for the small arched doorway on the right whence an iron stairway ran up to the organ loft. Nigel followed at his heels, his thoughts unpleasantly full of the recollection of John Kettenburgh ... 'There had been teeth and bones, and a great many of these appeared to be broken ...' The stairway was dark and chill, running up through an unpierced well of damp stone, and once he looked back over his shoulder.

They arrived in the organ loft. It resembled many another such. There were framed photographs of other organs – St Paul's, Truro, King's, Cambridge – cases and shelves of music and hymn books, an old comfortable chair for moments of inactivity, a primus stove on which Donald had been accustomed to make tea during the President's rather lengthy sermons.

What else he had expected to see, Nigel never knew. What they did see was Donald Fellowes, lying across the organ stool with his throat cut from ear to ear, and a blood-stained knife on the floor near him.

The next few hours had for Nigel, in retrospect, the proportions and inconsequence of a nightmare. He remembered Fen saying, in tones of bewilderment utterly uncharacteristic of him: 'I couldn't have known! God help me, I couldn't have known!'; remembered the words of the Benediction, rising up out of infinite stillness: *The Grace of our Lord Jesus Christ, the love of God, and the fellowship of the Holy Ghost ...*'; remembered his whispering, in a voice that he could not prevent from trembling a little: 'Could a woman have done this?' and Fen's grim but abstracted reply: 'It has been known.'

Then there was the business of getting rid of the choir when they returned to the vestry, of informing the college authorities, of keeping away unwelcome sightseers, of telephoning the police. Fen went immediately and interviewed the boy who had fainted during the service. His story was incoherent, but they were able eventually to elicit the main facts. He had entered the vestry at the chapel end and found it in darkness; the light switch was by the outer door. He had been about to walk over and put it on when he had heard a slight movement in the darkness, and someone, or something, had whispered to him an invitation to come in and shake hands, a thing which he had felt little inclined to do. He had stood for a moment in a fright, and then run back again into the chapel, after which he remembered nothing more. Asked whether the voice had been that of a man or a woman, he replied reasonably enough that when a person was whispering it was impossible to tell, and added that he thought it had been neither. At which Fen, who had recovered something of his normal manner, went away snorting with annoyance and deploring the influence of M. R. James on the very young.

The Inspector, the doctor and the ambulance arrived in a very short time, and immediately afterwards Sir Richard Freeman appeared apocalyptically from nowhere, somewhat to the Inspector's annoyance. Their investigations proved to be of little value; Nigel remembered Fen showing them a few faint but unmistakable red stains on a copy of the Respighi Prelude which lay open on the organ desk, but at the time he did not realize their significance; he remembered, too, a casual, irrelevant remark on the oddness of the registration which Donald had prepared for the last hymn. The time of death, even apart from the doctor's contributory evidence, was easy to establish; it had been somewhere between the anthem and the last hymn, that was to say, somewhere between 6.35 and 6.45. The Inspector inquired how it was that no sound of a struggle had been heard, but Nigel, who had visited the organ loft several times during his undergraduate days, remembered that in fact very little was audible even from immediately below, and a few experiments proved this to be correct.

As to the weapon, its provenance was easily discovered. It belonged to the kitchen, situated near the chapel, which served the Senior Common Room, and was a sharp, thin-bladed affair of a fairly common type. The kitchen had been left unattended since 5.30 that afternoon, and there were no fingerprints on the knife except some old ones belonging to one of the kitchenmen. On the iron staircase some traces of rubber-soled shoes were found, but they had been partly obliterated by Fen and Nigel, and it was impossible to tell either their type or their size; in the vestry, apart from a few smears made by someone wearing gloves, there was nothing. Fen turned the loft inside out in a fruitless search, and then asked the Inspector:

'When did you take your guard off Fellowes' room?'

'At 4.30 this afternoon.'

'Then,' said Gervase Fen, 'I fancy we shall find that has been searched too.' (*Quaeram dum inveniam!* thought Nigel). Investigation proved him to be right, but they discovered nothing to help them there any more than they had elsewhere.

The porter was questioned as to the presence of strangers in the college that evening. He had seen no one, but he pointed out that there were half a dozen side entrances by which anyone could have come in unobserved. Those undergraduates and dons who had been in college but not in chapel were then assembled in hall and asked if they had seen anyone in the college between five and seven whom they did not know, but again with negative results. This series of frustrations was beginning to harass the Inspector exceedingly; Sir Richard maintained a gloomy silence; and Fen, while following the proceedings with sufficient attention, seemed little concerned about the outcome.

The culmination of the Inspector's troubles came with the visit to the dress-rehearsal which they made towards eight o'clock. Conveniently enough, all the possible suspects were there, including Nicholas, who had come to watch; inconveniently enough, none of them could be eliminated, since not a single one had an alibi which would bear investigation. A few who claimed immunity were rapidly shown that they had nothing of the sort. Most of them had not arrived at the theatre until 6.45, and some later; and as the theatre was only five minutes' brisk walking from St Christopher's, nobody could be freed from suspicion. When Robert assembled the company on the stage at the end of the first act to give them his notes, they were told what had happened, but apart from a manifest unease there had been no special reaction; only Jean gave a little strangled cry of dismay and went straight to Fen, remaining talking to him incoherently for some time. Nigel had no opportunity to see Helen alone, but he read the fear and dismay in her eyes. It was a dispirited little party that returned to St Christopher's.

Back in Fen's room, the Inspector frankly admitted himself at a loss. There was no more talk of suicide, and obviously all he now cared about was getting the whole business cleared up and done with as soon as humanly possible. He appealed direct to Fen.

'We've absolutely nothing to go on, sir,' he said, 'and if you can't help us, nobody can. In its own way, this is a perfect crime; not a handle anywhere.'

'Yes,' said Fen slowly, 'a perfect crime because a lucky crime. The murderer entered the college by a back way – unobserved; took the knife from the kitchen and went up to the organ loft, frightening away that boy on the way – still unidentified; then killed Fellowes and left – still unobserved. The murderer had fantastic luck, and if it had been a murder in isolation, I think it would have been insoluble. Whoever killed Fellowes saw to it that his (or her) buttons were properly sewn on before leaving, refrained from smoking, and failed to catch his (or her) clothing on projecting nails. All very excellent. But because of the murder of Yseut, there's no doubt at all who that person was.' He mused. 'It's my fault that Fellowes was killed, but I couldn't have foreseen it; it was impossible to foresee. Only, if I'd acted sooner, I could have prevented it.'

Sir Richard said: 'Then the murderer was – ?'

'I'll tell you,' Fen replied, 'and I'll tell you the way in which Yseut Haskell was murdered, on one very simple condition. You'll excuse us, Nigel? I'd rather you didn't know just yet.'

Nigel nodded glumly and went out to smoke and walk in the garden. For half an hour Fen talked to Sir Richard and the Inspector in a low voice, explaining, emphasizing, illustrating. As he talked, Sir Richard tugged at his moustache, and the Inspector's face fell. Then they went away.

'Nigel,' said Fen an hour later as they sat together in his room, 'it appears that my scruples have been a trifle imbecile.'

'I'm afraid,' said Nigel, 'that I've been in a state of super-stitious terror over the whole business.'

'Superstitious terror? Oh, you mean Wilkes' fairy tale. It's time that particular college ghost was laid once for all. I've taken the opportunity of investigating the business, and I've discovered a dirty bit of work, which you may have guessed at. As I suspected, the President at that time wasn't at all the sober, more-things-in-heaven-and-earth character that Wilkes led us to believe, but simply an old fool who'd got his position by nep-otism and influence. And you must remember that all the ghost part of it, apart from one or two easily explainable atmosphere incidents in the chapel, came from Archer, the dean; Parks, it seems, never mentioned his nocturnal "adventurer" to anyone else. And a very pretty piece of invention it was, too, though the business about John Kettenburgh and the chapel wall gave it a convenient *cadre*. The relationship between Archer and Parks was, it seems, of such a discreditable kind that in those puri-tanical times not a whisper of it could be allowed to come out. Then Parks decided to do a bit of blackmail, and Archer pol-ished him off, concealing the weapon heaven knows where before the others arrived.'

'Good God,' said Nigel, profoundly shocked. 'But how did you guess?'

'All that dog-latin, of course. What youth in his senses would bellow out a latin invocation for deliverance while being clubbed to death, even by a ghost? What he really shouted was the name of the man who was killing him. And as he was a church organist and not a classical scholar, I'm willing to bet he used the ecclesiastical pronunciation, and said *ch* for *c*. But I suppose that tale Archer spun, coming from a convinced ration-alist, shook them a bit, and as they weren't very bright and he was a highly respectable man, they didn't tumble to it. He must have had some uneasy moments, though. No wonder he turned churchman!'

'Supernatural, my dear Holmes,' said Nigel, who was in fact genuinely impressed; and added: 'In more senses than one. What about Wilkes' theory of the ghost operating through the living?'

'That,' said Fen, firmly and crudely, 'is all hooey. Anyone

who's not actually demented can prevent himself from committing a murder. Possession by demons is always a convenient way of shelving responsibility. And that reminds me – '

He took from his pocket the envelope he had addressed earlier that evening, tore it into small fragments and threw them on the fire. They watched in silence as the paper caught, flared, and shrank away into ashes.

'Tomorrow night,' said Gervase Fen, 'we go hunting.'

14. Horrible to be Found Out

No! will it not be yet? if this will not, another shall.
Not yet? I shall fit you anon – *Vengeance!*

Ford

By six o'clock, the queue for the unreserved seats already stretched a quarter of a mile down the road. At seven, the commissionaire went out, counted them, compared their number with the seats available, and informed those who would be unable to get in of the uselessness of waiting. The latter part of the queue broke up and dissipated, but a great many of its members continued to wait about, partly in order to see any celebrities who might be recognizable, partly in the hope that some of the reserved seats might not be claimed and that they might still be able to get in. Three policemen inefficiently but self-importantly regulated the increasing flow of people. Even those who had booked seats arrived early to claim them, fearful of not getting in, and having done so, hung about in small knots on the lawns in front, chattering excitedly. From every hotel in Oxford came agents, theatrical managers, actors, actresses, producers, critics, and fellow-playwrights. Some, who had not been able to leave town earlier on account of business, came direct from the station in taxi-cabs. The intelligentsia of the university arrived with habitual expressions of boredom. Dons arrived and made their way in with the practised ease and tranquillity of those in authority. Everywhere there was talk, talk, talk. A group of three eminent critics stood outside, talking spasmodically and glancing nervously over their shoulders. 'Shakespeare foresaw it,' said Nicholas gloomily as he passed in with the blonde on his arm,' "an agate vilely cut".' The electrician, Richard Ellis, Sheila McGaw and the stage hands stood in a bemused group in one corner, watching the ever-increasing flow of people as it came from all directions, and consumed with inner excitement. Robert strolled out to greet a group of friends who had come down from London, and was the object of interested, covert scrutiny. Black and white posters on all hands announced the first performance of *Metromania* with a sobriety somewhat out of keeping with the general furore. Rachel, in her dressing-room, performed the difficult double task of applying mascara to her eyes and running over her part in the book that lay open beside her. Jean conducted a last-minute survey of properties, even in her acute inner unhappiness not wholly unaffected by the prevailing atmosphere. Most of the men in the company were still in the 'Aston Arms', acquiring dutch courage under the minatory gaze of the parrot. Clive had already torn himself away from the arms of his wife, and was moving towards the theatre at all speed, probably to be in time for the performance. The bar, which had been provided with five extra staff and an emergency counter erected at one end, was packed to overflowing. Helen, entering the stage door with Bruce, looked at the crowds in alarm and spent the next three-quarters of an hour trying to forget them. Robert's publisher made a gloomy mental note to raise the royalties in the contract for *Metromania*. Robert himself remained cool and grave, but inwardly felt more nervous than he had ever been in his life before.

Fen said, as he, Nigel, and Sir Richard walked towards the theatre: 'The last time I went to this theatre, I swore I'd never go again. Yet here, apparently, I am. I hope, by the way,' he added to Nigel, 'that my actor friend turns up in good time. I should like to take him round to meet Helen before the show.'

Nigel nodded; he was too excited for words.

'And,' said Fen in a lower voice to Sir Richard, 'I suppose all the arrangements are all right?'

'The Inspector and his people will be there in plenty of time. There are a number of them now, of course, dealing with the crowds. I'm sorry' – said Sir Richard a little absently – 'that you had to spoil the evening by making this arrangement.'

'God knows, I'm sorry too,' said Fen, 'but you know it couldn't be helped. I don't really see why it need prevent us from enjoying ourselves.'

Sir Richard looked at him curiously. Then he squared his shoulders. 'It's certainly not going to prevent *me*,' he said resolutely.

'You might,' said Nigel, 'tell me what you're up to.'

'At the end of the show,' Fen replied, 'we're going to call a little meeting, and an arrest will be made. All very quietly, of course, when the excitement has died down. Only the people chiefly concerned will be there.'

'Oh.' Nigel was silent. Then he said: 'It seems a pity.'

'Throat-cutting and shooting are also a pity,' said Fen drily. They walked on in silence.

'God, what a crowd!' Nigel exclaimed, as they approached the theatre. 'I suppose,' he said to Fen, an ugly suspicion rising up inside him, 'that you've got the tickets?'

Fen felt in his pockets, and an expression of alarm appeared on his face. 'Oh my ears and whiskers!' he said. 'I've left them on my desk.' Nigel groaned.

'So you did,' said Sir Richard equably. 'So I took them. I trust you no further than I do your opinion of Charles Churchill. Come on, Gervase, for heaven's sake. Don't sulk.'

They forced a passage through the throng, Fen waving cheerfully to friends and acquaintances. He seemed, Nigel thought, to know an extraordinary number of people. After some difficulty he discovered the Eminent Actor, and bore him round to the stage-door to see Helen. Nigel and Sir Richard, thinking discretion the better part of valour, ploughed their way through a sea of mackintoshes, feet and programmes to their seats.

The Eminent Actor was discreet, charming and business-like. 'It's cruel of us to disturb you,' he said to Helen, 'at a time like this. I know I'm always terrified out of my wits on these occasions.' He smiled. Helen, somewhat flurried, admitted she was nervous, and said agreeable nothings. Fen wandered about the dressing-room, experimentally smearing his face with sticks of grease-paint.

There was a knock on the door. 'Five minutes, please!' came the dismal voice of the assistant stage-manager; and further down the corridor, a series of echoes: 'Five minutes, please!'

'Good heavens!' said the Eminent Actor, 'we must go. For heaven's sake take that stuff off your face, Gervase. No, don't rub it with your handkerchief, you ass; you have to put grease on it first. There! Now wipe it off with this towel.'

Fen, somewhat chastened by these proceedings, merely grunted.

'There's really no need to hurry,' said Helen. 'With all these people we're sure to go up late, and I'm not on till the second act.'

'None the less,' said the Eminent Actor, 'I think we should go. I'll watch the first act for the sake of Robert, and the last two for the sake of you. Good luck!'

In the auditorium, the footlights went up, bathing the lower part of the curtain in a subdued white glow. Fen, after taking leave of the Eminent Actor with the remark: 'Remember that time you pushed Cumber of the Lower Fourth into the Lake,' joined Nigel and Sir Richard. Nigel, looking about him, saw the Inspector, in plain clothes, and accompanied by two solid-looking companions, sitting some way behind. Sheila McGaw was at the back of the one-and-six-pennies; Nicholas and his blonde two rows ahead; Robert and his party in the front row. Backstage the beginners trooped down from the dressing-rooms. The assistant stage-manager settled down by the prompt copy. Jane gave a last professional glance at the set. 'Lights!' she said. A series of clicks from the electrician's gallery, and the stage was lit from floods, spots and battens. The beginners settled down in their places. 'House lights!' The auditorium was darkened; the doors were barred against gate-crashers, late-comers, and other pests; the chattering died. Clive, suddenly beset by the conviction that something was amiss, rushed off the stage, retrieved a newspaper, and returned to his place, where he opened it and gazed at it in an interested manner. 'Curtain!' The press-button in Jane's hand clicked. And with a soft, insinuating hiss, the curtain went up on the first performance of *Metromania*.

From the first moment there was no question but that it was going to be a success. Nigel, with the inner cautiousness born of his Scotch ancestry, had wondered whether the build-up would not be too much for the play; but he need not have troubled himself. From Robert the audience had expected great things, and in a literal sense, they got them; from the company they had not expected much, and it was the more pleasing to have that expectation disappointed. Even Sheila grudgingly admitted that they had never worked so well together before. Timing, climaxes, curtain-lines were all perfect. It was a performance no one in the company ever forgot. From the beginning they knew they were working well together, and the audience was as perfect as an audience can be. As the play continued, those who were not on stood in the wings and hardly dared to speak about it, for fear of breaking the spell. Rachel, it goes without saying, was the heroine of the evening. She moved through the play with a fluent, lissom grace, exquisitely controlling and focusing the whole structure about her; the others, though acknowledging their dependence, yet lived and moved in their own right, and when Helen had been on the stage five minutes Nigel could have shouted with excitement. Without question it was performance in a million; the gradual heightening of the tension left everyone, actors and audience alike, in a state of emotional exhaustion at the end of the evening.

But it was the play itself which was responsible. As he watched it, Nigel found himself marvelling at its revelation of a unique and particular genius. In the first act, it might have been nothing more than a particularly witty and eccentric comedy, were it not for the extraordinary ease with which every character insinuated his or herself into the comprehension of the audience. The second act was at once more serious and more impressive. There was less frank laughter, and there was an ever-growing sense of uneasiness, impossible to set aside. The people of the first act, without losing their identity, became less humorous and more openly grotesque. It was not that they personally developed; it was that more and more was shown of their real selves. The last act was played in semi-darkness, under the shadow of an impending physical disaster. Now everyone except Helen and Rachel seemed degenerated into monstrous puppets and automata, mouthing words that were a terrifying parody of their former selves. It was done without expressionistic effects, in the frame of an ostensibly naturalist play. But as they lost their hold on the sympathy, and faded into mere talking shadows, so Helen and Rachel stood out more and more as real persons. At the end it was as if there was a sudden gust, and the shadows were dissipated, leaving these two alone. On a note of sudden personal tragedy, delicately and movingly hinted at, the play ended.

There were twenty-three curtains. At the fifth Robert appeared, holding the hands of Helen and Rachel. There were flowers by the thousand. At the fifteenth curtain Robert made a speech. He said:

'I don't expect you'll want to hear another speech by me tonight. But I should just like to say thank you for being such a delightful audience, and to express my very heartfelt thanks to the company and technicians of this theatre for attempting – and achieving so magnificently – the herculean task of putting on a new play in the course of a week. Any applause which there has been this evening should be theirs.'

The riot in the theatre redoubled. They had to take eight more curtains before they were allowed to go. It had been a glorious evening.

And it was then that Nigel remembered, with a cold chill of foreboding, what was still to come.

He read it in the changed look of Fen's eyes, in the glance which Sir Richard threw at the Inspector as they went out. He saw the Inspector move across and say something in a low tone first to Sheila McGaw and then to Nicholas Barclay. The excitement of the evening began too rapidly to ebb, and a feeling of depression took its place. True, there was still a good deal of commotion going on around him. When he reached Helen's dressing-room, for example, he found the Eminent Actor already there and the offer of the London job already made. But although he was sincerely glad, he could not wholeheartedly rejoice with this other thing still on his mind, and he was relieved when the remainder of the company left the theatre, chattering noisily, in search of supper to be followed by a first-night party, when the staff finally cleared up and left, and the theatre was given over to an incongruous and empty silence. He left Helen to finish dressing and went to the bar.

Fen, Sir Richard, the Inspector and Nicholas were already there. The others joined them at intervals. Robert was obviously tired and exhausted; Nicholas pale and unusually silent; Jean insignificant, suddenly drained of colour and personality. Nigel thought there was a look of sheer animal fright in Sheila's eyes. Helen and Rachel were the last to arrive, Rachel quiet and obviously distrait, Helen still keyed up to a high pitch of nervous tension. She came across and took Nigel's hand. They stood in a silence, intensified by the sudden small noises from the rest of the theatre, stood among the wreckage and ghostly remains of an unprecedented evening, waiting for the curtain to go up on the last act of another play.

Gervase Fen said:

'I'm extremely sorry to have to close a, for me, unforgettable evening' – he bowed slightly to Robert, who gave him a tired smile in return – 'in this disagreeable way. But I think you may all' – he checked himself – 'that some of you may be glad to see the business of this double murder finally off our hands. It would be in the poorest taste for me to explain to you now the reasons which have decided us to take action. But I should like just to say that I personally very much regret having to be an agent in the matter at all. To anyone of sensibility and imagination' – he smiled a little wryly – 'an occasion like this is not a subject of congratulation. It's a Pyrrhic victory.' He paused.

And unexpectedly, there slipped into Nigel's mind at that moment the one cardinal fact he had been looking for for so long. In retrospect, he decided that had it not been for the peculiar mental strain he was undergoing, it would never have come to him at all. But after it, the rest fell into place with ever-increasing momentum; all pointing to one person; all spelling out the letters of one familiar name . . .

Helen suddenly gripped his arm, so violently that it hurt. 'Nigel!' she whispered. *'Where's Jean?'* He looked round. Jean Whitelegge was gone.

He bent a confused mind on hearing what Fen was saying.

' – Finally it might be as well for me to say that every entrance to this theatre is guarded, and that there is no chance of anyone's getting out.' He paused, seemingly at a loss. 'Perhaps, Inspector, if you would –'

He stepped back with a little gesture of resignation. His face wore an expression of worry and depression. He, and the Inspector, and Sir Richard were looking at someone who stood in a corner by the door,

And as Nigel followed their gaze he saw that in the hand of that person was a squat, ugly little automatic, like a toy.

'Don't move, anyone,' said Robert Warner.

The first shock was succeeded by an immense wave of relief, almost of exhilaration. This is the point, thought Nigel rather light-heartedly, at which, the police having bungled their job of arresting the criminal, I leap in and disarm him before the admiring eyes of my beloved. However, he added comfortably to himself, I am going to do nothing of the sort. He waited with interest to see what the next development would be, and a moment later was feeling acutely ashamed of childishness in harbouring such thoughts. He held Helen's hand more tightly.

'That's very foolish, Warner,' said Sir Richard mildly, 'because I'm afraid you can't get away.'

'I shall have to risk that,' said Robert. 'This melodramatic final exit is in the worst of taste, but I fear it can't be helped.' He turned to Fen. 'Thank you for allowing me this evening,' he said. 'It was considerate of you. Possibly if I ever come up for trial I shall have time to write the successor to *Metromania* which I contemplated.' His voice was bitter. 'But somehow I think not.' He backed to the door. 'It would be inexpedient for me to linger here giving you explanations and justifications of my conduct. But in case I never have the chance to say it – I bitterly regret having had to do what I did, not for the sake of my own skin, but because Yseut was only a misguided little fool and I had no grudge against Donald at all. For the benefit of posterity, let it be put on record that I quite realize I've behaved like an imbecile. And I think' – he drew himself up a little, not in arrogance but in reasonable confidence – 'that posterity will be interested in anything that concerns me.'

He turned to Rachel. 'And you, my dear. I'm afraid our nuptials will have to be – postponed. I shall never be able to make an honest woman of you.' He smiled lightly, and his voice was affectionate. 'And now' – stepping back another pace – 'I leave you all. I must warn you that if anyone – *anyone* – attempts to follow me, I shall shoot without hesitation.' He glanced quickly round the gathering and was gone.

It seemed an age before anyone moved; actually, it was a matter of seconds. The Inspector dragged out a gun and raced down the stairs, with Nigel, Fen, and Sir Richard at his heels. The foyer was empty, but they reached the back of the auditorium in time to see Robert scrambling on to the stage in front of the curtain. He turned as he heard them come in, and levelled his automatic. There was a sudden deafening report in Nigel's ear. Robert dropped the gun, clutched at his leg, twisted and dropped like a broken doll. As they ran towards him they saw that even in the extremity of his pain he was groping for his glasses, which lay broken a little way out of his reach. It was oddly and terribly pathetic.

But they saw more. There was a movement at the top of the proscenium arch, and they saw the safety curtain dropping its whole weight with the speed of a guillotine down to the place where Robert, blinded and hurt, lay. Even as Nigel ran for the door which led backstage, he knew it was too late. Even as he ran up the little flight of stone steps, the blood pounding in his ears, he heard the shattering, sickening thud which seemed to shake the whole theatre. In two leaps he was up into the electrician's gallery and had reversed the switch. The curtain slid up again as the others clambered over the orchestra pit towards the shapeless thing that lay below.

He looked at his companion in that narrow steel place. But Jean Whitelegge stared at him for a moment without comprehension, and then slid fainting to the ground. He made no move to help her; instead, he gazed down at the little group beneath him. As if out of an infinite distance, he heard Fen's voice:

'I'm afraid there's nothing we can do now.'

15. The Case is Closed

Live we for now,
Time is unstable;
Vain is the vow
Broken the fable . . .

Maxwell

'And the key to the whole thing,' said Gervase Fen, 'was simply this: *the shot we heard was not the shot that killed Yseut at all*.'

He, Helen, Nigel and Sir Richard were once again in the room looking out over the garden and the quadrangle. It was two days later. They had just returned from an excellent dinner at the 'George' (for which Helen, to the embarrassment of Sir Richard and the delight of Fen, had insisted on paying) and were now settled comfortably to listen to the Post Mortem. Fen lay sprawled in an armchair and made precarious gestures with his glass.

'It was our easy assumption to the opposite effect,' he pursued, 'which made the whole business seem so impossible. And I realized the truth, as I told you, three minutes after we were in the room. Williams assured us that no one had come in or out; we ourselves were quite rightly convinced that no one could have shot the girl, faked the suicide, and got away in the time; accident or suicide were equally impossible, for reasons which we discussed. So what other alternative was there?'

Nigel swore gently under his breath. 'But if there was another shot,' he said, 'where did it go? And how on earth could he fire it and *then* put the girl's fingerprints on the gun?'

'Of course he didn't fire it from that gun at all. He used an ordinary blank-cartridge pistol, *after* he'd finished faking the gun. That had the additional advantage of leaving a nice fresh smell of burnt powder on the air; and it also provided the burns on Yseut's face which suggested that she had shot herself, or been shot, at close range.'

'Then she wasn't shot at close range?'

'Certainly not. How could she have been? She was alive when she went into that room, and no one followed her in.'

'I see a difficulty,' said Helen. 'This man Williams was in the passage outside, so she couldn't have been shot from there; Donald and Nicholas were in the room opposite, so she couldn't have been shot from there; and Williams watched Robert on his way up here, so he couldn't have done it then. So how did he do it? It seems as impossible as ever.

'Ah yes,' said Fen. 'That, I agree, is the next point. You understand that immediately after the murder I had no ideas about that. At the time I only knew enough to be able to identify the murderer for certain. There was only one person who could have faked the suicide and fired the decoy shot, and that was Warner. No one entered the room from the outside; no one left this room except him. Therefore there was no alternative. He pretended to go to the lavatory, made such arrangements as were necessary, fired the shot, and slipped back to the lavatory before Williams appeared (you understand that Yseut was already dead before he went down). Or he may have hidden behind the screen in the sitting-room and gone back after Williams reached the bedroom. Then he came out again and met us as we came down. As it was reasonable to suppose that only the murderer would have faked the suicide, then obviously Warner was the murderer. A lavatory, by the way, is a very good alibi: one doesn't like to pester a man with questions about it. And it probably served another purpose as well – I imagine there's a pair of light gloves and small blank-cartridge pistol somewhere in the sewers of Oxford at this moment.'

'What things did he rearrange?' asked Nigel.

'He shut the window, wangled the fingerprints, put the gun by the body, and slipped on the ring. Then he fired off the blank-cartridge pistol, holding it to the dead girl's head to make the burns. It can't have taken him more than three or four minutes in all – probably less. One contributory point: you remember I drew your attention to the fact that nothing was touched in the room until at least a quarter of an hour after we arrived? That meant that nobody felt the gun to see if it had, in fact, been recently fired. If it had, it would have been warm. Doubtless Warner relied on our good police training to prevent us

193

touching anything; and as the matter was already obvious enough, I deferred to the good old convention.

'We now come to the problem of how the girl was actually shot. You, Helen, have put the difficulties about that pretty lucidly; so there again a process of elimination was the only way. Actually, the solution was given to me by a chance remark of Nicholas', to the effect that he and Donald had been performing the anti-social act of listening to the wireless with all the windows open. *All* the windows open! That gave the game away, with a vengeance.

'It meant that the *only* way Yseut could have been shot was from the west courtyard, through three sets of windows, two in the room occupied by Donald and Nicholas, and the bedroom window in front of which she was kneeling as she went through the chest of drawers.

'If you look at a plan you'll see that such a thing was perfectly simple.* The two windows of the room opposite are practically parallel with the window of Fellowes' bedroom. There's no furniture in the way. And Fellowes and Nicholas were, I ascertained, sitting well out of the line of fire, in front of the fireplace.

'Finally, there was the fact that the wireless was making a lot of noise – playing the *Meistersinger* overture, in fact (you remember *Heldenleben* didn't begin until immediately before Warner joined us). I imagine there's little doubt that he used a silencer on the gun, and detached it afterwards. Even that would make a certain amount of din, but if he chose his moment well – say the *fortissimo* re-entry of the main theme just before the contrapuntal section where all three themes are played together – there was little chance of its being heard – as it undoubtedly would have been if he'd shot her when he went down from this room. And then of course he could stand well back to avoid being seen by the two in the room he was firing through.'

'What an extraordinary idea!' exclaimed Sir Richard. 'To fire from the open air, *through* a closed room, out into the open air again, and into another room. No wonder I never thought of it.'

* See page 71.

He appeared to be offended that such a thing should ever have been expected of him.

'Exactly. At that point, then, it was fairly easy to see what had happened. The acquisition of the weapon presented no difficulties. Warner told Jean at the party that he wanted a revolver for next morning's rehearsal, and probably guessed that she would somehow contrive to get hold of Graham's gun; even if she didn't, it hardly mattered, except as an additional safeguard to himself – he could easily have taken it if she hadn't, and the good old traditional flourishing of the weapon before all the suspects was a tolerable alibi in itself. As it happened, she did go back, and as he told us, he saw her (doubtless he was on the lookout). What he didn't tell us was that he slipped in immediately afterwards and removed the cartridges – I'm assuming this, but it seems the most likely thing – so that when you, Nigel, looked in the drawer, the whole lot was gone. After that he'd only to take the gun from the property room, which he did the next afternoon.

'On the Friday evening, then, he saw Yseut going to Donald's room, or knew that she was going. And provided with the silenced gun, a pair of gloves, and the blank-cartridge pistol – which, by the way, he took from the property room along with the real gun; it was used as an effects instrument offstage, and as I thought there was sure to be one in the theatre, I asked Jean if it had gone, and found that it had – ' He stopped abruptly. 'What was I talking about?'

'He'd seen Yseut enter the college,' Sir Richard prompted gently.

'Oh, yes. Well, he entered the west courtyard by the door from the street, did his bit of shooting at the convenient moment, went out again the same way, probably deposited the silencer somewhere temporarily, then came in at the lodge and up here as we know. At an appropriate moment he went down and did the faking. You see now, Nigel, why your timetable was so revealing. Not only did it show that he was the *only* person who could have done the faking, but it also showed that his time of leaving the hotel was unconfirmed, and that it might have been as late or as early as he pleased. By itself that wouldn't have mattered, but he bungled the whole thing by trying to make a cryptogram out of it, and faking that improbable suicide. *Anyone* – you, Helen, Rachel, Sheila, Donald or Nicholas – could have done the shooting from the west courtyard; if he'd left it at that, he'd still be as safe as houses; but as I've said, only one person could have done the faking.

'I may say there was also some casual evidence which by itself would have been highly suggestive, though not conclusive. For one thing, there was the fact – of which you informed me, Nigel, and which I subsequently verified – that Warner had deputed Jane to understudy Yseut. Now even I know enough about repertory to realize that for very practical reasons it contains no understudying – and certainly not of parts as small as that which Yseut was to play. But his anxiety for the success of his play led him to make that elementary blunder. Again, he told us that he had to ask his way to this room at the lodge – that he had never been in the college before; yet in conversation with my wife, immediately after the murder, he suggested that the killer might have come in through the west courtyard, of whose existence, if his other assertion was true, he could not have been aware. That was another blunder resulting from a tendency to elaborate too much.

'I confess, though, that certain things didn't seem to me at first to fit in with this simple and quite obvious statement of the facts. And one of them, Nigel, was given me by you. You emphasized a good deal the *lack of surprise* with which Donald received the news of Yseut's death. But whereas you seemed to regard this as a sort of abnormal unmotivated psychological state, I was inclined to look at it more simply. It meant either (a) that Donald had known the murder was going to be committed, or (b) that he had seen someone he knew prowling about the place prior to the discovery of the murder – and someone who hated Yseut – and on hearing the news instantly jumped to the conclusion that that person had done the killing. Now (a) was very unlikely. Robert would certainly not have confided in Donald, and the likelihood of Donald's having discovered Robert's plan (which depended in any case a good deal on chance) was so small as to be discounted altogether. That left (b). It was in the first place possible that Donald had seen

196

Warner himself. But in that case why should he have kept silent about it? He disliked Warner, and regarded him as a potential rival with Yseut. Having heard of the death – he was infatuated with her, remember – he would if he had seen Warner certainly have revealed the fact. Yet there was somebody he was protecting: who was it? Jean Whitelegge was the *only* person. And I assumed quite provisionally that he had seen her in the west courtyard (which was the only place she could have been) and probably while doing the black-out on that side of the room. In such circumstances I also assumed, first that he would have spoken to her, and second, that as she was there at the time she would probably have seen the murderer if not the actual murder – remember the black-out must have been put up only a very short time afterwards.

'This, at the time, was the merest speculation. But it seemed to me to be worth while following up, for my own amusement and satisfaction if nothing else (the main facts of the case were settled already beyond all possible dispute). And I went first to Nicholas, getting out of him without much difficulty the fact that Donald had met and talked to someone that evening, though Nicholas refused to say who it had been; that didn't matter as I was already pretty certain. Even by being severe with Donald, I got nothing out of him; he was being too chivalrous for words – I think to some extent he was relieved by Yseut's death, and not inclined to let Jean, who he still imagined had committed the murder, suffer for it. Jean herself, who I tested as regards the second part of my theory, was more helpful. By dint of casting asperations on the quality of the murderer's mind, I produced a fine outburst of rage and indignation. As it seemed unlikely that she was admiring the crime *in vacuo*, it was obvious that she knew who the murderer was. And as she had at that time no idea of the facts of the case and couldn't have made the deductions I made, it was reasonable to assume that she had actually seen him. That she should have been determined to protect him, by the way, was not surprising. She had no reason to love Yseut, and as we know, she had a tremendous admiration for Warner's work; her scruples were no doubt the same as mine – a strong disinclination to deliver a great creative artist not yet in his prime into the hands of the hangman. Hence her refusal even to admit that she was in the college that evening.

'I suggested to her that she should come and tell me privately what she knew, and when Donald was killed she did in fact do that. It appears that she followed Warner into the courtyard and actually saw him commit the crime. As with most of us, her first instinct was to hide, and she slipped into an archway and waited until he had gone. It was when she came out that Donald saw her and talked to her. In the circumstances the conversation on her side must have been pretty strained, and no doubt that gave him additional grounds for suspecting that she was the killer.'

'I imagine,' said Sir Richard slowly, 'that after the death of Donald Fellowes she wanted to go straight to the police and tell them what she knew. How did you stop her? I hear that she and Fellowes had been reconciled and were intending to marry.'

Fen groaned. 'Lord, yes,' he said. 'She was practically demented with grief, poor child. But at the same time,' he added rather irritably, 'I seemed to be the only person who had the slightest idea of what was going on, and I wasn't going to have my plans interfered with. I intended the first night of *Metromania* to go through without a hitch – as, in fact, it did.'

Sir Richard grunted. 'Yes,' he said, 'that was your condition for making us privy to the secrets of your remarkable brain.'

Fen scowled at him suspiciously. 'Anyway,' he said, 'I lied to the girl for all I was worth, and invented the most fantastic tales to prove that the murders had been committed by different persons. I half convinced her – enough to keep her quiet for a while; but only half. She realized in the end, with the result – ' He made a gesture. He was disinclined to remember what had happened.

'And now for heaven's sake,' said Nigel, 'what about the *motive*? Surely he didn't kill her just because she was making a nuisance of herself and sending Rachel into temporary tantrums? You've been liable to gnomic utterances on the subject of motive. Explain yourself.'

'My gnomic utterances,' said Fen severely, 'reduce themselves to three: that I do not believe in the *crime passionnel*; that the motive for murder is almost always either money, vengeance or security; and that none the less it is sex which is at the root of this business. I'll explain just how those assertions are justified.

'The *immediate* motive was without any question that mysterious something for which both Yseut and the murderer were searching. And my first clue to its identity came from the admirably lucid account which you, Nigel, gave me of the morning after the party. In it, you described without any apparent sense of incongruity two people behaving in odd and inconsequent ways, and attributed their antics to the probability that Yseut had slept with Warner the previous night and was intending to make a song and dance about it. Let me capitulate what happened – you must correct me if I go astray –

(1) Yseut came into the bar, carrying her handbag and a thin red notebook, which she threw down somewhere.

(2) Robert, on seeing her, appeared first angry and then uncomfortable.

(3) Yseut regarded him with "triumph and defiance".

(4) She chattered to him about "blackmail" and "revelations".

(5) Donald picked up his music and left, while

(6) Yseut went with you to the bar, keeping her eyes on Robert all the time.

(7) Her attention was diverted by you emptying a glass of brandy over her.

(8) She returned with you to the table, "stiffened and flushed" suddenly, and flounced out.

(9) Robert gazed after her with "genuine bewilderment".

'Now all this, I thought to myself, is extremely odd, and indeed only explicable at all on the assumption that it's the red notebook which is the centre of the furore. You had seen Yseut come out of Warner's room with it earlier that morning; on the strength of (2) and (4) I assumed that it was something of great importance to Warner and probably something which seriously incriminated him. The rest then fell into place, Yseut's attitude, her talk about blackmail (doubtless blackmail for West End jobs rather than money), the watch she kept on him; while the last two items in my summary were particularly revealing. They obviously meant, first, that Yseut had turned back from her diversion to find that the notebook had gone, and second, that it was not Warner who had taken it.

'That, you see, fitted perfectly. It explained why Yseut was searching Fellowes' room; and it explained why she was killed. Despite the fact that the actual proof was out of her hands, she knew too much to be left alive. (There is your motive: security.) It was obvious to me, as later it became obvious to her and as it was almost immediately obvious to Warner, that it was Fellowes who had gone off with the notebook, gathering it up carelessly with his music (he could not have taken it on purpose, since he could not have known what it contained). It was at that point, however, that my logic went entirely to the winds, and I made the fatal mistake of assuming that Warner had found the book among Donald's music, unlooked-at, when he killed Yseut – or rather when he went to fake the suicide. In fact, he did nothing of the sort. He had no time to make a search when he faked the suicide, and after that the room was under guard until 4.30 on Sunday. Then he looked round, failed to find it (as I failed to find it when I looked earlier, and thought he already had it) and went on up to the organ loft. There's little doubt, I think, that by that time Fellowes had discovered the thing, looked at it, and realized its implications – apart from anything else, it provided the only real motive for the killing of Yseut. And as a matter of fact there were a few faint red stains on one of his pieces of music, where the cover had smeared against it. What his feelings were when he saw Warner, God only knows. But Warner realized he knew – had gone up prepared for that, in fact – and took the only possible course. Before he died, Donald left us the identity of the murderer in the only way he knew, hoping against hope that someone would notice it. You remember my remarking on the curious mixture of stops he'd left out? The Inspector thought that some tedious musical irrelevancy, but it was not. On the right-hand stop-jamb, the stops were out in the following order: Rohrflote, Oboe, Bourdon, Euphonium, another Rohrflote (on the Choir), and Tierce. They haven't been touched since, so you can go and look for yourself.'

'But I don't quite see,' said Nigel, 'where the music, and the notebook, were, if not in Donald's room.'

'They were in the organ loft, of course; the obvious place. As to the contents of the notebook, I could only guess. But I remembered Warner had been in South America several times before the war, and I thought it just possible that he might be remotely connected with the industry for which that part of the globe is notorious – procuring. I rang up a friend on the secretariat of the League, and learned from him that Warner had in fact been suspected of complicity in the matter, but that nothing could be proved against him. That was before the war, naturally; nothing of that sort can be carried on now. But I claim no credit for that part of it; it was the merest fluke. But that was what I meant when I said that the questing beast was in fact, at the root of this business, though the actual motive was security. I'm afraid I wasn't able to whip up much indignation about Warner's goings-on. It's always seemed to me that unless these girls are actually shanghaied, they're less sinned against than sinning. It seems an extraordinary sideline for a great playwright, but there was a sort of ironic twist in Warner's character, a kind of deep fatalism, which forbade him to take anything seriously. Even the murders he didn't take seriously; they were both brilliant, chancy affairs.'

There was a long silence. Then Helen said slowly:

'I'm glad the play couldn't go on after that one performance, even if Rachel could have done it. It – it seems somehow *right* that there should have been just one – and a perfect one.'

Fen nodded. 'A magnificent final exit, I agree,' he said. 'But a final exit, none the less. The world is the poorer for it.'

'What has happened to Rachel, by the way?' Nigel asked.

'She's gone off to the country. And Jean has been sent home to her parents. In the circumstances we couldn't possibly have proceeded against her, as she was "helping to apprehend an escaping murderer". Not that he ever had any chance to escape – and least of all when that thing crushed him.' Fen's voice was hard.

They all looked at him. As he smoothed back his unruly hair, he seemed suddenly old and tired. 'It has been an abominable business,' he said, 'and we are all the worse as a result. There will be no more *Metromanias*. And I for one cannot thank God for it.'

16. Epilogue: The Gilded Fly

Whether we fall by ambition, blood, or lust,
Like diamonds, we are cut with our own dust.

Webster

The journey from Oxford to Didcot (and thence to Paddington) involves difficulties of a different kind from those experienced in travelling in the inverse direction. The train, once it gets started at all, moves at a uniform if unspectacular pace. The problem is to know when it is going to start. Nicholas always insisted that the first train to leave in the morning was deliberately made ten minutes late, that this made the next train even later and that the process went on cumulatively throughout the day. At a certain stage in the day, however, he averred, the train behind caught up with the one in front – the 12.35 left at 1.10 and the 1.10 at 1.35, so that at the end of the day there were probably several trains which never ran at all. Be that as it may, it is certain that if you reached the station in time for your train you had to wait at least half an hour, whereas if you relied – as you reasonably might – on its being even ten minutes late, it invariably left on time and you missed it. It was this which led Nicholas to insist that the blind god of Chance wore the uniform of the G.W.R.

The six people who travelled up during the week of 19–26 October 1940 were, however, little affected by this difficulty. One way and another they were all too happy to care.

Nicholas, who was seen off by his blonde at the station, was pleased at the melodramatic conclusion of the case; also, he thought it had enlarged his conception of certain Shakespearean characters. Goneril, for example, should always be played by a young woman with red hair.

'Fen is a clever devil,' he said grudgingly to the blonde, after they had discussed the case *ad nauseam*, 'despite the fact that he considers me a fascist.'

'Aren't you a fascist?' said the blonde in apparent surprise.

'Certainly not. I'm an earnest supporter of this war; that's why I'm going back to town.'

'What are you going to do when you get there?'

'Find a war job. Not, heaven help me, in a factory with odious machines and odious jazzes blaring away half the day from mechanical contrivances, but something civilized and useful.'

The train came in. He climbed into a first-class compartment and leaned out of the window. The reluctance of most trains to start, he reflected, makes the pleonasm of one's carefully prepared parting phrases rather tedious. He said:

'There's no need for you to wait now,' to which the blonde replied:

'I'm not going to wait. I'm coming with you. Look out of the way.' She climbed in, and Nicholas gazed at her severely.

'Why,' he asked, 'this sudden decision?'

'Sooner or later I intend to marry you, for the purposes described in the Order of the Solemnization of Holy Matrimony. I'm sorry to be so pushing, but I'm really rather fond of you, and you're such an ass that you'd never succeed in getting married on your own initiative.'

'Oh, dear,' said Nicholas. 'I must re-read *Much Ado*. My situation becomes more Benedickian every moment.' Then he grinned. 'But do you know,' he added, 'I think I should find it rather pleasant.' The train moved out towards London.

Fen and Sir Richard travelled up together. Fen had practically forgotten about the case already, though if tackled on the subject he would have strenuously denied it. His interest in what was going on around him was so intense that it really precluded any very prolonged recollection; he was a man who lived almost entirely in the present. At the moment he was engaged in a strenuous dissertation on the merits of Wyndham Lewis, and at intervals trying to dissuade Sir Richard, with well-calculated rudenesses, from writing the critical and appreciative volume on Robert Warner's work which he contemplated. He was as happy as a schoolboy on a half-holiday, and commented in penetrating whispers and with increasing offensiveness on the physical appearance and probable vices of the other persons in the compartment.

Helen and Nigel, married four days previously, were more or less oblivious to everything except each other. They had spent their all-too-brief honeymoon cycling in the countryside round Oxford, and now Nigel was returning to his work and Helen was going to begin rehearsals with the Eminent Actor.

'Good-bye, Oxford!' said Helen, looking out of the window as the train moved away from the station; then, turning to Nigel: 'You know, I'm sorry to be leaving.'

Nigel nodded. 'Oxford is a wearing place,' he said. 'The idle, free-and-easy, unconventional life is too stern a test of character for me. I always loathe it at the time. And yet – I can never resist the temptation to go back.'

She took his hand. 'We'll go back one day and have a little private requiem for the dead. Not for Robert, because – I don't think he needs it.'

They were silent for a while, thinking of many things. Then Helen said more lightly:

'I think it was sensible of Sheila to get another play into rehearsal straight away. And she did it well, too. Did you see the Inspector and his wife, two rows in front of us?'

'Yes, good heavens. She looks exactly like Hedy Lamarr. What a capture! "White as the sun, fair as the lily." An odd comparison. Is the sun white?'

'Don't be dismal, Nigel,' said Helen practically. 'I can't understand,' she added, returning to her copy of *Cymbeline*, 'why a man of "so fair an outward and such stuff within" should get drunk and make such a silly bet in the first place.'

'By the way, did you go and say good-bye to Gervase?'

'Yes, of course I did. We talked about gardens and food and the state of Christ's church militant on earth. He had on his extraordinary hat.'

'There's been too much Shakespeare in this case already,' said Fen gloomily.

He and Nigel had met in the bar during the first interval of a performance of *King Lear*, and Nigel, tortured by the recollections of a problem still unsolved, had taken the opportunity to ask him about the ring – the Gilded Fly.

'Too much Shakespeare,' Fen repeated, as though fascinated with the phrase. 'I'm preparing a new anthology "Awful lines from Shakespeare". "Alas, poor Gloster? Lost he his other eye?" will have pride of place.'

'The ring,' Nigel persisted. Fen drank deeply; he appeared unwilling to be reminded of the subject.

'Purely a baroque flourish on the main structure,' he said eventually. 'A little cynical personal touch. I didn't recognize the reference until I happened to mention the Gilded Fly in the same breath with Mr Morrison's slogan. It was partly, I think, an ironic salute to Yseut's main interest in life, and partly an intimation of "measure for measure". By sex she lived; by sex, or because of sex, she died – a poetic retribution. The ring just happened to be a handy symbol. Few murderers can resist decorating.'

'But what is the reference?' Nigel asked.

'These people have cut the play about so badly,' said Fen, 'that one doesn't know *where* it will turn up. But if I remember rightly, it's in Act IV, scene 4.'

The second bell rang. Gervase Fen finished his drink with reluctance.

'I can't understand,' he said dismally as they moved towards the door, 'why they allow foreign actors to play in Shakespeare. One can't make out a word they're saying half the time . . .'

FOR THE BEST IN PAPERBACKS, LOOK FOR THE 🐧

In every corner of the world, on every subject under the sun, Penguin represents quality and variety – the very best in publishing today.

For complete information about books available from Penguin – including Puffins, Penguin Classics and Arkana – and how to order them, write to us at the appropriate address below. Please note that for copyright reasons the selection of books varies from country to country.

In the United Kingdom: Please write to *Dept E.P., Penguin Books Ltd, Harmondsworth, Middlesex, UB7 0DA.*

If you have any difficulty in obtaining a title, please send your order with the correct money, plus ten per cent for postage and packaging, to *PO Box No 11, West Drayton, Middlesex*

In the United States: Please write to *Dept BA, Penguin, 299 Murray Hill Parkway, East Rutherford, New Jersey 07073*

In Canada: Please write to *Penguin Books Canada Ltd, 2801 John Street, Markham, Ontario L3R 1B4*

In Australia: Please write to the *Marketing Department, Penguin Books Australia Ltd, P.O. Box 257, Ringwood, Victoria 3134*

In New Zealand: Please write to the *Marketing Department, Penguin Books (NZ) Ltd, Private Bag, Takapuna, Auckland 9*

In India: Please write to *Penguin Overseas Ltd, 706 Eros Apartments, 56 Nehru Place, New Delhi, 110019*

In the Netherlands: Please write to *Penguin Books Netherlands B.V., Postbus 195, NL–1380AD Weesp*

In West Germany: Please write to *Penguin Books Ltd, Friedrichstrasse 10–12, D–6000 Frankfurt/Main 1*

In Spain: Please write to *Longman Penguin España, Calle San Nicolas 15, E–28013 Madrid*

In Italy: Please write to *Penguin Italia s.r.l., Via Como 4, I-20096 Pioltello (Milano)*

In France: Please write to *Penguin Books Ltd, 39 Rue de Montmorency, F-75003 Paris*

In Japan: Please write to *Longman Penguin Japan Co Ltd, Yamaguchi Building, 2–12–9 Kanda Jimbocho, Chiyoda-Ku, Tokyo 101*

FOR THE BEST IN PAPERBACKS, LOOK FOR THE

PENGUIN CLASSIC CRIME

The Big Knockover and Other Stories Dashiell Hammett

With these sharp, spare, laconic stories, Hammett invented a new folk hero – the private eye. 'Dashiell Hammett gave murder back to the kind of people that commit it for reasons, not just to provide a corpse; and with the means at hand, not with handwrought duelling pistols, curare, and tropical fish' – Raymond Chandler

Death of a Ghost Margery Allingham

A picture painted by a dead artist leads to murder . . . and Albert Campion has to face his dearest enemy. With the skill we have come to expect from one of the great crime writers of all time, Margery Allingham weaves an enthralling web of murder, intrigue and suspense.

Fen Country Edmund Crispin

Dandelions and hearing aids, a bloodstained cat, a Leonardo drawing, a corpse with an alibi, a truly poisonous letter . . . these are just some of the unusual clues that Oxford don/detective Gervase Fen is confronted with in this sparkling collection of short mystery stories by one of the great masters of detective fiction. 'The mystery fan's ideal bedside book' – *Kirkus Reviews*

The Wisdom of Father Brown G. K. Chesterton

Twelve delightful stories featuring the world's most beloved amateur sleuth. Here Father Brown's adventures take him from London to Cornwall, from Italy to France. He becomes involved with bandits, treason, murder, curses, and an American crime-detection machine.

Five Roundabouts to Heaven John Bingham

At the heart of this novel is a conflict of human relationships ending in death. Centred around crime, the book is remarkable for its humanity, irony and insight into the motives and weaknesses of men and women, as well as for a tensely exciting plot with a surprise ending. One of the characters, considering reasons for killing, wonders whether the steps of his argument are *Five Roundabouts to Heaven*. Or do they lead to Hell? . . .'